SLEIGHT OF FANTASY

SASHA URBAN SERIES: BOOK 4

DIMA ZALES

♠ MOZAIKA PUBLICATIONS ♠

Copyright © 2019 Dima Zales and Anna Zaires
www.dimazales.com

Published by Mozaika Publications, an imprint of Mozaika LLC.
www.mozaikallc.com

Cover by Orina Kafe
www.orinakafe-art.com

e-ISBN: 978-1-63142-387-1
Print ISBN: 978-1-63142-386-4

CHAPTER ONE

THE STUPID DOORBELL BLARES.

Through my still-closed lids, I see the sun rays peeking into the window. Which means that though I feel like I've only just gone to bed, it's already morning.

Whoever is at the door isn't being as unreasonable as they seem.

"Felix!" I shout without opening my eyes. "Can you get the door?"

"He left for work," Fluffster states in my head, and I can almost hear him wanting to add, "Unlike some people."

"How about you?" I pull the bedsheets over my head. "Can you get that?"

"Me?" Confusion replaces Fluffster's attitude. "I can't open the door with these tiny paws."

We both know his "tiny paws" can turn into gigantic claws that rip and kill, but I don't argue.

Instead, I grudgingly open my eyes and pull the blanket down.

Yep, it's daytime.

Grumbling, I get up, put on a bathrobe, step over Fluffster, and trudge to the front door.

As I walk, the reason for my grogginess becomes clear.

Despite my hopes, my sleep was *not* dreamless. I had nightmares about mind-controlled gangsters trying to kill me. Worse, some dreams featured me and my boss in compromising positions—and I'm not talking about the stocks in our portfolio.

"Who is it?" I ask the door hoarsely.

"It's Rose."

The peephole verifies the truth of that statement, so I unlock the door.

"What time is it?" I ask, rubbing my eyes.

"Oh my." My elderly neighbor flutters her heavily mascaraed eyelashes. "Did I wake you?"

"It's eight a.m.," Fluffster says, presumably in both of our heads. "Sasha's going to be late for work."

Dang it. With everything that's happened, I totally forgot to set my alarm.

"Nero is going to kill me," I mutter. "I'm going to be late on my first day back."

"Oh." Rose looks crestfallen. "I wanted to ask you something…"

Adrenaline attacks my drowsiness. "What's up? Did something happen?"

"No, nothing like that." She looks guiltily at me,

then at Fluffster. "How about you stop by my apartment before you leave for work, and I'll feed you breakfast?" she suggests. "You need proper nourishment."

I bite my lip, cognizant of the time. "I know there's no such thing as a free breakfast."

"You make me sound so Machiavellian." She chuckles. "I just wanted to ask for an itsy-bitsy favor."

"Fine. Give me a minute." I do have to eat.

She shuffles away, and I close the door.

"What do you think that's about?" Fluffster asks me as I head to the bathroom to get ready.

"I have no idea," I tell him. "Whatever it is, I hope it's quick."

Closing the door before Fluffster can get in, I take care of all my washroom business, finishing with a splash of ice-cold water on my face.

I'm awake now, but deeply disappointed.

I hoped that a good night's sleep might clarify last night's events, but here I am, in the morning, and nothing makes any sense still, particularly that kiss...

"So, what happened after you left?" Fluffster asks as I make my way to my room.

"Didn't Felix tell you?" I begin to get ready.

"He did. But he also said you hung up on him, so I was wondering if—"

"Not much happened after I hung up," I lie. "I got out of there and came home."

The chinchilla tilts his head in an oddly human gesture. "Well... I'm here if you want to talk about it."

Did Fluffster's mental message sound extra sage in my mind, or is it my imagination?

"Thank you," I mumble.

Of course, I'm *not* planning to discuss the kiss with Nero with my fluffy domovoi.

Or Felix.

Or anyone, really.

I guess I could see myself talking to Ariel about it if she really pried, but she's in rehab for her vampire-blood addiction and won't be talking to me anytime soon.

I sigh. I already miss Ariel, and I'm still really worried about her, even if she's finally getting the help she needs.

The guilt, though, is the worst. It's lurking just under the surface of my mind, ready to suffocate me—the way Ariel nearly choked me while under Baba Yaga's control.

Shaking my head, I glance at myself in the mirror and frown.

It figures.

Working purely on autopilot, I'd put on my leather pants, black bracelets, the black vinyl vest, and the rest of my restaurant getup.

Well, so what?

When Nero so brutally negotiated my comeback, he didn't stop to discuss the dress code—so I can wear whatever I want, even if I look like I'm headed for the nearest goth club rather than a hedge fund.

Hurrying out of the room, I stop by the door to put

on my steel-toed boots and then make my way to Rose's apartment.

She opens the door before I ring her doorbell and rewards me with a wide grin.

"Come in," she says, leading me into the kitchen.

My stomach rumbles as I inhale the aroma of freshly baked muffins and jasmine tea.

"Sit. Eat," Rose says, pointing at the head of the table —where she set up my breakfast.

"I only have time for a quick bite." I look at her wall clock and cringe. "Nero doesn't like tardiness."

"I'm sure he'd rather face you when you have eaten," Rose says, a smile touching the corners of her eyes. "Otherwise, he's the one you might bite."

I fight a flush. "I'm not sure what you're trying to imply there." I blow on my tea as casually as I can.

"Okay, tell me then," Rose says. "What happened after Vlad took you to the facility in Gomorrah?"

So I do. I tell her about my spying on Nero, and how it revealed an ancient Russian contract between my boss and the man who turned out to be my biological father: Grigori Rasputin. As Rose's eyes widen, I go into how Nero fulfilled his side of that bargain—by keeping tabs on me my whole life and interfering whenever he saw fit. I stop just short of telling her about the kiss, but the way she moves her eyebrows during the part where he caught me with the folder in my hands makes me wonder if she guessed it anyway.

"So your birthday isn't in the summer?" she asks when I stop talking.

I nearly choke on my tea. "*That* is your reaction to everything I told you? Not that I'm over a hundred years old, sort of? Or that Nero did what he did? Of all the million things, you're worried about my birthday?"

"I need to know when to get you your gift," Rose says, her eyes twinkling. "Gifts are important."

"I'll still celebrate my summer birthday," I say, fighting the urge to roll my eyes. "It marks the day when my adoptive parents found me at the airport, and I don't see any reason not to celebrate it as I've always done."

"Great," Rose says. "I have that in my calendar."

I bite my delicious blueberry muffin and sip the tea.

She just sits there, watching me.

"You're not outraged at Nero's behavior? You don't think it was a big deal that he—"

"Nero's bad behavior is the reason you are alive—Vlad too," she says, her tone now somber. "Unlike you, I make it a habit not to look a gift horse in the mouth."

"Well, you're welcome to this horse," I grumble and hurry to finish my muffin so I can skulk away. Rose clearly doesn't understand the perversity of the situation.

"I have my own wonderful horse that I can ride, thank you very much," Rose deadpans. "And besides, I don't think you mean it. I doubt you'd want another woman to mount that—"

"I'm late." Face burning, I jump to my feet. "What was that itsy-bitsy favor you wanted?"

"Wait. Please don't run away like that."

Chastised, I sit back down, mentally blaming my rudeness on Nero.

"I'm sorry if I upset you," Rose says when I pick up my tea cup again. "It's just that I saw the way Nero looked at you when Isis put you in that healing sleep yesterday."

"Sure. Like Scrooge McDuck at his gold-filled swimming pool."

"The way you talk about him betrays you, you know. You want him, but you think it's inappropriate, so you're unwilling to give it a chance."

I catch myself squeezing the cup so hard it's a wonder it doesn't shatter. "You only have one thing correct. That atrocious scenario *would* be inappropriate."

"Oh child." Rose's blue eyes take on a distant look. "I understand your situation far better than you think."

"You do?"

"Of course." Rose stares at the tablecloth as though determining the thread count. "I, too, find myself in a relationship that is the very definition of inappropriate, and when it started, I was in denial, like you, and likely for the same reasons."

I feel a strong urge to shout that Nero and I are *not* in any kind of relationship. I also want to storm out of the room and slam the door behind me, teenager style. I don't let myself do any of that, though. Rose is finally delving into the mysterious waters that are her relationship with Vlad, and I'm too curious to stop her.

Staying silent, I raise my eyebrows slightly.

It may have come off looking like a nervous tic.

"My beloved's lifespan is theoretically limitless," Rose says quietly. "Meanwhile, I have only a few decades of life left."

I hold my breath, worried that even an exhalation might spook her.

"We could never have children—and I wanted a daughter so desperately..." She keeps staring at the table as though it were a movie screen replaying her long life. "His blood has the same effect on me as Gaius's blood has on Ariel," she says in an even softer tone. "We always have to be extremely careful."

Unable to hold my breath any longer, I let it out.

Either that barely audible sound or some memory seems to bring Rose out of her strange reverie. Looking up, she catches my gaze and her lips twist. "I guess that's a long way of saying that no matter the circumstances, it's always worth it to have love in your life."

"I'm not going to argue with that," I say. "I'd consider myself lucky if I found someone who'd mean as much to me as Vlad clearly means to you. Big emphasis on *if*."

She smiles, then sheepishly glances at the clock. "I'm going to make you late. Do you want me to wrap you a muffin to eat on the way to the office?"

"Sure," I say. "That would be great."

I finish my tea as she gets up, slowly walks up to the oven, and gets a muffin out.

"So, about that favor," she says as she wraps my treat. "Vlad wants to take me on a little vacation again…"

"That's great." I stand up. "You two should enjoy yourselves."

"Right," she says. "Here's the thing." She hands me the brown bag without meeting my gaze. "Luci finds our vacations stressful. And she felt so comfortable in your house yesterday. I was hoping—"

"You want me to babysit your hell spawn?"

"She's in her carrier already," Rose says defensively. "And she's been washed."

I take in a deep breath.

Rose deserves a vacay. Vlad too. After the way he risked his life for us yesterday, I should be willing to even bathe the cat for him. Without any protective gear.

"Where is she?" I ask, resigned.

Rose leads me into the living room and picks up the carrier.

Lucifur is sleeping inside, looking like a feline angel.

Rose either drugged the beast, or Vlad used his glamour on her—if it works on cats or demons, that is.

Not wanting to lose a limb, I carefully pick up the crate and bring it to my apartment. Rose comes along.

"Do not kill the cat," I tell Fluffster when he stares at the cage with a dumbfounded expression.

"Another mouth to feed?" The chinchilla looks at Rose indignantly.

"I'll bring her food and toys over," Rose tells him. "Sasha, you should run. Nero awaits." She winks.

"Thanks," I say, suppressing the urge to roll my eyes. "You enjoy your vacation."

"Will do," Rose replies and goes back to her place to get cat accoutrements.

The elevator is still broken, courtesy of my driving into it, so I take the stairs.

When I get into the cab, I take out my muffin and start chewing it.

Nope.

The food does nothing to suppress the hungry butterflies that seem to have taken up residence in the pit of my stomach.

Really? Am I worried about facing him?

That's just silly.

Yet the anxiety increases as we get closer to the fund. Questions swirl through my head, each more difficult than the other.

How should I act when we meet?

Do I pretend like the kiss never happened?

I could probably manage that, though it would be like standing in the rubble of one's house and acting like the tornado that destroyed it didn't happen.

Choking down another bite of the muffin, I replay the end of last night's encounter in my head like a broken record.

Then I catch my fingers touching my lips and snatch my treacherous hands away.

One thought keeps nagging at me.

Kissing the real Nero was completely unlike my experience with Kit pretending to be him. With fake Nero, I remembered that he was my boss, and knew the whole time how wrong any liaison between us would be.

Not so with the real deal.

It's as though my brain took a break and let my hormones ride my body last night—despite the fact that the boss/Mentor aspect is now just the tip of this mountain-sized iceberg of inappropriateness.

Nero is old enough to be my distant ancestor, my weird century-ago birth aside—and he watched me grow up.

Doesn't that make him something like that Humbert guy from *Lolita*?

Then again, I *am* in my twenties.

Wait, am I actually defending him? Did Rose's words bewitch me, or did the kiss give me permanent brain damage?

"This is you," the cabbie says, pulling me out of my confused thoughts.

I pay, stuff the rest of the muffin into my mouth, and sprint to the elevators.

Getting to my floor, I nod at a few coworkers, most of whom are looking at me strangely, and head over to my desk.

Except, my desk is missing.

And not just my desk. My chair, my computer—it's all gone.

Instead, there's a hand-written note—a rarity in this paperless office.

It's lying boldly on the now-empty floor.

The impeccable penmanship states in strong, masculine strokes:

Come see me first thing.

-Nero

CHAPTER TWO

STORMING BY AN OUTRAGED VENESSA, I barrel into Nero's office unannounced.

He has his sit-to-stand desk in the standing position and is blissfully typing away, seemingly unaware of my arrival.

He's dressed in a striped shirt and has his sleeves rolled up to his elbows—a lot like magicians do in order to prove we have nothing up our sleeves.

What a load of crap.

I would trust Nero as much as anyone should trust a magician. As in, not at all.

I clear my throat.

He doesn't acknowledge my presence.

"Where is my desk?" Though he's fully clothed, I can't help but see the image of him naked—no doubt his exposed forearms are to blame. "How am I supposed to work without a chair or a computer?"

"You're finally gracing us with your presence?" Nero stops his typing and looks me over, his gaze lingering on my leather pants. "Is there such a thing as a casual *Monday*?"

"Is fashion advice part of your famous Mentorship training?" I plop into his visitor's chair without an invitation. "If so, I could use some makeup tips."

"You don't need any makeup." Nero's eyes scan my face as though he's making a 3D printer plan for it.

I frown. "Was that a compliment?" If he meant to distract me with that statement, he succeeded admirably.

Nero lowers his desk and sits down in his own chair, bringing our eyes to the same level.

"Tell me everything," he states imperiously.

"42," I say. He raises his eyebrow, so I explain, "That's the answer to life, the universe, and *everything*."

"I've met Douglas Adams, you know—the author of the book you're now referencing." Nero's lips curve sardonically. Before I can pepper him with questions about such a bombshell, he says, "Let me make myself clear. How did you get into that mess with Baba Yaga?"

"That doesn't seem to be work related." I slowly cross my leather-pant-clad legs—channeling *Basic Instinct*.

My maneuver works as intended. The limbal rings in Nero's eyes seem to grow, and for a moment, he looks like he's about to leap at me from his chair.

Wait. Why would I want that? My heart rate

speeding up, I uncross my legs and sit forward belligerently. "Why should I tell you?"

He gets himself under control in an eyeblink and with annoying calmness asks, "Because you don't want to piss me off?"

I'm about to give him a wholehearted, "Yes, I do want to do that," but he must realize my intent because he gives me a knowing shark's smile and says, "Never mind that. I'm your Mentor. It is my prerogative to know such things in that capacity, so you *will* answer. Is that clear?"

Sighing, I explain how the search for my heritage led me to Baba Yaga—and what the evil witch wanted in return for giving Fluffster a memory of belonging to Rasputin. When I get to the part about her wanting me to have sex with Yaroslav the bannik, Nero's face turns so dark I worry his orc-tearing claws might come out.

I rush to explain how said bannik sex did not happen, and wasn't ever going to happen to my conscious body, and Nero relaxes slightly. I then mention my escape, and how I learned about Ariel's kidnapped state. Finally, I tell him about the rescue all the way to the part when I called for his help.

"It was all your fault," I say in conclusion. "You've always known who my father is. If you'd just told me that, I wouldn't have met Baba Yaga."

"You're going to see Lucretia next." Nero pulls out his phone and looks at the screen. "In two minutes."

"You're changing the subject, just like that?" I resist the urge to leap to my feet.

"Seeing Lucretia is going to be part of the Mentorship, and therefore, the time you spend with her isn't going to be subtracted from your work allotment."

Work allotment? Is he kidding? What about giving me some answers?

"Who is my mother?" I demand. "And where is—"

"Lucretia will be seeing you in her office." Nero puts his phone away.

"I'm not going anywhere until you tell me about my parents."

"We made a bargain," Nero says coolly. "When it comes to Mentorship and your job here at the fund, you will do as you're told."

"Is it the secrecy clause in that stupid contract?" I cross my arms. "Can't we figure out a way to bypass that? Maybe you can write me an email; that wasn't invented in 1916."

Nero looks at me, then pointedly gazes at the door.

"Please, Nero." Dropping the attitude, I make puppy eyes, hoping he's susceptible to the trick that always works on Felix. "Imagine if someone hid *your* family from you. If—"

I stop speaking because Nero's face turns terrifyingly dark. The skies above Mordor didn't look this bad. Then he blurs into the supernatural motion that preceded the orc massacre, and a fraction of a second later, he's standing by the door.

"Out," he growls, jabbing at the exit with his thumb. "Now."

Something in his voice makes me obey without question.

Leaping to my feet, I sprint out of the office as though something extremely dangerous is about to chase me.

And for all I know, that might've been the case.

CHAPTER THREE

"PLEASE HAVE A SEAT," Lucretia says when I enter her office.

I plop onto the brown leather chaise, stretch my legs out, and practice relaxing breathing as she herself had taught me.

She watches me with seemingly infinite patience.

When I calm down enough, I reexamine my surroundings.

Now that I know Lucretia is centuries old, the traditional feel of this office makes more sense. She might've owned that antique bookshelf since it was new, and watched her book collection turn yellow and pricey-looking over the years.

Then again, Nero is ancient too, yet his office is ultra-modern.

She gets up and closes the intricate curtains that cover the glass walls of her office.

"You think that gives us privacy?" I say. "Nero no doubt has monitoring equipment all over this room."

"We have a contract, Nero and I." She walks over to the bookshelf, grabs something, and approaches my chaise. "What happens in this room *is* private."

"If you don't mind, I'm going to assume that man is a liar and a cheat." I look around but see no hidden devices—but that just means someone did their job well.

"It's a written, binding contract." Lucretia hands me the object she's holding—some sort of an ancient doll. Am I supposed to squeeze it for stress relief? Before I get a chance to ask, she adds, "Such contracts cannot be broken."

"He can steal your notes." I squeeze the toy. Definitely stress relief. "He did it to my mom's therapist."

"Privacy of my notes is in the contract." She lowers herself into her throne-like chair.

"Well, okay, but for all I know, you might report everything I say to him yourself."

She exhales sharply, looking as though she's been gut-punched.

"I'm sorry." I drop my gaze to the doll in my hands. "I'm not exactly in a trusting mood today."

"Why don't you tell me about that," she says softly. "Pretend like we indeed don't have any privacy. Surely there are topics we can still discuss?"

"You're right." I straighten in the chair and look at her. "How much do you know about my situation?"

"Not much. Why don't you run me through everything from the beginning?"

So I launch into my story—the TV performance gone wrong, the zombie attacks, the visions, the Council, teaming up with Ariel to deal with a necromancer named Beatrice, Nero's orcs, Beatrice's succubus girlfriend Harper, and Harper's revenge.

I then start telling her about the mess with Baba Yaga, and she moves to the edge of her seat when I get to the part about the bannik.

Why does that, of all the horrific things that happened to me, get special attention?

"Do you know Yaroslav?" I ask, going on a hunch.

She fidgets, and a hint of color spreads over her cheeks. "When he had more autonomy, Yaroslav was a client of mine. We still meet from time to time, but less formally, given his new situation."

"You still meet him?" The idea of the bannik seeing a shrink seems odd, but then again, I'm seeing her myself, so why not? In fact, if *I* were under Baba Yaga's thumb the way Yaroslav is, I'd sure need loads of therapy.

"Why shouldn't I meet him?" Her blush deepens. "I'm allowed to treat myself to a spa treatment from time to time, so why not chat with someone who happens to already be there?"

"I figure Baba Yaga might mind," I say.

"She can't mind what she doesn't know about." Normal (for a pre-vamp) paleness finally returns to Lucretia's face. "We only converse when no one else is in his sauna. The banya is open to anyone willing to pay, and Baba Yaga takes pride in the profits the place makes. It's actually very popular in the Cognizant community, especially with the vampires."

"Seriously?"

"Why not?" She lifts her eyebrows. "Vampires like spas too. I saw Gaius there on numerous occasions, and some other Enforcers too. When I was there last week, there was a—"

"You were there last week?" I nearly get up from my chaise.

"Sure. But before your unfortunate adventure." She bites her lip. "I can't tell you more details, though—client confidentiality, you understand."

"But—"

"Please, Sasha," Lucretia says. "Let's talk about you."

I sigh. She's clearly back in her shrink mode and won't say more about this intriguing topic.

I can't stop my mind from wondering, though.

Does Lucretia also have an inappropriate relationship? With a client, no less? Yaroslav *was* extremely easy on the eyes, so I can't blame her for—

"Please tell me the rest of the story," Lucretia says, leaning forward to gaze at me intently.

Oops. Did my emotions somehow betray what I was just thinking about?

She *is* an empath.

"I was almost near the end," I say and proceed to tell her about the bannik's vision-based plan for my escape and what followed it. I then conclude with how the search for my parents revealed Nero's role in my life last night.

Though I don't tell Lucretia about the kiss, I get the same feeling as with Rose: that the shrink might've deduced it somehow.

Her expression appears far too knowing.

"That is a lot to handle," Lucretia says when I fall silent. "Your emotions are all over the map. Nero was right to suggest that you see me."

"He didn't suggest." I squeeze the doll. "He commanded."

"Well." She gives me an enigmatic smile. "At least his heart was in the right place."

"His heart is probably a hunk of metal he keeps in some underground bunker," I grumble.

She chuckles. "In any case, you're here, so you might as well get some benefit from the situation."

"I guess."

"Why don't you choose a topic. Any topic. We can then simply talk about it as friends," she suggests.

"I honestly don't know where to start." Somehow, she's putting me at ease by just being in the same room—a strange effect I noticed the first time we met.

"I sensed a lot of guilt when you were telling me your story," she says, "and guilt is a heavy burden to carry. So unless it has something to do with the forbidden topic of Nero, why don't we talk about what's making you feel that way?"

Do I have any Nero-related guilt?

I did spy on him using Felix's gizmo, and I also broke into his house.

Nope. No guilt on that score.

If anything, I'm almost proud.

The only thing I may regret is kissing him back. Maybe. Still, I don't feel *guilty* about it.

If anyone should feel guilty about the kiss, it's Nero. Hanky-panky wasn't part of the deal he made with my father, I'm pretty sure.

"We can talk about something else entirely," Lucretia says when I remain silent. "There were some very complex emotions I detected toward the end of your story, and—"

"Guilt is a good topic," I say quickly. No way am I digging into the emotions surrounding the kiss. "I feel extremely guilty about Ariel's predicament."

"Vampire blood addiction is a horrible affliction." Lucretia steeples her fingers. "I actually worked at that rehab facility early in my career. It's excellent. If Ariel really *wants* to get better, they will be able to help her."

"I don't know if she wants to get better." I pull my legs to my chest and hug them. "I hope so."

"Hmm." Lucretia stares at me unblinkingly, as if she's peering into my soul. "I know logic doesn't fix situations such as this, but it might be a good place to start."

"Logic?"

"You didn't drag Ariel to fight Beatrice," Lucretia says. "It was the other way around. She was going to face the necromancer, and you forced her to bring you along. Yet you're acting as though she was hurt because you made her go."

"She was protecting me from my problems." I lower my legs and hug the squeeze toy against me, as I would Fluffster. "If it weren't for me, she wouldn't have gotten hurt and thus tasted vampire blood."

"Do you realize that one drink from Gaius should *not* have made her an addict?" Lucretia says.

"No?"

"No." She winces. "I know this from personal experience. I was hurt some time ago, and by coincidence, Gaius saved me in a similar fashion. I didn't become addicted in the slightest. It's a lot like getting morphine after a horrific injury; any chance of euphoria is miniscule."

"Even if what you say is true, I suspect she got hooked because of her PTSD."

"You say that as though *that* is your fault," she says. "You didn't send her to war. You didn't—"

"Still, I could've done more." I catch myself nearly choking the poor doll and loosen my grip. "I could've suggested that Ariel come see you, for example."

"Do you think that would've worked?" she asks. "Isn't she in denial about her PTSD?"

"It would've worked if I'd tried hard enough," I say stubbornly. "Besides, the addiction is only a part of it all. I also failed to notice that my friend was kidnapped."

"You said she'd stopped coming home before the

kidnapping. How were you supposed to know that she wasn't just out with Gaius?"

"I guess." I lower the doll to my lap. "Still doesn't make me feel that much better."

Actually, that's a lie.

Somehow, I *do* feel a little better.

"We can talk more about this later," she says—no doubt sensing my relief with her empath powers. "Were there any other guilt-related issues you wanted to discuss?"

"Maybe," I surprise myself by saying. "Or more precisely, my lack of guilt."

She gives me an encouraging look, and I feel a strong compulsion to squeeze the damning words out.

"I shot and killed Baba Yaga's men." I grab the doll again. "And I didn't feel any remorse about it. I kept on shooting them," I whisper, recalling it with a shudder. "And I didn't give their deaths much thought until this very moment. Beatrice and Harper's deaths, too. Granted, I didn't personally—"

"I can feel how much those actions bother you," Lucretia says, frowning.

I bite the inside of my cheek. "Well... I'm worried I'm some kind of monster."

"Don't be. I've known real monsters in my life," she says sharply. Then she inhales a big, calming breath and seems to shake off whatever oddness came over her. "You're not like that," she says in a steadier voice. "Your very questions demonstrate that you're capable of remorse." She smiles thinly. "Monsters don't bring up their sins to their therapists. Monsters aren't conflicted."

"I wouldn't say I'm conflicted." I put the doll on the coffee table next to my chaise. "What you're sensing is probably due to a certain someone I sometimes *want* to murder."

The smile spreads to the corners of her eyes. "The source of your angst might feel the same way."

I frown. "I'm not sure he—I mean, the source—is capable of feelings."

"You'd be surprised," she says, then glances at the drapes. "When it comes to feelings, the hypothetical person might be just as afraid as you, even if your reasons are different."

"Afraid?" I'm tempted to reach for the doll again, but instead, I just stare at her in confusion, unsure of what I find more impossible: the preposterous things she's implying about me, or that Nero can be afraid of anything.

"I think I'd rather you arrive at these insights over many sessions." She looks down. "I'm not being a good therapist by bringing this up in the first place."

"But now that you did, you have to elaborate," I say. "As a friend."

She glances at the door.

"You said we wouldn't be overheard," I remind her. "You can't use that as an excuse when it suits you."

"Fine." She faces me. "You haven't had a relationship for a long time. Nor did you ever have one where you felt emotionally vulnerable. Am I right?"

Wait a second. I never told her about my dry spell, or the brief, unsatisfying relationships that preceded it.

Did she really just figure this out using some Hannibal Lecter-like shrink methods?

The magician in me wants a simpler explanation, so I ask, "Did you pull that info from the files Nero keeps on me?"

Her blue eyes take on a sorrowful look. "I knew this was a bad idea."

"No." I unclench my hands, realizing they'd turned into fists. "You're right about my past, but so what? It's just bad luck. I was focused on school and then my career. There's no sinister deeper meaning."

She tilts her head. "You fear being abandoned by the person you fall in love with."

"Well, duh," I say. "Doesn't everyone?"

"Not me," she says. "Not Vlad and Rose. Not—"

"Fine," I say testily. "Even if what you say is true, which it isn't, it has nothing to do with why I shouldn't develop feelings for the hypothetical person we were talking about before. It's perfectly normal to be wary of evil, manipulative bastards." I realize that my voice is starting to rise, so I take in a deep breath and more calmly add, "What's *he* afraid of?"

"That another person he cares about would die," she says somberly. "But don't ask me for details because they're not mine to share."

As though waiting for that exact moment, Lucretia's stomach growls like a bear roused from hibernation.

She covers her belly with a delicate hand and chuckles mirthlessly.

"Saved by the stomach," I mumble, still overwhelmed by the topic we stumbled upon. Swallowing, I square my shoulders. "Should we end the session?"

"If you wish." She nods.

I stand up. "How about I buy you breakfast before I go face a certain someone again?"

"Deal," she says, getting up from her throne. "But you have to promise to come back."

"I doubt I'll be given a choice," I say as we step out of the office.

I, too, could use a visit to the cafeteria.

To face Nero again, I need to consume enough espresso to make a rhino bounce off the walls.

CHAPTER FOUR

JITTERY FROM ALL THE CAFFEINE, I storm into Nero's office for the second time in one day.

This time, he stops typing instantly and looks me up and down.

"That was quick," he says. "I never said you had to make your therapy quick."

"I'm here to deal with my 'work allotment,'" I say. "I'm dying to know what that is, and how I can accomplish it without a desk."

"Follow me," he says and marches out of the office.

By the time I catch up with his long-legged strides, he's already summoned the elevator.

Surprising me with a gentlemanly gesture, Nero holds the elevator door from closing. "After you."

Is he mocking me?

My heart rate elevated for some reason (no doubt the brisk walk), I slink inside and lean against the back of the car.

Nero saunters in and stops by the elevator buttons, his side to me.

I grit my teeth in annoyance. The guy manages to look great even from the profile.

My throat feels uncomfortably dry as I realize we're confined together in a small space.

Does he always take up more room than the laws of physics dictate?

Oblivious to my discomfort, Nero takes out some unusual-looking card and swipes it over what I would've guessed to be the fireman's override on the elevator button console.

The elevator dings approvingly.

Nero presses the button labeled B01—one of several that don't work when a mere corporate peon presses on them, no matter how curious said peon is.

We ride down in a silence that gets progressively more uncomfortable. "Are we headed to your secret underground lair?" I ask, only half-jokingly.

The persistent rumors about Nero having a cave filled with money and riches often feature these off-limits basement floors.

Nero raises an eyebrow but doesn't answer.

"I'd sure like to take a swim in gold," I say.

"No time for that today, I'm afraid," he says, his expression unchanging. "Your task is simplicity itself. You are to provide me with a stock recommendation. Just one. That is all."

"That doesn't sound so bad," I give him a relieved smile, and he smiles in return—but something about it isn't right. It seems like he's laughing at me, not with me.

The elevator dings.

We exit into a long, poorly lit corridor that reminds me of the secret passages that lead to the gate hub in JFK airport.

As I follow Nero down a few forks, the resemblance grows stronger.

Just in case, I sneak my phone out and make notes on the turns we take—just like I did in the JFK labyrinth when Ariel was leading me.

We turn right, and the corridor ends with a metallic door.

There's a digital screen on the front of the door.

Nero reaches for it, and I prepare to nonchalantly spy on what he types in.

As though *he's* the psychic, Nero uses his body to block the keys he presses from my sight.

The only thing I get a good look at is his backside—not bad as far as consolation prizes go.

"Is that a safe?" I ask when the door swings open. "Is this where your money is stashed?"

Nero just gestures for me to enter, so I do.

The safe isn't a safe.

It's a furnished room.

A fuzzy carpet with a modern-art motif is on the floor, with a comfortable-looking meditation cushion in the middle of it. My old chair is here too. It's standing to the side, but there's no desk or computer. However, there is a couch in the back.

Could the computer be in one of the adjacent rooms? I do see two doors inside, so perhaps that's where the workstation is kept?

The only monitor-like screen is a keypad identical to the one outside.

Nero again blocks what he types into the keypad, and when he's done, 8:00.00 shows up on the screen above the number pad. A second later, the clock changes to 7:59.59.

Wait a minute.

He can't mean—

"This is the work allotment," Nero says, pointing at the digital countdown. "You are to put in eight hours of work every weekday."

"This is outrageous." I look at the metallic sheen of the walls, then at my boss.

Nero lifts an eyebrow again. "You're going to be the only person at the fund putting in so few hours, and you know it. Even you used to work more."

"I'm talking about this." I wave around the safe-like contraption. "This is every claustrophobe's worst nightmare."

"It's nine hundred square feet, which makes it the second largest office in this building." Nero crosses his arms. "And you don't have claustrophobia."

"After eight hours in this cage, I just might develop it," I mutter.

"If you convince Lucretia that you genuinely 'developed claustrophobia,' I will swap offices with you," Nero comes toward me.

I back away from him. "Why are you doing this?"

"This room is soundproof, and no one will be able to interrupt you." To my relief, he stops a couple of feet from me. "Can you think of an environment more conducive to your visions?"

I want to smack myself for not getting it sooner.

Of course.

This *is* the perfect place for meditative contemplation—in a way that, say, a cave in the mountains might be.

Then again, it's also very similar to solitary confinement, which is usually a punishment that's worse than mere incarceration.

And it all comes down to the stupid visions.

How could I forget that?

Grigori Rasputin—or I should say *my biological father*—gave Nero a prophecy that listed all the notable events in the years between 1916 and 2016. Like Biff, the villain in *Back to the Future II*, Nero has turned Rasputin's foresight into obscene wealth.

So now that we're outside the list's timeline, Nero is going to use *me* to keep the money flowing.

Perhaps I'm lucky he plans to let me leave this cage after eight hours.

At least I assume he does.

He turns toward the door.

"What about lunch?" I ask quickly.

He walks up to one of the doors and opens it. Metallic walls aside, the room looks like a high-end kitchen, with a microwave and regular oven, a toaster, and a giant refrigerator with glass walls.

Inside the fridge are enough gourmet dishes to feed an army of the pickiest foodies.

Some stuff looks so good I almost wish I hadn't eaten all those muffins.

"What about a bathroom?" I ask, my heart falling further because I see where this is going.

Nero takes me to the other door, and of course, there's a huge fancy bathroom behind it—with a shower stall and a Jacuzzi. Most disturbingly, he opens a closet, and I see it filled with my favorite brands of cosmetics, shampoos, soaps, and even feminine products.

"What if there's an emergency?" I ask, in large part to keep myself from wondering how he knew which products to get.

"Press 911 on the keypad," Nero says. He must see some glint in my eyes because he adds, "If you do so when there isn't an emergency, your work allotment for that day will be doubled."

I stalk out of the bathroom.

He follows me out. "And don't try to guess the password and claim you meant to type 911. If a wrong password is entered at any point and for any reason, I will know it—and your work allotment will double for a whole week. Is that clear?"

"Crystal." I give him a baleful glare.

How could I have kissed such an insufferable man?

I must've been insane to find him appealing on any level.

"I will see you when you're done," he says and walks to the exit.

"You expect me to give you a stock recommendation without doing any actual research?" I ask, frowning at his back. "Without using any technology?"

"I believe in you." Nero turns and taps his forehead. "Now get to work."

He leaves, and the thick metal door locks with the finality of a tax audit.

"You suck!" I yell, but I doubt he can hear me over the thickness of the metal.

Yep. No reply comes. In fact, the room is so quiet it's eerie for a New Yorker like me.

In the dead silence, I hear my rapid breathing.

The nerve of that guy.

How does he expect me to have visions if he's going to piss me off like this?

Then again, he miscalculated.

He didn't explicitly say I must have a vision to provide him with the stock tip.

I could in theory tell him to buy whatever stock pops into my head.

We've never invested in CAKE, for example, which happens to be the ticker for The Cheesecake Factory. Nor did we ever buy EAT—a company that owns several other restaurant chains.

No, that might be my stomach talking. There was cake in the fridge.

Alternatively, maybe I should offer up BOOM, which is a metalworking company that uses explosives. The investment in that stock would also go boom.

I smile, Grinch like, getting into the spirit of the exercise.

Maybe I should tell Nero to invest in Harley-Davidson Motorcycles? That would suit him: their ticker is HOG, and Nero *is* being a pig.

Or is he being a dog? There is WOOF for that case —a veterinary medicine company.

No.

Too obvious.

I'll tell him to invest in Majesco Entertainment, a videogame company that has the ticker "COOL."

Unless that makes him think that we're "cool," which we are not.

My smile falters.

What happens when I tell him one of these fun stock names, and he loses a ton of money? Will that also double my "work allotment?"

I sigh.

Now that I'm calmer, I should try to get Nero a stock tip based on a vision—regardless of how much I would've enjoyed the petty revenge of having him invest in purely random stocks.

Parking my butt on the meditation cushion, I close my eyes and attempt to get into Headspace.

When my breathing evens out, my mind goes blissfully blank. All I notice now is my breathing.

I hover in that wonderful state for an indeterminate time, until my palms get warm.

This is it.

Lightning shoots from my palms into my eyes, and I spiral away.

———

THE USUAL BODILESS strangeness of Headspace surrounds me once again.

I float there, trying to readjust to the foreign set of senses unique to this place.

Soon, I become aware of the surreal shapes all around me—shapes that represent visions.

Okay, now what? I have no clue how to locate the shapes that will make Nero money.

Should I seek out green and minty shapes? Or ones shaped like coins or diamonds?

Better question is, why do I *always* have to figure out these things on my own?

Why did Nero have to scare Darian away from me?

Despite all his faults and obvious agendas, Darian has saved my bacon plenty of times now—and I doubt I'd have reached Headspace so soon without his Jubilee gift of the videotape.

Good old manipulative Darian.

Where is he now? Is there a way he could talk to me without risking Nero's wrath?

I can almost picture him now, evading my questions, sounding all British-royalty proper—

Suddenly, something extremely odd happens—that is, odd even for Headspace.

A moving shape appears next to me.

A shape so different from the others it might as well be a different species.

No, it's more like comparing a concrete physical object (like a pickle or a skunk) to something ephemeral (like honor or justice).

Besides the Headspace attributes I've labeled temperature, colors, taste, and music, this apparition has millions more—most without sensory parallels.

Yet that's not what's most strange about it.

It's the conviction that its appearance was triggered by my thoughts about Darian.

That, and the fact that it's sentient.

I don't know how I know this. I just know that *it* is like *me*. I bet if I magically turned my Headspace attention inward, I'd probably see the same awesome complexity.

Expectation (for lack of a better term) pulses from the entity.

"What do you want me to do?" I want to ask it, but don't know how.

The entity kaleidoscopes the myriad attributes impatiently.

I float there, pondering what to do.

Then it hits me.

Why don't I try the usual?

When it came to regular shapes, I had to sort of extend myself and metaphorically touch them to activate a vision.

Will it work in this case?

I try it.

The entity pulses in excitement and seems to reach for me just as I reach for it—which is when a vision-like black hole sucks me in.

CHAPTER FIVE

I'M STARING at a playing card in my hand.

My fingers look strange—bigger and without nail polish.

How odd.

I try to move, but find that I can't.

Huh?

"Two of Diamonds," thinks a male voice inside my head with a noticeable British accent.

"Darian?" I reply. "What are you doing in my head?"

No answer.

Instead, my eyes move from the card to take in my surroundings—which is when I realize I'm unable to control my body.

The surroundings are startlingly familiar.

This is the restaurant where I had performed my magic until I was forbidden from doing so—only everything is washed out, for lack of a better term.

It's as though everything was filmed with an ancient

camera, and then someone turned that footage into a virtual reality environment.

The people at the other tables are indiscernible, and even color is drained from most objects.

Without meaning to, I pick up a beer bottle from the table and take a swig.

To my surprise, the dark lager tastes yummy, not bitter as usual.

"'Two of Diamonds," a female voice that sounds like me says, but not out of *my* mouth.

I look up.

There I stand, holding a deck of cards in my hands and grinning.

Is this another trick by Kit?

It's possible, though this *me* doesn't exactly look like me—and Kit was pretty accurate.

This person looks like my much-hotter sister who had some major plastic surgery and was then photoshopped for a few years.

I zoom in on that face as though she's about to sprout an angelic halo.

"How did you do that?" I say to the other me in Darian's voice.

Wait, even my voice is Darian's?

"Very well," the supermodel version of me says with a seductive wink. "Now you try it." She turns to the woman on my right.

Wait a second.

I know what's about to happen.

The woman is about to choose a card under

extremely fair conditions, and I will reveal it to her.

Of course.

This is some strange replay of the day when I first met Darian—the meeting that led to the fateful TV performance and the rest of the madness.

But why am I seeing this memory in such a strange manner?

"She's so fiery," Darian thinks inside my head. "Just like Matilda was."

"Who the hell is Matilda?" I try to ask, but he doesn't reply—probably because I lack a mouth with which to speak.

The outside me guesses the woman's card correctly, then names another card chosen under lab-experiment-fair conditions, then another, and another.

"She is so bold," Darian thinks. "So adaptable and creative."

My doppelganger names his card. He claps and thinks, "So playful with the audience, so brave… and so bloody gorgeous."

"Thanks, pal, but seriously—"

My restaurant self hands over the deck and asks me to cut it.

When her hand-model-smooth fingers brush mine, I feel a strange sensation in my groin.

Wait.

What?

Since when do I have that kind of plumbing?

Did I develop some sort of narcissistic schizophrenia? Because this is beginning to remind me of that scene from *Being John Malkovich* when the titular John Malkovich gets inside his own head.

Then it finally dawns on me.

Somehow—and I have no idea how—I'm inside Darian's memory of our meeting.

It is *his* very masculine arousal I just felt.

That makes sense—in as much as such a thing could make sense.

This is why everything around us looks so odd. Memory isn't a perfect recording of events, and so Darian must not remember all the nitty-gritty, like the colors of things or who else was eating at the nearby tables.

For that matter, this is why the card selection was so much fairer than when I had actually performed this effect. He remembers what I wanted my spectators to recall later, not what *really happened*.

This also explains why the me in his memory looks so perfect.

It's *me* but seen through Darian's beer goggles—

The scene around me swirls and disintegrates like a mirage, only to be replaced by a new one.

CHAPTER SIX

I'M STANDING in front of a bathroom mirror, trying to wake up.

Against my will, my eyes look at myself in the mirror and confirm my theory.

A shirtless Darian stares back at me.

Wow.

Either Darian is rewriting history, or he was working out rather vigorously at this point in his life.

"Something is wrong," Darian thinks inside my—his own—head. "Where is she?"

A wolf howl pierces the air.

"She must be upset," Darian thinks. "But why—"

The door bursts open, and a naked woman rushes in.

A pregnant naked woman.

Darian looks her over and playfully whistles.

His memory must be playing tricks again, as mere mortals do not look as perfect as this lady. Her flawless skin resembles white chocolate melted over silk. Even her small baby bump somehow looks like it was designed by Leonardo da Vinci.

Darian smiles. "Great. Why bother with pesky clothing?" Then something about her face makes him stop talking.

Despite the fury in her features, as well as their almost supernatural beauty, something about the woman's face is distantly familiar to me.

Darian clearly knows her intimately, but where have I seen her? On a cover of *Maxim* magazine, maybe?

"How could you?" she shouts in a melodious voice.

"What's going on, love?" Darian clears his throat. "Did something happen?"

She slaps him/me on the cheek.

It stings.

"Matilda!" He rubs his cheek. "What is this?"

"So, this is the Matilda you compared me to in the restaurant?" I ask, knowing full well Darian isn't going to answer. "Why did you say she *was* fiery?"

"*I know*," she says, packing a novel's worth of meaning into just two words. "Stop the farce."

"She can't know," Darian thinks. "How could she know?"

The fear that accompanies that thought is stronger than any I've experienced myself—and I thought I was an expert on this subject after everything that's happened.

Then again, memory-fear might get stored stronger

than when you experience it firsthand. Especially if something horrific is about to happen to burn this episode into Darian's memory.

"I'm still not following," he lies.

"I can believe *that*," Matilda says, her jaw tensing. "You've had trouble 'following' me for some time now, haven't you?"

The fear solidifies into an iceberg in the pit of Darian's stomach. "You didn't—"

"I did," she says. "I asked Chester to shield me from seer eyes."

"Insane woman," Darian thinks. "Your husband isn't stupid. He will guess—"

The look on her face short-circuits Darian's thoughts.

"You wouldn't tell me what was wrong," she grits through her teeth. "So I shielded myself from your power, just long enough to hire a dream walker to find out what you're hiding."

Darian's negative emotions are hard to tell apart at this point.

Distantly, I recall Felix mentioning a dream walker friend who works for the rehab facility where we left Ariel. He said they can enter other people's dreams and manipulate their surroundings.

Sounds like they can also steal secrets.

"You're going to trust some charlatan?" Darian says, forcing outrage into his voice, but he knows how desperate he sounds.

"Don't." If looks could sever heads, Darian would've

lost his.

"Did the dream walker tell you *why?*" Panic creeps into his voice.

"Why?" She spits out the word. "Why you didn't tell me my baby will die, you mean?"

He cringes as though she slapped him again.

"I can guess," she says. "You know this is *his* baby. No doubt you saw a future where I finally stopped our —whatever this was—for the sake of my baby. No doubt you—"

With the speed of light, Darian concentrates in a manner I can't quite understand, and finds himself instantly in Headspace.

Wow. How did he do it so fast and without any meditation?

He does something else too quickly for me to comprehend—and enters a vision.

Which for me makes it a memory of a vision— which is kind of trippy.

Darian is standing on the edge of a graveyard.

"Lurking and hiding, like a coward," he thinks to himself through the grief.

Chester and a bunch of other black-clad people are standing near the freshly dug-up grave.

Chester's usually jolly, satyr-like face is furrowed with deep sorrow.

Sorrow that's nothing compared to what Darian feels—

The vision is over, and we're back in the bathroom, with the naked and furious Matilda saying,

"—rather the baby died, so you could have me to yourself—"

"The future is changed," Darian thinks, ignoring her words. "She dies now, unless—"

The scene around us swirls and disintegrates again, replaced by yet another one.

CHAPTER SEVEN

DARIAN IS IN HEADSPACE.

He reaches for a nearby shape, and a vision starts.

And what a vision.

Wow.

This is definitely TMI.

I feel the pleasure as Darian penetrates a woman from behind.

If I had my own face, it would be the color of an overripe tomato right about now.

Darian grabs onto the woman's narrow waist.

She moans.

"So this is what it's like for a guy?" I ask no one in particular. "Does it always feel this awesome?"

No.

Can't be.

This is no doubt another trick of memory.

Yep. Let's focus on *that* instead of his grunts and her moans.

Best to focus on the metaphysical aspects of this—
the trippy overtones and all that.

I mean I'm currently inside a guy while he's inside
someone else—

No. That way lies madness.

Maybe I should busy myself with the mystery of the
woman's identity?

She's on all fours, looking forward, so I can't tell
who she is—just that she's having a good time.

Darian's mind is completely overwhelmed by the
pleasure, so he doesn't think some useful thought, like
her name.

Though she looks too pale, I still hope it's Matilda
from the prior memory.

Maybe he found a way to prevent that graveyard
vision? Maybe she's left her husband and worked out
her differences with Darian—and her baby is alive?

Then a realization hits me as strongly as an orgasm
must hit Darian's current partner. At least, I assume
this is why she arches her back and makes sounds like a
cat in heat.

I already know what happened with Matilda.

And why her face was slightly familiar.

And who the baby is.

Gaius told me a version of this story before the Rite
—only his version was different from what seems to
have been the truth.

When explaining the feud between Chester and
Darian, Gaius told me that Darian had delivered a

prophecy to Chester's wife, telling her she would be the cause of her daughter's demise—and that it was that prophecy that drove the mom to kill herself.

He called her "a werewolf wife"—which explains that howl I heard in Darian's memory, and her nudity.

I later learned that the child in question is Roxy, my bitchy classmate.

This is why Matilda's face looked so familiar. Roxy inherited a lot of her mom's features.

The full story is so very different from what Gaius had told me, though. It looks like it wasn't a case of Darian having a vision and telling Chester's wife about it.

As far as I can tell, she—Matilda—and Darian had an affair, and then he had the vision about Roxy dying but *didn't* tell Matilda. However, she sensed Darian keeping a secret and contrived a way to pull the truth out anyway—with disastrous results.

If I had lungs, I'd sigh.

Had Chester known about the affair?

Given that Matilda asked him to shield her from a seer's view—and taking into account the lingering animosity between the two men—I bet Chester had put some of it together.

If I had a head, I'd shake it in frustration.

No wonder Chester wanted to kill me.

He must've thought Darian was romantically interested in me—and wanted to hit his nemesis where it would really hurt.

His motivation wasn't just about preventing a seer from getting recognized, as he claimed at Earth Club.

This also explains why he's left me alone since his initial strike. He must've decided that Darian wouldn't be with me because of Nero and all that.

Or maybe he's left me alone because I'm Nero's mentee?

Does self-preservation overrule revenge?

Of course, all that assumes that Chester has actually left me alone, which I don't know for a—

Ecstasy hits Darian's brain, completely ruining my attempts to ignore what is happening.

Whoa.

Is it my prolonged abstinence, or was that better than anything I've ever felt?

Darian leans in and hugs the woman, and she laughs and turns around.

I stare at her face, wishing I had a mouth so it could gape.

That's *my* face.

"I love you," what-better-be-Kit says in my voice and grins at Darian stupidly.

"I love you more," Darian says to her/me.

In his thoughts, he adds, "I love you almost as much as I loved Matilda—and I was able to save you when I couldn't save her."

He saved me?

What from?

Hopefully, he's thinking of the saves that have already happened. Like that time when he texted me on my way to work after the TV disaster—an action that he later claimed stalled me just enough to enable me to survive. Or he might be talking about yesterday's warning, when he said, "Beware the red light."

More interestingly, he actually means the lovey-dovey sentiments.

Now that he's *not* in the middle of coitus, the rest of his thoughts turn saccharine toward the sexed-out Sasha in front of him.

Which is when I finally put two and two together.

When we danced at Earth Club, Darian told me he'd seen a future of us together.

And this memory started in Headspace—so it must be a vision of some future.

I want to smack my missing forehead, but instead, I stare at the naked me through Darian's eyes.

This Sasha looks sinfully happy to be in his arms.

A part of me rejects what I'm seeing, but another part wonders if this future would be such a bad thing.

Don't I want to be *that* happy one day?

No, wait. What am I thinking?

Is this a side effect of literally f-ing myself?

You can't develop feelings for someone based on what happens in their memory of a vision of a future that may or may not come to pass.

That would be a paradoxical self-fulfilling prophecy.

Also, even in this rosy future, Darian seems to be comparing me to his Matilda.

Do I want to always compete with a ghost?

More importantly, might I be happier with someone else? Someone like, say—

The scene around me disintegrates again, and I find myself outside Darian's memories—in a place unlike any I've seen.

CHAPTER EIGHT

THIS MUST NOT BE regular Headspace because I seem to have normal vision. All around me is vacuum-like blackness, and in the middle of it is a hologram, for lack of a better term.

A hologram of Darian.

If those green brain synapses from my biology class were to make up a ghostly person, this is what that would look like.

Darian's translucent form seems to be attached to the uncanny shape-entity that dragged me into this Headspace misadventure. However, I don't see that connection with my eyes.

I sense it with that special Headspace awareness.

The same awareness tells me that the entity seems to have grown.

No, that's not right. It got entangled with another entity.

This is when I look down and realize that I'm a

spindly synapse-hologram myself, only attached to the second shape-entity thingy.

"Don't be alarmed," Darian says.

Did he say those words in the traditional sense?

His ghostly lips did move, but I have a strong suspicion there's no air here to vibrate. And his translucent ears look like they lack eardrums—so I assume mine do too.

"What is this?" I ask him.

Cool. I can hear myself in my head as though I spoke in the real world.

"You thought of me inside Headspace." His ghostly figure floats up. "I was also in Headspace at the same time, so here we are." He points his finger at where the intertwined entities are.

"Sure," I say sarcastically. "That explains it all. Thanks."

He floats in my direction, but I instinctively float backward.

Neat. I can float too.

He hovers down so our eyes are parallel. "Allow me to explain. Did you think that Headspace is a space inside your own head, like the rather unfortunate title suggests?"

I shrug. I actually thought it might be some other dimension, but I haven't dwelled on it much after the initial conversation with Felix.

"Well, this encounter clearly disproves that common misconception." He nods in the direction of the otherworldly entities. "In actuality, it is the 'space' part of the term that's key. Headspace is a type of, well, *space*, that seers can all visit." He spreads his arms. "One is shared for all. And, in case it's not clear"—he again points at the two thingies we're hooked up to—"those are the manifestations of you and me as we appear in Headspace. Our current translucent bodies are but figments of our imaginations, used to facilitate conversation."

My head spins pretty well for being merely imaginary.

First, there were the Otherlands—which are essentially parallel universes. Now a confirmation that Headspace is another realm altogether—one completely alien to our usual three-dimensional one.

"It shouldn't be that huge of a surprise," Darian says, misunderstanding my silence. "You'd have to be outside time to see the future."

"I guess," I mutter, still processing the whole thing. "I just find the idea of 'outside time' difficult to wrap this translucent brain around."

"I can't blame you for that." He winks. "Seers more powerful than I failed to fully grasp Headspace. They simply learned to use it—for visions and to secretly communicate as we are doing now. Only it can be dangerous to communicate this way—which is why I accepted your summons today. I wanted to warn you."

"Dangerous?" I try to cross my arms across my chest, but they simply go through each other, like those of a ghost.

"It can be bad for one's sanity, for starters," Darian

says, his face the very definition of earnestness. "Seers sometimes experience hallucinations when first connecting this way. The more powerful the seer, the stronger these hallucinations can be—and the greater the danger. You should've been okay today, being new to your power and all that, but still, with that TV-powered raw talent, the risk was there." He looks at me intently, and as offhandedly as possible, he asks, "You didn't experience any strangeness, did you?"

"No," I lie—hopefully as seamlessly as he just did.

And lie he must have—with a skill rivaling that of a magician.

Unless… could it be that those memories I just saw were indeed hallucinations?

If so, why was I Darian in them, and more importantly, how come they fit my prior knowledge so well?

The memory/hallucination from the restaurant was exactly as I myself recall the events, and the one about Matilda fits the feud between Chester and Darian. Even the one of Darian and me in bed was something he once claimed to have seen in a vision.

In any case, if I *were* going to hallucinate about sleeping with someone, it would be with a partner even less suitable than Darian. Like, say, my boss…

Darian hovers an inch closer and with suspicious relief says, "I'm glad to hear you were spared the unpleasantness."

"Lucky, I guess," I lie. "How about you?"

He looks like he's trying to suppress a smile. "I was not as immune to the dreadful things as you."

Oh no.

Did he see one or more of *my* memories?

Is that why he looks on the verge of a smirk?

Please let it not be that time my period started in the middle of geometry class, or the time I slipped and fell down wet subway stairs. In a skirt. In front of the whole lacrosse team.

Then I realize there are worse things Darian could've witnessed, like anything involving Copperfield—my "massager."

All the myriad scenarios replay in front of my eyes, each worse than the next, like the times I fantasized about Criss Angel while using Copperfield... or that time I was thinking about Nero after Harper sexed me up.

For that matter, I hope he didn't see my memory of last night's kiss with Nero—though something tells me Darian wouldn't be in a humorous mood in *that* case.

"I hope it didn't drive you mad, your hallucination," I force myself to say with a straight face.

"Not yet." He finally lets his grin out. "But madness isn't the only danger from a chat such as this." His face grows more serious. "If one isn't careful, a more powerful seer can drain one's powers during an encounter in Headspace."

"Oh?" The curiosity makes me feel buoyant, and I catch myself floating up, just a little.

"In case you didn't know, longer visions are more

draining than shorter visions." He floats up so we stay on the same level.

"I noticed." As though in response to my irritation, I float down an inch. Why did he not warn me about power drainage in his tape? He easily could have.

"Talking this way is similar to having a vision." He again evens our gazes. "The longer we talk, the more power we use up."

"Crap." As though in response to my concern, I float down again.

Do positive emotions literally lift me up here and negative ones bring me down?

Darian seems to be able to float at will.

I will myself to float down and grin when it works.

"Yes." He looks at my bobbing up and down more patiently than I might've done in his shoes. "Another thing to bear in mind is that this type of conversation can only end when both of us wish it, or if someone runs out of power, or if a seer is willing to give up a huge burst of power to disconnect. So a more powerful seer can drain a weaker one this way."

"Sounds like a nasty trick." I catch myself floating down and will my hologram to stay on the same level. "Is that what you're doing now?"

"I'm actually trying to accomplish the opposite." He bobs up and down, like a float on a rippling lake. "I want to give you information as quickly as I can so we can both leave. Keep in mind that when it comes to raw power, I'm not sure you're the weaker seer here. Nor do I have any reason to drain you, in any case."

"If this form of communication is so dangerous, why would seers ever risk using it?" I let myself float up.

"Let's say you and I wanted to have a secret negotiation." He floats to my level. "Let's further assume we agreed to meet someplace on Earth, or in some Otherland at a given time in the future."

"Sure. Let's."

"Another seer can in theory have a vision of that conversation—annulling the secrecy of our meeting."

I float down but don't say a word.

He joins me and continues. "More importantly, if only one of us foresaw the conversation, he or she would have the upper hand in the actual negotiation."

"I think I understand." I steeple my fingers—only to discover that they go through one another like a fork through mist. "Even if we both saw visions of this hypothetical meeting, we could then see a new vision of the new future where we both know about the meeting, then another set of visions, recursively."

"Exactly. That is, until one of us runs out of power." He shakes his head. "You have a devious grasp of this, which confirms my long-held suspicion: you're becoming a seer to contend with."

"So, let me guess." I float up. "Headspace conversations cannot be foreseen."

"Exactly." He again floats up to my level.

"And that's why a weaker seer would be willing to take the risk associated with such a meeting," I say. "At least like this, they can be sure what they say isn't already known to the more powerful seer."

"That and total privacy." He looks at me intently with his strange holographic eyes.

Something clicks and I try to smack myself on the forehead—just to have my hand go through my imaginary head.

"This is why you're talking to me, despite Nero's ultimatum," I say. "Even if he had a seer on his payroll, that seer wouldn't know about this meeting. No one ever could."

"Unless you turn out to be a tattletale." He floats down, then catches himself and floats back up. "Even then, I'd see the ripples of your intent to tell him—like, say, me getting skewered in all foreseeable futures."

"Interesting." I catch myself before floating up and stay even with him. I need to learn to hide my emotions in this place. "I guess I won't tell on you... at least if you keep behaving like a gentleman."

"You won't find a more authentic gentleman," he says, his British accent thickening. "Now, I'm sorry to rush this, but I must."

"I understand," I say quickly. "I just want to ask you a few more questions."

What I leave unsaid is that by his own admission, he needs my willing participation to end this metaphysical chat without a huge expenditure of power.

"Proceed," he says, his face unreadable.

"Do I merely think of a seer I want to talk to in Headspace to initiate a call such as this?"

"It's more like you need to evoke their essence," he says. "But it will only work if the other seer is also in Headspace, which in itself is a tricky feat. It will also require that seer to *want* to accept your summons—and few will without a prior agreement."

"How can they reject my call?" I ask. "Do they simply not touch my shape in return?"

"It's more of a willpower thing," he says. "Though willing participation is usually required, some very powerful seers can force the call to happen. The safest action is to leave Headspace when any hint of a call is about to transpire, which is basically when you see anything but the vision shapes."

"Leave Headspace?" I float up. "How do I do that?"

"Oh, that is simplicity itself." He floats up too, a smile touching the corners of his ghostly lips. "You just need to touch yourself." He says this deadpan, but I can tell he's suppressing another annoying smile. "I'm confident you can figure *that* out."

I float down almost a foot.

He must've indeed seen my memory pertaining to Copperfield—what else could he be implying with that?

Hey, at least I have never thought of *him* during my sessions. Or have I?

Wait, I need to focus on the important part.

It sounds like I can leave Headspace without having a vision by *metaphysically* touching myself.

As in, doing what I do to shapes to myself—nothing dirty about that.

If this works the way I suspect, it could be very useful when it comes to my Headspace practice—

"Time is of the essence," Darian says, and I suspect that if he had a watch, he'd look at it just then.

"Fine, but can we do this again?" I will myself to float back up so we're on equal eye level. "I want to learn more—"

"I'm sorry." He looks down at the darkness below us. "I fear we will not be able to talk again anytime soon. Either in this fashion or in person."

As disappointing as that statement is, there are interesting implications there. It might mean we just used up so much of his power that he will need to recover for a while. If true, and assuming I don't completely lose my powers for just as long, this could allow me to gauge which of us is a more powerful seer.

Or he could simply be low on power now because he used some earlier today.

"Don't be so glum," he says. "Distance makes the heart grow fonder and all that."

"Sure. Keep dreaming." I bob up and down like a feather in the wind. "How am I supposed to learn to be a seer then?"

"Not from Nero, that's for sure," he says, his ghostly features darkening. "Speaking of him, I wanted to tell you something of dire importance." He slides down a noticeable distance, then floats back up. "Do *not* fall for Nero... I'm telling you this as a seer, not as a man."

I nearly choke on the million possible replies that range from, "It's none of your business," to, "That was never going to happen anyway, so don't worry your pretty little head over it."

I settle for something in the middle of those extremes and with exaggerated sarcasm say, "I'll take that under advisement. Any *other* pearls of wisdom you wish to impart?"

"Practice your seer powers," he says. "It's a matter of life and death in a much nearer future."

I drop two feet down. "What do you mean by that? Whose life or death? What is going to happen to them? Is there something specific I need to worry about?"

"Yes," he says. "Your priority is your—"

I don't hear what Darian says next because in that very moment, our conversation short-circuits.

CHAPTER NINE

"NO!" I try to scream, but there's no way to scream when you're exiting a vision—which is what just happened.

I find myself sitting on my meditation cushion, back in Nero's metal cage.

"Your *what?*" I shout, but to no avail.

He could've been about to say "your friend" or "your mother" or "your unborn child."

I punch the cushion beneath me in frustration.

That was clearly an important warning.

Plus, I had so many more questions.

Did Darian know my father?

If so, did he also know my mother?

I launch to my feet and start pacing from metal wall to metal wall.

Why did the conversation end so abruptly? Did Darian lie when he said it couldn't be ended by him without my consent, or did one of us run out of seer juice after all?

If it's the latter, I hope it wasn't me, or if it was me, I hope I recover soon so that I can practice my powers, as he advised.

Not that I need that advice. I was going to practice my powers in any case.

Something tells me it wasn't me who ran out of power. I had that multi-hour vision about playing video games with Felix and recovered in a few days. Our conversation lasted a few minutes at the most.

Unless those conversations use more power than visions do.

I stop pacing.

I need to calm down and try to go into Headspace again.

If it works, it probably means Darian ran out of power.

Does this mean I'm more powerful?

No.

Like I surmised before, he could've had a long vision recently and was running low on juice when he got my call.

I catch myself pacing again and stop next to the screen with Nero's digital countdown.

I've only completed an hour of my eight-hour allotment.

Any hope of relaxation bursts when I realize how cooped up I'm already feeling.

I pull out my phone to check on my emails.

At first, it seems that I have none, but then I see it.

No cell connectivity or Wi-Fi.

Now this is just cruel, even for Nero.

Am I supposed to be like some modern-day Robinson Crusoe, stuck on this uninhabited island without internet access? Actually, I'm more of an Edmond Dantès —put in a horrific prison by a traitorous enemy.

I take a deep breath.

I have to seriously figure out a way to calm down.

Then I recall that Nero left me some comforts that Count Monte Cristo lacked in his cell at Château d'If.

Going into the bathroom, I turn on the faucet for the shiny new Jacuzzi.

Leaving the hot water to pour, I navigate my way into the kitchen and fix myself a gourmet snack.

Impossibly, the escargot is even better than it looks.

Did Nero's private chef make this?

I go for seconds, then thirds.

Hmm. I'll have to watch my weight if I stay in this room for eight hours every day. With food this yummy and no place to exercise, I might easily balloon out of control.

Done with food, I head back into the bathroom. The water in the Jacuzzi is just right, so I close the door, pray Nero isn't watching, and take off my clothes.

The jets in the tub are almost as good as a massage therapist, and I soon find myself relaxing, especially when the food coma arrives.

Once I'm good and pruney, I gingerly leave the tub and dry off.

Now I'm ready to meditate.

I assume the position and start the breathing.

Soon after, I find myself in Headspace.

I FLOAT AMONG THE SHAPES, musing.

Seems like I had some seer power still in the tank.

I sense my surroundings as though for the first time.

This is a *place*.

A location.

If any seer, anywhere in the multitude of Otherlands, is currently trying to get a vision, they're here somewhere, also surrounded by shapes not unlike these ones.

Could I meet one by chance?

How big is Headspace?

If my intuition is right, Headspace might be vast—a whole universe size or larger, making a chance meeting unlikely.

Which is probably for the best, given what Darian told me.

I wonder... could I chat with him again so soon?

Thinking about Darian makes me recall the happy look on the face of Sasha from the strange future—a future where she seems to care for Darian.

I refuse to think I would've ended up in that position otherwise—pun intended.

Do I want that future?

The shapes around me change as I ponder this question, but Darian doesn't show up.

Well, I didn't expect him to. Clearly, he's the one who ran out of mojo.

Suddenly, an idea occurs to me.

My biological father is a seer.

Could I call him in Headspace?

Pulsing with excitement, I think the word "father" over and over to myself.

Nothing happens.

Crap.

I might need to evoke his essence, whatever that is —which might be tricky to do, given that I know nothing about him.

"Grigori Rasputin," I think over and over.

No luck.

I try to recall everything I've read about the man.

Zilch.

I dwell on fictional accounts, like his villainous roles in the *Anastasia* cartoon and the *Hellboy* franchise.

This time, I'm glad it doesn't work. If his essence were anything like those fictional depictions, I'm not sure I'd want to meet him.

When I tire of futilely summoning my biological father, I contemplate using the same method to summon my biological mother—assuming she's also a seer.

I try my best, but it doesn't yield any fruit.

Then something occurs to me.

I shouldn't "Headspace call" important people like Rasputin when my powers are as drained as they are; else what happened to Darian will happen to me.

If I want to practice my powers today, I think I'd better focus on the concept of leaving Headspace that Darian mentioned.

Right.

That might let me leave and come back here over and over, until I learn to activate visions as smoothly as Darian did in his memory.

If I had lungs, I would sigh.

All I now need is to touch myself.

CHAPTER TEN

OKAY, Darian definitely made this task harder by turning the idea dirty.

At least I think that's why I'm having trouble with this.

I don't even know where to start.

When I activate a shape here in Headspace, there does seem to be some sort of an appendage involved, but I have trouble feeling it now—especially in reference to myself.

The problem is that I don't know where I am. What passes for my senses doesn't have the capacity to "look at self."

Wait a second.

Maybe this works like those calls?

In that case, maybe the first step is for me to think of my own essence?

Easier said than done, though. What the heck is my essence?

Darian thought of me as bold in his memory—and I might agree, to a point. I'm definitely bold when it comes to the methods of my magic, but I'm less sure about my boldness outside that context.

He also called me adaptable and creative—but I'm not sure how much of that is true either, at least outside my performing persona.

I do get playful with the audience as he suggested, but is that something that can be considered my essence?

I'm not sure I'd think of myself as brave either—which is something else he thought. There are spheres of my life where I'm not brave at all. My love life is a great example.

As to the idea of me being, and I quote, "bloody gorgeous," that is ridiculous. I'm cute, at best, and more importantly, I don't see my appearance as part of my essence at all.

My bout of introspection doesn't yield any results. Does that mean I need to dig deeper into my essence?

Who would've thought that "touching yourself" could feel so much like a therapy session with Lucretia?

I'm sneaky, I'll admit *that*. I try to channel my mischievous deviousness into my illusions, but it doesn't always work. Sometimes Felix ends up with a keyboard that sprouts greenery, or super-sour cake—

Something finally happens.

Wow.

Trippy.

This is what those out-of-body experiences must feel like—except I didn't have a body to begin with.

Metaphysics aside, I sense the shape I was connected to during the Headspace chat with Darian.

Somewhere in my nonexistent gut, I know that this is *me*.

Now I just have to figure out a way to "touch" her/it.

This part is easy, though.

I do what I've done with shapes—and Darian's version of the entity.

First things first, however. My Darian-dirtied-up mind demands I change some earlier terminology. Henceforth, what I dubbed my metaphysical and nebulous *appendage* is going to be called my *ethereal wisp*.

Because if I'm going to "touch myself," I'd rather do it with that than anything that brings to mind tentacles of a Lovecraftian monstrosity.

So, using my ethereal wisp, I finally touch myself.

And feel as though I implode—straight out of Headspace.

I look around the metal cell that is now my office.

I did it.

I left Headspace without having to see a vision.

Did that use up any seer power?

The best way to find that out is to try to go into Headspace again.

Before I do so, I take out my phone and find a playlist Felix made for me. I locate a song on it by

Divinyls called "I Touch Myself" and press play, grinning the whole time.

The meditation goes better to the upbeat music, and I return to Headspace faster than ever.

I stumble a little when it comes to summoning my Headspace self once again, but I do get it to work—after which point I touch the summoned me with the ethereal wisp and find myself back in Nero's metal cage.

I repeat the whole ordeal over and over, until my legs cramp up.

Getting up, I fix myself another snack.

I can now exit Headspace almost seamlessly—though I'm far from Darian-proficient when it comes to entering it.

I should probably train some more. It's not like I have anything better to do with my jail-like "work allotment."

I sit on the chair and get into Headspace, then swiftly get out.

I do this over and over until I do it as well on a chair as in a lotus pose.

Next, I try doing it standing—which works out, just takes somewhat longer.

So I practice getting into Headspace standing until my legs really hurt.

I'm now just as good doing this standing as I was sitting.

I check Nero's countdown.

I have an hour left.

Time really flies when you set yourself a task.

Mastering Headspace reminds me of the years' worth of hours I put into learning sleight of hand. That practice also made the time fly.

Standing by the digital pad, I get inside Headspace once more but do not exit.

I should at least try getting the slave driver his stock tip.

Thinking green and minty thoughts doesn't work, so I try to think of happy Nero instead, figuring making money brings him joy and all that.

A shape shows up in front of me.

It's a room-temperature, red, caviar-tasting snowflake-ish thing with safe melodious music emanating from it.

Seems like my life isn't in danger in the vision—else the music would be less friendly.

That's a great sign. Stocks tips aren't usually dangerous. At least not to one's immediate survival.

I zoom in on the shape a few times to make sure the resulting vision will be nice and short. I don't want to use up too much of my power supply all at once.

Happy with the size of the shape, I will my ethereal wisp to touch it—and tumble into a vision.

———

TIME SEEMS to slow as I focus on Nero's face, blocking out everything else.

My fist flies forward and, to my utter shock, smacks

into his jaw.

Even through the glove, my hand screams in pain.

Nero, however, doesn't seem to care. It's like I just gave him a boring stock tip instead of committing aggravated assault.

No. There *is* emotion on his face; it's just well hidden.

Does he look satisfied?

What—

———

I OPEN my eyes and find myself still standing by the digital screen.

I furtively stare around the room as though Nero could've somehow spied on what just happened inside my mind—or wherever the visions occur.

That is what I got when I tried to summon a vision of him happy?

Me punching his smug face?

Does that mean he's a secret masochist? If so, given how much he keeps pissing me off, perhaps that vision I saw was us reaching a mutually beneficial arrangement?

Jokes aside, though, what was my future self thinking in that vision? Who punches the boogeyman of the Cognizant community—not to mention her Mentor and boss?

Between Darian's wet dream and this, I'm beginning to get the feeling that my future self doesn't think before she does things—not as much as I would in her shoes. Whatever happened to being older and wiser?

I check the work allotment timer.

Not done yet.

I sit back on the cushion and try to get into Headspace.

And fail.

I try it once more and fail again.

Looks like I ran out of juice after all—at least for now.

Hopefully, I'll be as good as new tomorrow.

Making my way into the kitchen, I eat again, then spend the rest of my time with a deck of cards in my hand, rehearsing my favorite moves.

When the hated timer finally reaches zero, the big metal door swings open, revealing Nero.

I walk up to the door, but he blocks my way.

We stare at each other like two cowboys about to draw their guns.

I blink first. "Can I go?"

"The stock suggestion," he says. "Give it, and you can leave."

I take a breath. "You should go long ML Macadamia Orchards." Fighting to keep a serious expression, I add, "Their stock ticker is NUT."

"Oh, I know *that*," Nero says, his expression unreadable. "What I want to know is: did you use your time in the room productively?"

"Sure," I say, trying not to think about the Jacuzzi

session. "Totally."

He frowns. "Let me be more specific. Did you utilize your powers?"

"I made some very good progress with my powers today," I say carefully.

I can't forget the man is a walking polygraph exam.

The frown upgrades to narrowed eyes. "Let me be even more specific. Did you use your power to guess the stock market for me today?"

"Yes," I say. "I did."

Of course, I only did it for a little while, and failed at it, but hopefully, it doesn't make my affirmative statement register as false to his truth-recognizing ears. If he then assumes I got the NUT recommendation using my powers, and not because he is driving me nuts, that is his problem, not mine.

He relaxes.

I exhale a breath I didn't realize I've been holding.

"Why is this so important to you?" I ask, though I'm not sure why I care.

Looking noticeably *less* satisfied, he raises an eyebrow.

"To lock me up, I mean." I stand up straighter. "All so that you can get richer when you're already rich as sin."

He steps toward me. "Giving you a chance to use your powers isn't—"

"Please don't make this about me." I step back.

"Your car is waiting," he says and turns on his heel.

"Wait, what car?" I ask, but he's already ahead.

Annoyed, I follow him as he walks with those long strides.

I'm huffing and puffing by the time we get into the elevator. But hey, at least I'm burning off one of the snacks.

He presses the button for the lobby, and I notice he doesn't need his special card to get us off the secret floor, only to get *to* it.

We ride up in sullen silence.

Then, without turning, Nero says, "It's not about wealth."

"Making money isn't about wealth?" I'm shocked my earlier question is actually getting answered.

The muscles in his back tense up. I fight the urge to give him a little backrub because—what is wrong with me?

"It's about power," he says, still facing away. "And power is survival."

The elevator dings before I get a chance to follow up.

Nero strides out so fast you'd think he's running away from me.

Confused, I follow. Power is survival? What does that even mean?

Lost in thought, I exit the lobby... and slam into Nero's hard body with a loud smack.

If this were a cartoon, I'd slide off him into a puddle on the floor, but in this very real reality, he just gently grabs me by the shoulders, as though to make sure I'm steady on my feet.

And all I can do is stupidly ponder: when did he stop his brisk pace and turn around?

"Are you okay?" he half whispers, half growls.

I recover enough of my wits to look up at him and mutter through my dry throat, "Fine."

The gleam in those blue-gray eyes makes it clear he detected my lie.

"This is your car." Nero gently turns me toward the road, and I see a sleek limo standing there. "It will be taking you home."

A limo?

That's new.

What—

"Wear something sporty tomorrow," Nero says from behind me.

"Excuse me?" I turn around to stare at him.

"You're going to meet me in the gym at seven a.m.," he says. "Do not be late."

"What?" I look at him for signs of amusement and find none.

"A sports bra would work nicely," he says—and this time, there might be a hint of mirth touching his eyes. "Perhaps yoga pants?" He looks me up and down. "I'm sure you can figure it out."

I inhale a lungful of air, preparing a tirade, but before I get a chance to unleash it, Nero turns and stalks back into the building.

Was he serious?

Workout clothes? Gym?

Unless… could he also be worried that I'll put on

weight with all that sitting around inside his gourmet-food-stocked cell? If so, that's so wrong, and probably illegal too.

An orc-sized driver exits the limo and opens the door for me.

I examine the guy carefully, trying to decide if he's actually an orc.

There's no aura, but the orcs who worked for Nero didn't have one either. But the driver also has no makeup on his face—a much better clue.

Tentatively, I decide he's just an extremely beefy human.

"Thanks," I say when I get inside the car.

He just nods and closes the door.

Is he unable to talk?

I wouldn't put it past Nero to give me a driver with damaged vocal chords or a missing tongue.

Since the partition to the front is raised, I don't get a chance to test his ability to speak further. Instead, I explore my surroundings.

The limo is impossibly fancier inside than it was outside.

I eat a spoonful of black caviar, pour myself a glass of $100 per liter Vieille Bon Secours beer, then watch the big-screen TV as I relax on the super-comfy loveseat that turns out to be a full-featured massage chair.

A girl can get used to this kind of commuting.

We stop sooner than I'd expected. We must've been driving faster than it seemed.

The big guy opens the door and even offers me his hand.

Deciding to ignore the hand, I climb out and say thanks—but he doesn't talk back.

Approaching the building, I'm shocked to see that the place looks completely repaired.

My usual key opens the new door without a problem, and the elevator works just as well as it did before I crashed into it.

Pondering Nero's power over repairmen and subcontractors, I make my way to the apartment.

The image that greets me when I enter makes me want to rub my eyes in disbelief.

The cat and the chinchilla are sleeping snuggled together in the hallway—like the proverbial lion lying with the lamb.

I wonder which of them is the lion, though: Lucifur, being the cat, or Fluffster, being the one that can rip you into little pieces?

Tiptoeing over the odd pair, I walk into the living room.

Noises from Felix's room make me curious, so I gently knock.

"Come in," Felix says.

A computer chip crunches under my foot as I step in.

"Dude," I say. "What the hell?"

The room looks like Intel's biggest factory exploded into a random collection of transistors, cables, and other assorted hardware.

Felix puts down his soldering iron and looks at me with a smile.

"Did you rob a RadioShack?" I ask. "Or was it the Apple Store?"

"I smuggled some of this from Gomorrah," Felix whispers conspiratorially. "I was visiting Ariel and—"

"Ariel?" I shriek so forcefully that Felix cringes. "How is she doing?"

"Hard to say. They're using various methods to keep her comfortable, but the side effect is that it's unclear how aware she is."

"I'd like to see her," I say. "Can we go together next time?"

"Sure," Felix says. "I'll be home early tomorrow, so we can go then."

"I'll try to get home early too," I say, then frown. "Nero is very strict about me putting in the eight hours, but I figure if I start the day extra early, I should make it."

Matching actions to words, I pull out my phone and set the alarm. A visit to Ariel aside, I don't want to find out what happens if I don't show up at the gym at exactly seven, as Nero demanded.

"About Nero." Felix looks down at the various computer parts littering the floor. "What happened after you hung up?"

"Nothing," I say, and suddenly develop my own fascination with the hardware Armageddon on the floor. "You're pretty much up to speed as far as that's concerned."

Felix is the last person I'd tell about seeing Nero naked, or about the kiss.

"Oh." He looks up. "It seemed there was more to it."

"Nope. Good night."

I escape before Felix asks anything more. Getting to my room, I prepare my cutest tank top. Then I choose a particularly nice pair of fishnet-stockings-inspired yoga pants from my closet—ones with holes on the sides that show a decent amount of skin.

Will this be "sporty" enough? Hard to say without knowing what Nero has in mind for me tomorrow.

Whatever it is, I have a feeling I won't like it.

Oh, and if Nero is just playing a joke on me with this outfit, my payback prank will be more devastating than the legendary fish brains I once left in a bully's locker in high school.

I know just the thing, too. I'll buy a durian fruit in Chinatown and leave it to rot in some nook and cranny of Nero's office. The stuff smells so bad that an Australian university once evacuated five hundred people when they mistook the pungent odor for a gas leak.

Getting in bed, I smile as I imagine the expression on Nero's face when he first notices the malodorous development.

Does his super speed come with super smell? That would be even better.

The evil thoughts lull me into sleep, but once in the arms of slumber, my dreams about Nero morph from vengeful into X-rated.

CHAPTER ELEVEN

MY ALARM BLARES.

A furry creature whooshes under my blanket.

"Fluffster?" I rub sleep from my eyes.

Checking under the blanket, I see that it's *not* Fluffster.

Lucifur looks at me sternly, with eyes that seem to be saying, "This royal blanket is Our Majesty's property. What is a peasant like you doing trespassing?"

The door to the room creaks, followed by the pitter-patter of tiny feet on the floor.

The cat hides her head under the blanket.

Fluffster jumps onto the bed, squeaks, and jumps after Lucifur.

Confused, I swiftly extricate myself from the whirlwind of furry activity under the blanket.

"Fluffster, what the hell?" I say as I start putting on my athletic outfit.

"We're playing hide-and-seek, like you and me did back in the day," he says in my mind. "If I don't keep this beast busy, she'll destroy every expensive piece of pottery in the house."

As though to punctuate his words, he rushes from under the blanket, with Lucifur literally on his bushy tail.

"Sure," I say under my breath when the excited hissing and squeals navigate into Ariel's room. "You're just doing it out of domovoi duty, not because you *love* hide-and-seek."

Fluffster doesn't reply, so I finish dressing, then stumble into the kitchen and set up food for the two hide-and-seekers.

Grabbing a quick sandwich to eat on the way, I head out.

I'm not surprised to find the limo waiting for me. I wouldn't even be that shocked if I found out it stood here all night.

"Morning," I say to the mute driver as he holds open the door for me.

He nods and closes the door behind me.

Ditching my sandwich, I attack the snack bar.

The limo delivers me to the office just as I finish my feast.

Wiping remnants of truffle oil from my lips, I exit my ride.

A few former floormates give me strange looks when they see me climb out of a fancy limo, and a few more do the same when they notice my outfit.

When I press the button for the gym floor, the elevator neighbors seem to nod in understanding. They must think I have a proper outfit stashed in a locker.

It's 6:59 a.m. when I arrive at the gym's entrance.

Nero is standing there, staring at his watch.

Like me, he's dressed in exercise clothes, and they look just as right on his muscular frame as his usual button-up shirts and dress pants. If I didn't know he was in finance, I'd guess him to be either a swimmer or a gymnast… or maybe a martial arts champion. All in all, he looks way too nice to—

"Cutting it a little close," Nero says without looking up, dispelling the "nice" sentiment.

How did he know it was me without looking up? Did he smell me?

"Good morning to you too," I reply evenly. "What's on the agenda today?"

Nero looks up from his phone and gives me a once-over from sneakers to ponytail.

He steps toward me.

I step back.

His nostrils flare, and the limbal rings in his eyes do that widening thing.

"You said to wear something sporty," I say, fighting a strange panicked feeling.

A man clears his throat behind Nero.

My boss turns so fast he startles both me and the newcomer.

The new guy has a Cognizant aura and looks like Po—the hero in the *Kung Fu Panda* franchise. Those

Uncle Fester-like dark circles around his eyes further add to the impression, as does the rounded belly visible though his black-and-white tracksuit.

"I'm ready when you are," the new guy says, and he even sounds like he looks.

Is there such a thing as a werepanda?

Without waiting for a reply, the stranger walks back into the gym.

"Let's go," Nero tells me over his shoulder as he follows the guy.

The gym is empty as we walk through it. Did Nero clear it for us?

We stop next to the room where yoga and the other classes usually meet.

"Put these on." Nero hands me knee pads, a boxing helmet, a mouth guard, and a pair of gloves that look vaguely familiar.

I don the gear and examine the room.

Someone put a thick mat on the floor there, and the panda guy stands on the mat, legs apart, in a martial arts stance not unlike the one his bear counterpart would assume in the cartoon.

"Sasha, this is Bentley," Nero says. "Bentley, this is Sasha."

I give Bentley a beauty-pageant wave with my glove, and he smiles a round-cheeked grin at me.

Nero gives him a stern look, and the man's face turns serious.

"Bentley will be your martial arts trainer," Nero says, facing me. "You have a penchant for getting into trouble, so as your Mentor, I decided to arrange for you to be able to take care of yourself."

Wow. You know your shenanigans are out of control when Nero is finally forced to fulfill his Mentor duties.

"Okay," I say with nervous excitement as I step onto the mat. "How is this going to work?"

"Assessment first," Bentley says, his grin coming back with a vengeance. "Hit me. If you can."

"Okay, Morpheus," I mutter and walk toward my opponent. "You asked for it."

I swing a fist at Bentley's copious tummy.

My hand whooshes through empty air.

Grinning even wider, Bentley stands two feet away from where he was a moment ago.

Though I expected him to do something like that—him being a teacher of martial arts and all—I still underestimated him. It's a mistake I don't intend to make again.

I put my fists in front of me as misdirection and aim a kick at Bentley's shin.

My magic-inspired attack fails.

Bentley's leg isn't where I thought it would be.

"I said hit, not kick," he says jauntily. "But either would—"

I swing at him before he finishes his sentence.

He moves before my fist connects with his temple.

"Stop *trying* to hit me and hit me." He winks at me.

Did he hang out with Felix before he came here?

That's a second quote from Felix's favorite scene in *The Matrix*.

I attack—and fail.

Then again.

And four more times.

Sweat beads roll down my forehead as I pant.

To my chagrin, Bentley looks less winded than a panda eating a bamboo leaf.

The next time I try to hit him, he catches my wrist and with the most miniscule move makes me faceplant onto the mat.

The fall hurts my pride slightly more than my face.

Groaning, I roll to the side and get on my feet, panting like a marathon winner.

In my peripheral vision, Nero looks annoyed.

"That settles it," Bentley says. "I think I'm done assessing you."

I look at Nero for a reaction, but his earlier annoyance has been replaced with a careless, stone-cold expression.

"I'm going to start by teaching you a fighting style used by the nuns in the Jinto mountains," Bentley says.

I struggle to catch my breath. "Geography isn't my strong suit, but I've never heard of mountains by that name."

"You haven't?" He looks at Nero with a "what have you been teaching her?" look. "They're the tallest, most sacred of the dead volcanos on Voikomlya."

I shrug. "Still doesn't ring a bell, I'm afraid."

"It's one of the Otherlands," Bentley says with

exasperation. "The nuns in question are into two rather mutually exclusive activities: self-defense and fasting." He rubs his belly as though in defiance of the very idea of skipping a meal. "That's why I think the style would be perfect for you. Though not as emaciated as the nuns"—he looks me up and down—"you're pretty puny, and their style of fighting should fit you perfectly."

Nero nods approvingly. Does *he* think I'm puny? Because I'm totally not.

"First, let me teach you the stance," Bentley says and walks up to me. He stops so near I can smell the cookie-dough on his breath.

"Put your leg like this," he says, grabbing my yoga-pant-clad leg and pulling it forward.

As he positions my other leg, his sausage-like fingers tickle my skin though the holes in my pants, and I can't help but giggle.

Nero folds his arms across his chest, his expression turning stormy.

"Now your hands," Bentley says and positions my arms in an insectoid pattern that I doubt I'll ever be able to replicate on my own.

He then gets into the same pose—which makes him look like a black-and-white lovebug standing on its hind legs.

"Thrust your arm out like this." He executes a tai-chi-like maneuver.

I repeat his gesture to the best of my ability.

"No." He grabs my wrist and moves my arm as though I were a marionette. "Like this."

Nero's expression grows darker. He must think I really suck.

Ignoring my boss, I repeat the gesture—doing my best to mirror the movement required.

"That's better," Bentley says. "But it should be more like this."

He grabs my wrist once more and shows me the proper arc again.

Nero looks on the verge of ripping apart orcs.

Damn. Someone *really* wants me to get good at self-defense double quick.

Doing my best to avoid somehow triggering my boss's ire, I repeat the motion as carefully as I can.

"Good. Finally," Bentley says. "Now do this with your other arm."

He shows me a new move that looks even trickier.

I fail.

Bentley walks over and grabs my wrist.

"Enough," Nero growls so viciously that both Bentley and I flinch.

"Your own pose is lacking," Nero says to Bentley. "You're supposed to stand like this."

He assumes the pose Bentley was teaching me, and I have to admit, the pose looks much more natural when my lean, fit boss does it.

"I didn't realize you knew the technique." Bentley smiles nervously at Nero. "I just—"

"Watch me," Nero says and walks onto the mat.

Shuffling his feet, Bentley goes to where Nero stood earlier, while my boss takes the stance again.

I do my best to replicate it and find it is easier to do so now that I'm copying Nero. Perhaps because my eyes enjoy roaming over the grooves of those muscles and the—

"Move your left leg an inch back," Nero barks at me. "And lift your right hand two inches."

Though I'm tempted to tell him that a "please" would be nice, I just do as he instructs.

"Now." Nero walks over to me and stands within slapping distance. "Do the strike from before, but like this." He performs his own version of Bentley's maneuver, and as he does it, it looks like a cobra striking a fluffy mouse.

"I'll hit you if I do it now," I say uncertainly.

"If you do, I'll deposit ten thousand into your savings account." He smirks. "If you couldn't hit Bentley, I'm pretty safe."

Bentley clears his throat. "I'm not sure you're paying me enough for verbal abuse."

I don't wait for them to settle their differences.

My only chance to make the ten grand is a sneak attack—though I don't know the fancy move well enough. Then again, Nero only said "if you hit me." He didn't clarify that it had to be a strike in the proper Jinto-nun style.

I make my hands into fists as time seems to slow. Blocking out everything else, I focus on Nero's smug face.

My fist flies forward and, to my utter shock, smacks into his jaw.

Even through the gloves, my hand screams in pain.

Wait a minute. I saw a vision about this yesterday.

Just like in my vision, Nero doesn't look the least bit hurt.

Also like in the vision, there's a hint of satisfaction on his face.

He looks meaningfully at Bentley.

Bentley shrugs. "She didn't use the move."

"But she landed a hit on *me*," Nero says. "With proper motivation—"

"Do I get the money?" I ask.

"A deal is a deal," Nero says. "Now if you'd like, I'll give you a chance to make even more money. All you have to do is land another hit, but in the proper style, at least once this week. If you do, I'll give you ten times your winnings so far."

My breath catches. "And if I lose?"

"I keep my ten thousand," Nero says. "What do you say?"

"Deal," I say and try to sucker-punch him with my best imitation of the move Bentley showed me—hopefully before my words even reach Nero's ears.

My boss moves his head exponentially faster than Bentley.

My fist misses the target.

Then, with a touch so soft it feels like a lover's caress, Nero manages to make me lose my balance, and I plop onto the mat.

"Your form was atrocious." Nero extends a hand to help me up. I let him get me to my feet and pretend to be mildly concussed. "Though you do deserve some brownie points for trying to seize the element of surprise."

As suddenly as I can, I lash out with the move again.

Nero's head isn't where it was a second ago.

Somehow, I end up on the mat again, and as I lie there for a moment, a simple truth becomes clear: the bastard played me. He *let* me hit him that first time, knowing full well I will become like a gambler chasing that original dopamine high. And the worst part is that knowing about his scheme doesn't make it any less tempting to hit him again—and not just because ten thousand (or a hundred) are riding on this or because of the smug expression on his face.

I *want* to learn to defend myself.

He extends his hand again, and I lean on it as I get to my feet, then try to hit his midsection—figuring he never said I had to hit his face.

His torso isn't where it was a moment ago—and neither is his hand.

Losing the support, I fall.

This time, my back smacks into the mat at a strange angle, causing the air to painfully vacate my lungs.

"Ouch," I pant when I can make a sound. "I hope you have a chiropractor booked after this."

Nero kneels on the mat next to me and examines me closely, his expression unreadable.

Now would be a great moment to deck him, except I'm still catching my breath.

"Why don't you learn proper technique for a while,"

Nero suggests. "You'll then have an advantage when you execute your sneak attack—plus I'm less likely to see it if you lull me into complacency with good behavior."

It's annoying when Nero is right.

Whenever I need a new sleight-of-hand maneuver for an illusion, I rehearse the movements involved until they become instinctive. Hitting him isn't that different from fooling him with an effect, so my usual illusionist approach is the way to go.

Starting with this cobra punch, or whatever it's called.

Grunting, I roll over and start pushing myself up.

Strong hands land on my bare shoulders, helping me with the task.

My breath catches again, and warm electricity pulses through my body.

Oh no. Not going there.

Pushing away the unwelcome sensations, I assume the prerequisite pose.

Nero steps up and places his hand on my right leg— presumably to correct my stance.

Why, oh why did I wear yoga pants with holes in them?

I can feel Nero's calloused palms on the sensitive skin of my thighs, and martial arts are increasingly far from my mind.

Seemingly oblivious to my discomfort, Nero corrects my left leg next—leaving it tingly and aching for more touch.

"Bend like this." He places a big, warm hand on my lower back and gently pushes me forward. "You should feel tension in your core." His fingers brush against my abs—and I do indeed start to feel *something* in my core, but probably not what he meant.

"Now your arms," he says and touches my right shoulder, spreading liquid heat—

"Perhaps you two should get a room?" Bentley says, unzipping his tracksuit. His cheeks are flushed, and he looks like he'd rather be anywhere else.

This is what those pandas in zoos must feel—the ones forced to watch panda porn as motivation to propagate their dwindling species.

Nero steps back and glares at Bentley. "You're fired." His voice is sharp enough to skewer. "You did an acceptable job figuring out what style she should learn, so you'll get paid for that, but—"

Bentley bolts out of the room as though chased by a forest fire.

"Now, where were we?" Nero looks me over.

I clear my dry throat. "The position. You were showing me how to—"

"Right." He effortlessly assumes the prerequisite stance. "Hit the air this time around."

I do.

"No," he says. "Like this."

His muscular arm pierces the air with an audible whoosh. "Now you."

I try it as well as I can.

Nero winces. Approaching, he grabs my arm and directs my motion.

I swallow. Now that we're alone, I feel his touch all the more.

Am I screwing up my movements so that he touches me?

No. That's a silly theory.

"Focus," Nero murmurs, letting go of me. "Part of any martial art is being in the present moment—conscious and aware."

"Right," I croak. "Got it."

"Now do it again."

I execute the move.

He nods approvingly, walks over to the corner of the room, and pulls on a pair of punch mitts.

My guess is, they're there to make it easier on me rather than him.

"Now hit one of these that exact way," Nero says, putting his covered hands out. "Do your best to keep the form as you move."

I punch his right mitt, then his left.

A droplet of sweat rolls from my face into my sports bra, and I notice Nero's gaze following it.

I flush. I guess I'm not the only one affected by this.

Shaking it off, I try to focus. Nero is distracted, so now is as good a time as any to make that hundred grand.

Pretending I'm about to hit his mitt, I go for his face instead.

He ducks effortlessly, then smirks.

"Not bad. You may yet succeed. Now keep hitting the mitts."

I do as he says, channeling all my pent-up frustration into the pummeling.

As far as workouts go, this is a great one.

At least, I hope my skyrocketing heart rate is due to the physical activity and not someone's proximity.

After a few more minutes of this, Nero grunts approvingly.

Encouraged, I repeat the movement, over and over, until my muscles start to burn.

"You're getting better," Nero says after a few more minutes of grueling exercise.

I want to say, "Shall we test this theory?" but throw a punch at his face instead of at the soft mitt.

Before I even finish the movement, something similar to my driving intuition tells me this attempt will fail, so I follow with a punch with the other hand, aiming for where I think Nero might end up by dodging the first.

My first punch hits air and pulls me slightly forward.

The second stops a nanometer from Nero's surprised face.

Does it mean I *almost* got him?

I don't get a chance to figure out the answer because Nero taps me with his finger just as I regain balance after the second punch.

Flailing my arms, I start to fall.

If I'm going down, I'm bringing my tormentor with me.

Turning my hand into a grabbing claw, I grasp Nero's shirt on my way down.

There's a sound of ripped clothing, followed by a muffled curse.

My back hits the mat again.

Nero tumbles at me, but manages to gracefully land on top in a pushup position—arms straight and hands planted firmly on my wrists.

My pulse surges into the stratosphere, and my breathing goes from ragged to supersonic.

He bends his arms as though showing off his pushup skills.

Is he about to kiss me again?

He stops just outside kissing distance, his own breath fast and muscles tense under the large rip I made in his shirt.

"I think this is enough for today," he mutters, seemingly an hour of staring later. "We will resume this tomorrow at seven."

He leaps to his feet with supernatural speed, but I let myself lie there for a couple of seconds, mostly to catch my breath.

When I'm feeling semi-human again, I accept Nero's extended hand and get to my feet.

Do this again?

And to think, yesterday I worried about getting out of shape, of all things.

CHAPTER TWELVE

WE ENTER MY METAL CELL, and Nero sets the timer again.

"Eight hours?" I almost try my luck at making the hundred grand by punching him in the face right now.

"The martial arts training is part of your Mentorship." He walks toward the exit and over the shoulder adds, "Please have a stock tip ready for me when you're done."

He leaves the room, and a moment later, the impenetrable door seals shut.

I stare at the keypad on the door device, reminding myself of the severe penalty if I try to guess the password and fail.

At least Nero said *please* this time around.

I don't remember him saying that before.

Standing there, muscles aching, I even out my breathing in order to get into Headspace.

If this works, I can retest all of yesterday's accomplishments.

Before long, I find myself floating among the shapes.

That didn't even take much effort. My powers have clearly recovered, and I'm able to get into Headspace even when uncomfortable.

First, no doubt inspired by that "please," I do my best to initiate a vision about the stock market.

Just like yesterday, instead of a stock idea, I get a glimpse of my upcoming training with Nero.

It's a boring vision, since all I do is punch Nero's mitts over and over, just as I'd done today.

Exiting Headspace, I run hot water into the Jacuzzi and make myself a snack.

Can I get better at martial arts if I witness myself practicing inside a vision the way I just did? Logic would say no—part of practice is developing muscle memory, and I suspect my body today isn't affected by what happens to the body inside the vision.

After all, I've gotten hurt and killed in visions, but snapped out of them unscathed.

Then again, I once had a dream about practicing a card magic move, and upon awakening, I could swear I got noticeably better at the move's execution. At the time I called it placebo, but Felix dug up some articles about athletes practicing their sport in their dreams and improving.

Did I discount Felix's findings too quickly?

For that matter, was my card-move dream a vision

dream?

Any way I can speed up being able to punch Nero would be worth exploring.

Speaking of that, training my seer powers is probably my best route to making that hundred grand. All I have to do is get so quick at entering Headspace that I can do so during the sparring.

And why not? If Darian could do so during a verbal fight, it stands to reason I might figure out a way to do it during a physical fight.

Which reminds me... when Darian had that vision right in front of Matilda, how come she didn't realize it?

Or did she realize it but not say anything?

On a hunch, I set up my phone to record video and make myself go in and out of Headspace.

When I play the video, I get my answer.

Somehow, going faster into Headspace reduces or speeds up the lightning effect that hits my eyes.

I have to play the video frame by frame to catch a glimpse of it. A regular person wouldn't notice it was there at all.

That's good. It means when I master even faster Headspace access, I might be able to use my powers in front of regular people without breaking the Mandate.

After the snack and the bath, I return to Headspace and try to summon Darian.

No luck.

I then try to call Rasputin with the same lack of results.

Too bad Headspace doesn't allow voicemail or texting.

For the rest of my prison cell stay, I practice going in and out of Headspace and manage to further reduce my focus time by a few crucial seconds.

"What's the stock recommendation?" Nero demands when he unlocks the door.

"BioTelemetry," I say, fighting to keep the smile off my face. "They develop heartbeat monitoring technology."

"BEAT?" Nero narrows his eyes. "Did you use your powers for me *today*?"

"I did," I answer honestly, glad I made sure to try to locate a stock-related vision.

"Should we go long or short?" he asks, suspicion gone.

A flashback of the kiss flits through my mind, and I'm tempted to say "long." And maybe hard.

Reddening, I realize how many financial terms have sexual innuendo when you remember your boss naked. Aside from size, there's position, straddle, spread, market penetration—

"Well?" Nero asks, eyebrows furrowing.

"Short," I blurt out.

I figure if my heartbeats are suddenly fast and short, why not have the position in BEAT match that?

"Okay. Let's go," Nero says and leads me out.

Whew. Speaking of length—how long do I have before he loses money on my stock tips?

We get into the elevator, and he stands with his

back to me.

"Can you tell me *anything* about my parents?" I ask, figuring now is a better time than after he loses a bunch of money and is thus pissed at me.

The silence in the elevator is deafening.

Oh well, at least I can attempt to make some major cash once again.

Without any ado, I throw a punch at the back of Nero's head.

His head is no longer there.

My hand smashes into the metallic elevator panel, and my knuckles scream in pain.

"Ouch!" I yank the hand back, giving Nero a seething glare as the elevator screeches to a halt.

I must've hit the stop button.

"Let me see that," he demands, reaching for my wrist.

Gingerly, I extend my arm, trying to ignore the way his touch is making me feel as he clasps my palm in his big hand.

He examines my knuckles as carefully as a surgeon. Then again, how do I know he isn't one? After all, he managed to know a random fighting style Bentley seemed to pull out of his panda butt.

"You should be fine," Nero says with finality, letting go of my wrist. "But if it hurts tomorrow, you can have a leg workout instead of the usual."

"Please tell me something about my parents," I whisper, figuring I'd leverage this misery for some sympathy points.

Nero shakes his head.

Silly me.

Sympathy requires empathy.

"You can't tell me?" I say, trying another tack.

He nods.

"So, you *would* tell me if you could?" I ask, though I'm not sure why it matters. "Because I can come up with—"

"No." Nero turns away and fiddles with the panel, restarting the elevator. "Even if I could, I would not. Bring it up again, and I'll double your allotment for the following day."

We ride the rest of the way in angry silence. The only reason I don't try hitting him again is the pain in my hand.

Without saying goodbye, I stride out of the elevator and dive into the limo.

Grabbing some ice from the bar to apply to my injury, I pull out my phone.

I have a dozen texts from Felix.

They start by gently reminding me about our visit to Ariel's rehab, proceed to chastise me for not replying, and then chide me for being late. Finally, at seven p.m., Felix says he's going without me.

I text him my apologies but don't hear back for the rest of the ride.

By the time I make my way into the apartment, the throbbing in my hand has subsided and I can move my fingers without pain.

Lucifur greets me by the door with the friendliest

expression I've seen on her flat, furry face. "Honor befalls you, vassal," her eyes seem to say. "You get to feed Our Majesty Fancy Feast this eve. Go wash your filthy hands and get to it."

As I put cat food into the bowl, Fluffster joins me in the kitchen, so I feed him too.

"How was your day?" he asks mentally, so I tell him.

"You must hit Nero," Fluffster says as soon as I finish. "For that kind of money, you must do nothing but practice how to hit him. You have to—"

I tune the rest out, wanting to belatedly slap myself for mentioning money to my frugal rodent friend.

When Fluffster switches his attention to food, I go to Felix's room, on the off chance he's back.

The sounds in the room tell me he is, so I sheepishly knock.

"Yes?" Felix says. "Who is it?"

"Who can it be?" I pop my head in. "I'm sorry I didn't reply to your texts. My solitary confinement chamber doesn't have reception, and Nero—"

"It's not a problem," Felix says without looking up from his soldering. "You didn't miss much. Ariel is going to be under mind control for the rest of the week. They said they may let her think on her own this Saturday."

He looks up and studies me intently.

"I'm going to be there no matter what," I say solemnly. "I don't care if I have to—"

"Good," he says. "I'm sure Ariel would like to see some friendly faces."

"Yeah," I say and finally examine the mess in his room.

The computer hardware he had lying about randomly is beginning to coalesce in the middle of the room—though it's still unclear what the final result is supposed to be.

"I'm building something cool," Felix says, following my gaze. "Check this out."

He thrusts his hand out, and a blob of parts he was just soldering mimics his movement.

"It's like a skinless metal arm," I say, examining the mishmash of wires forming the arm's capillaries, a hydraulic servo that mimics muscles, and the thin metal struts that serve as bones.

"A majestic arm." Felix gives me a thumbs-up with his real hand, and the skeletal artificial arm repeats the gesture.

"You've gone full Skynet, haven't you?" I smile. "Whose mom is this Terminator going to go back into the past to kill?"

"If I were Skynet, I'd just have my robot spike her drinks with birth control pills, or—"

"But seriously," I interrupt, knowing full well Felix could play-act at being a malevolent AI for a while. "What is this thing?"

"I shall call it Golem," Felix says in his best imitation of Dr. Evil. In a normal voice, he adds, "It's a robot I plan to remote control."

"And you need a remote-controlled robot because...?"

"Because I don't think I can physically join you the next time someone gets herself kidnapped," he says, examining Golem's metallic intestines spread out at our feet. "I've been having really bad nightmares."

"Oh," I say, feeling like the crappiest friend ever. It didn't occur to me to ask how he's doing after seeing all that gore—and it should've. He's not a fan of blood, and there were rivers of it. "In that case, this is a great —though hopefully unnecessary—idea."

"Whether I need Golem or not, the work keeps my mind occupied." He makes a fist, and the robot arm parrots it.

"You should talk to Lucretia. Also, I'm always here for you, if you want to talk."

"I've asked my dream walker friend for help." He relaxes his fist. "She's confident she can make these nightmares go away—so I should be fine."

"Good," I say and suppress the urge to ask him if his friend could banish the X-rated images of Nero from *my* dreams. I'm not about to admit to Felix that said dreams exist. "I better go to bed. I have another long day waiting for me tomorrow." I yawn as I say the last words.

"Good night." Felix also yawns. Then he grins, and both he and his creation wave goodbye.

I get myself into bed as quickly as I can and drift off to sleep in record time. However, without the aid of a dream walker, Nero invades my dreams once again.

And it is triple-X this time.

CHAPTER THIRTEEN

OVER THE NEXT TWO DAYS, I spar with Nero in the mornings, and it's just as brutal of an experience as the first time. Whenever I try to hit him anywhere but the mitts, he catches my attempt with the stupid things. Eventually, he gives me lukewarm compliments on my improving form, but I still don't manage to catch him with a hundred-thousand-dollar punch.

The practice of my seer powers is also a mixed bag: summoning Darian and Rasputin doesn't yield any results, but I'm able to go into Headspace much faster. In fact, by the end of Thursday, I reach Headspace as easily as I did when using a Focusall pill, but au naturel.

On Friday morning, I decide to cheat. I take one of the remaining Focusall pills in the hopes that I will be able to reach Headspace during my sparring session with Nero—and thus have a chance to win the big cash prize.

Half an hour into our practice, I'm confident the

drug has kicked in. The improved focus makes me execute my moves so well Nero gives me his first genuine-sounding compliment.

"Thank you," I say, and hit his mitts with another perfect punch, then another, and another.

Nero smiles.

He actually smiles.

Dispelling the uncalled-for warm fuzzies, I dance around Nero until I put the wall clock behind him. Then I attempt to reach Headspace.

And fail.

"I'm going to hand over your training to a professional in a few minutes," Nero says, distracting me from attempting the Headspace entry again. "I'm flying out to Europe today and will only get back in the middle of next week."

I stop pummeling his mitts and raise an eyebrow. "If you're going to be away, who will lock me up in the cell?"

"You will use my office." Nero lowers the mitts. "I'll make sure Venessa makes all the arrangements."

I chuckle. Venessa will probably have an aneurysm when he tells her that a lowly analyst is going to camp out in the big office.

Then it hits me.

He's going to hand over my training to someone in a *few minutes.*

My chances of making the hundred thousand are about to fly off to Europe.

Then again, his hands are lowered right now, and I'm not actually punching the stupid mitts.

I stare at him, as though questioningly, but in reality, I will myself to get that Headspace focus with all my power.

Come on, Focusall.

Come on, tireless training.

Something in my brain clicks into place as I reach that elusive feeling, and I finally do it.

I jump into Headspace in the middle of fight training.

———

I FLOAT in Headspace and stare at the surrounding shapes.

Almost as a habit, I try summoning Darian and Rasputin, but I don't let myself fret when it fails.

I'm not here for that.

I'm here to make the hundred thousand—only I have no idea how.

Actually, that's not true.

I have a roundabout way of getting myself a vision where I fight with Nero. For whatever reason, it happened every time I tried to get Nero a stock tip.

Well, that's worth a shot then, but what did I actually do in those cases?

I think about minty and green shapes, then about happy Nero, or greedy Nero, or—

A cloud of shapes shows up in front of me. Each is a

variation on something room-temperature, orange, and fishy-tasting. Each can generously be called a snowflake, and almost all have safe melodious music emanating from them.

Great.

These are very similar to the shape that gave me the vision of punching Nero the other day. Could it be proof of something I long suspected: that the vision content and its Headspace representation correlate?

Not letting myself get distracted by metaphysics, I reach out with my ethereal wisp and touch one of the shapes.

―――――

NERO and I are having a staring contest.

It's 7:59 on the clock behind him.

I execute the move.

The mitts are down. My hope is that he dodges the hit, which is why I also hit where I think he will dodge to, as that was how I almost got him the other day.

Almost doesn't pay a hundred thousand, however.

Nero's darkly handsome face is an inch away from where my second hit whooshes through the air.

Just like the last time it happened, Nero does something with his super speed, and I tumble to the mat—

―――――

I EXIT the vision before I land on the mat.

Was that a vision from next week?

No.

Nero's mitts are down, and we're having a staring contest just as we did in the vision, plus the time on the clock is the same.

Without thinking, I punch him as I did in my vision, but on the second hit, I adjust to account for that critical inch.

My gloved hand barely taps Nero's face, but he looks as stunned as if I've managed to knock him out.

"I did it!" I shout, pumping my gloved fists in the air. "The money is mine."

He smiles again—setting some kind of record. "A deal is a deal," he says. "You deserve a bonus for the recent stock recommendations anyway."

"I do?" I almost blurt out loud. Is Nero mocking me with this? There's no way NUT, or BEAT, or the others have actually made him money.

I suggested those stocks as a joke.

Nero looks behind me, and his smile evaporates. Straightening his back, he says, "I knew if I gave her a proper motivation, she'd—"

Someone slow-claps in response.

I turn and face the newcomer.

It's a woman with a skeletal face.

She's looking at me with a twinkle in her brown eyes. Her aura marks her as a Cognizant, and her waif-like body can probably be found in medical texts under "anorexia." Twiggy at her thinnest would look chubby in comparison. Did someone curse her, like in the movie *Thinner?* The roughly spun crop top she's wearing is so see-through that her nipples are showing, and her bottoms remind me of what sumo wrestlers wear—though if a sumo wrestler ever got this thin, he'd probably commit hara-kiri.

"Sasha, this is Thalia," Nero says. "When things didn't work out with Bentley, I asked her to take over—and here she is."

Right. Was Nero trying to find the polar opposite of Bentley?

Thalia walks onto the mat rather spryly, considering how hungry she looks.

She gestures at Nero, then at her mouth.

"Apologies," Nero says to her and steps away from the mat. Looking at me, he says, "Thalia is under a vow of silence."

"You are?" I look at the woman, and she nods, eyes still twinkling.

"You don't like people talking, do you?" I look at Nero. "First, the limo driver who can't speak, now a martial arts trainer who refuses to."

"Kevin *can* speak." Nero folds his arms across his broad chest. "I told him he has to behave like a professional around you; I guess not talking is how he interpreted it."

"But who takes a vow of silence?" I look at Thalia, and then it hits me. "You're one of the nuns, aren't you? The ones who came up with the fighting style I've been trying to learn?"

Thalia nods.

"So besides fasting, you guys don't even talk." I shake my head. "Remind me *not* to sign up."

Thalia chuckles, then looks at Nero and gesticulates with her hands, pointing at her eyes, then at her Mandate aura, then at her mouth.

"I think she wants me to tell you that they wouldn't accept you anyway," Nero says, and Thalia gives him a thumbs up. "Only a Cognizant without powers may join the Jinto order."

"Oh no," I say sarcastically. "Poor me."

Thalia crosses her spindly arms across her chest.

"Leave it to you to upset your brand-new sensei," Nero says caustically. "Thalia decides when you get to go home today. I've suspended your work allotment as an extra reward for that punch."

The nun looks meaningfully at Nero, then assumes the fighting position I've been trying to learn.

Seeing her do it makes me doubt all my progress. When Thalia does it, her stance brings to mind those female insects who like to snack on the hapless males after coitus.

The nun proceeds to execute a couple of moves with a speed that rivals Nero's—except he's supernaturally fast and she allegedly isn't.

"I think she's saying she will let you go when she likes the progress you've made today," Nero says, deadpan.

Thalia nods sagely.

"There's no way you could've gotten that

information from what she just did," I say. "She wrote this out for you beforehand, didn't she?"

Looking impressed, Thalia fishes out a cell phone from her primitive-looking underwear and mimes texting.

"Clever," I say. "But doesn't it break the spirit of the silence vow?"

Thalia shrugs, then walks over to the corner of the room, puts down her phone, and pulls on a pair of gloves.

Uh-oh.

Those aren't punching mitts. Is she going to hit me back?

Then again, how hard can she actually hit? She looks like a strong wind could knock her down.

"I have a plane to catch," Nero says to us. "Have fun."

To my surprise, I realize I don't want him to go.

I guess I really don't like the idea of being left alone with this strange nun.

That's it.

No way would I miss Nero, of all people.

Thalia walks up to me and fist-bumps my gloves with hers in a ceremonial fashion.

She then takes the stance.

I do so as well.

She looks me over, shakes her head disapprovingly, and punches the air in the style I've been practicing all week long.

I repeat the gesture.

She shakes her head with slightly less disapproval,

lifts the gloves in front of her face, then points one at my face and the other at her own.

"You want to spar for real?" I ask.

She nods and pantomimes for me to start.

I cautiously try to punch her. On the one hand, I know how fast she is, but on the other, I'm worried that if my punch lands, she'll snap like the twig she resembles.

My worry is unnecessary. Her face is nowhere near where I hit.

She winks, then hits *me* in the face.

White blotches dance in front of my eyes before I collapse on the mat.

CHAPTER FOURTEEN

I COME to my senses and realize I'm not in my bed. This is the mat, and I was knocked out.

By a skinny nun.

I lie there long enough that if this were a boxing match, the referee would've easily counted to ten.

Did Nero lie about this woman's lack of powers?

How could someone with so little muscle tissue knock me out so easily—especially with padded gloves? What's even more mysterious is that I don't feel like anything in my face is broken.

It doesn't even hurt anymore—well, except for the deep wound to my pride.

I struggle to my feet.

She pantomimes a blocking movement.

"Neither Nero nor Bentley taught me how to block," I say.

She rolls her eyes and shows me how to block in slow motion.

I mimic her, and she executes her strike again—much slower and with less impact this time.

"Taking the punch on the block is a lot more pleasant than on my face." I smile at her.

She winks, then strikes again.

I try to block, but her hand smashes into my forehead anyway.

I plop onto the mat again, the white blotches dancing the same jig in front of my eyes, but I don't pass out.

Knees shaky, I struggle to my feet.

She shows me the block again, but then hits me before I can even hope to block her.

I get up. Again, surprisingly, my face doesn't seem damaged, but I'm starting to get a headache.

I wipe my nose and narrow my eyes at the nun.

If I had an AI speaker nearby, I'd request the "Eye of the Tiger" song, because I feel as though I've fallen into a *Rocky* movie—except with martial arts invented by nuns.

Thalia proves my point by repeating the whole ordeal of knocking me down at least ten more times. Each hit is slightly different from the other—so even when I manage to put my hands in a way that would've blocked the previous punch, it doesn't work.

Throughout all this, Thalia ignores my non-Rocky-like complaints about my growing headache.

On the twentieth fall, through the haze of what is now a migraine, I recall my powers and the Focusall coursing through my system.

I stand up and face her.

As she starts to wink, I attempt to go into Headspace.

Nope.

I hit the mat again and lie there for a second.

This really blows.

Even Rocky didn't get knocked down this often.

When I get up and try reaching Headspace again, I get punched in the face one more time.

Maybe I need to even out my breathing preemptively?

Though it's hard to do after so many hits, I slow my breathing and stand up again, facing the dreadful nun.

She starts to wink.

I reach Headspace mid-wink and just float there, enjoying the lack of headache that is a pleasant side effect of not having a head in this place.

Now that I'm here, how do I initiate a vision that will help me win this fight?

Do I think of the exercise room or my lithe torturer?

How did Nero even convince some nun from the mountains on another world to come train me? With their vows of silence and fasting, these nuns do not strike me as material girls. If not money, how did he entice her?

A set of shapes shows up, interrupting my musings.

These shapes look and smell different from the ones I used to deal with Nero, yet close enough to be their distant cousins.

When I touch the one closest to me with my ethereal wisp, I get exactly what I hoped for.

Tilting her body thirty degrees, the nun strikes me, and I start to fall.

I snap out before my back hits the mat in the vision.

My hands instinctively block the hit I just witnessed.

Her punch lands on my gloves, and she looks at me approvingly.

She pantomimes for me to hit her.

Given what she's been doing to me, I now really want to land a punch, no matter how fragile she seems.

Correction, I *hope* it hurts when I hit her.

The problem is that when I try to hit her, she doesn't even block it. She just dodges as fast as Nero did.

Well, I just have to use the same solution.

I start to hit her again and try to reach Headspace.

Sadly, Headspace eludes me, so my fist whooshes completely off the mark.

She sticks out her tongue at me, like a five-year-old.

If someone had told me I'd so desperately want to hit a nun in her stupid face, I wouldn't have believed them.

I attempt to reach Headspace yet again as I throw another punch.

Again, nada.

I take in a deep breath. Being pissed-off isn't very Headspace conducive.

Exhaling the breath, I focus with all my might... and end up in Headspace once more.

Repeating all my thoughts from the last time I was here, I summon nearly identical shapes without much effort.

The closest one does the trick. I see where the nun will be when I try to punch her.

As soon as the vision ends, I do to the nun what I earlier did to Nero—except my glove smacks her square in her until-that-moment-smug face.

She looks stunned.

Crap.

Did I overdo it?

I hope she doesn't need 911, and if she does, I hope—

She grins at me.

If my punch hurt her in any way, she doesn't show it.

Are the other nuns in her order this freaking tough?

She pantomimes for me to defend myself.

I do, and get smacked like before, over and over, until I finally manage to use my powers to block her.

She then makes me hit her, which follows the same script.

This loop of blocks and hits continues for what seems like twenty of the worst hours of my life.

She ignores it when I complain about thirst, and she scoffs when I gripe about hunger.

"I have to use the bathroom," I lie after I block her punch one more time.

She pantomimes getting hit in the face five times.

"If I hit you five times, you'll let me pee?" I ask, not hiding my annoyance.

She shakes her head and points at the door.

"If I hit you five times, you'll let me leave for the day?" I say with a lot more hope in my voice.

She nods.

"Okay." I steady my breathing and reach Headspace —which lets me score my first hit.

The next three hits follow the same basic formula, but something goes awry on the fifth.

I'm unable to reach Headspace no matter how hard I try.

Oh no.

Did I use up my power already?

I do my best to hit her without using my powers.

After a hundred failures, all I accomplish is that I'm barely standing on my feet from exhaustion.

My muscles are frozen lead bricks, and the air around us seems to have turned into molasses.

Is this the hunger and thirst playing tricks, or did swinging my arms get me this tired?

Worst of all, though I lied about needing the bathroom before, my bladder feels like it might explode any second now.

My agony must show on my face because the sensei rolls her eyes and lifts her gloves tauntingly.

If she could speak, I bet she'd say, "You're worthless. Fine. Hit me and leave."

I tap her gently this time.

She rolls her eyes and walks off the mat. Taking off her gloves, she picks up her phone.

Her thin fingers dance as though she's about to text someone as she walks over to me.

Smirking, she shows me the screen.

You'll have to do better on Monday.

"I'll do my best," I say. Under my breath, I mutter, "I'll also make sure to eat an extra big breakfast, drink like a camel, and probably wear adult diapers as well."

"That's the spirit," she writes, her expression unchanged. "I'll see you next week."

I beeline for the bathroom with the gym gloves still on and learn how hard it is to take off one's pants with such a handicap. Cursing, I pull them off, do my business, and then attack the water cooler, nearly choking on the blessedly cool liquid.

When I come back to leave the gloves, Thalia is no longer at the gym.

Not willing to test my luck, I rush to the limo.

"Hi, Kevin," I say to my apparently capable-of-speech driver when he opens the door. "You know, it wouldn't be very professional of you not to say hi back to me."

"Hi, ma'am," he deadpans, his expression as blank as a moment ago.

I don't believe making a client feel old is professional either, but I decide we can argue that point when I'm less starved.

Leaping inside, I attack the food bar with one hand

as I hold a paper towel filled with ice to my face with the other.

By the time I stumble into my apartment, the Bluefin tuna sushi I gobbled in the car reaches my belly, making me want to crawl into bed and pass out.

I check on Fluffster and the cat, then say hello to Felix using my last ounces of energy.

"Do you want Golem to carry you?" Felix offers when he sees my sorry state.

The half-finished robot in his room now resembles an old-model Cylon from *Battlestar Galactica*. Metal carapace covers its torso, arms, and legs, but it has no head yet—which is among the many reasons I refuse Felix's generous offer and get into bed of my own accord.

At least something good comes out of all this brutal exercise.

My sleep is blissfully dreamless—and thus Nero-free.

CHAPTER FIFTEEN

I WAKE up at eleven a.m. and stumble into the bathroom.

Though I feel no pain in my face, I check it for bruising.

I find none.

Did Thalia's gloves shield me from getting marks?

No. That doesn't help boxers.

Either the nuns developed a kind of non-damaging fighting style, or Thalia somehow took it easy on me. That's a scary idea in itself, though. I'd hate to see what she can do if the gloves come off, both literally and metaphorically.

I'm just about done with my morning routine when someone rings the doorbell.

I tie the strap of my bathrobe and go answer it—only to find that Felix has already beaten me to it.

"Hi, dears," Rose says to us, smiling. "I'm back, and I'm here to get Luci."

As though waiting for that exact moment, the cat strolls into the hallway with her furry head held high.

Fluffster follows her, his shoulders down.

"Does she have to go?" he asks mentally.

"I'm afraid she does," Rose says kindly. "She misses me like crazy."

I look at the cat's placid expression and back at Rose's super-eager one, but keep my mouth shut.

For the next hour, Rose, Felix, Fluffster, and I turn into cat herders as we try to put the beast into her carrier. We manage it with no fatalities, but the casualties include a cut on Rose's wrist and a self-inflicted bump on Felix's forehead.

"I owe you two brunch," Rose says to me and Felix after the monster is tamed. "And I'll bring you the amazing walnuts I got on the trip," she tells Fluffster.

"Deal," Felix says. "You'll have to also tell us about your vacation."

Poor naïve Felix. Does he *really* want to hear about Rose and Vlad's sexcapades? Because I bet that was probably the core of their vacation.

"Let's get dressed for the trip to rehab, so we can go there right after we're done at Rose's," I tell Felix as I turn to go to my room.

"I'll need a few minutes," Felix says to my back.

"Sure," I say over my shoulder and enter my room.

After I dress, I use the few spare minutes Felix gave me to contemplate a magic effect I can perform for Ariel in order to cheer her up—assuming she's conscious and is in any condition to enjoy such things today.

To really impress her, it has to be something big.

Something I've been saving for the TV show that will never happen now.

I scan my drawers until an almost psychic intuition draws my eyes to a pin cushion filled with sharp, shiny needles.

Bingo.

The effect in question is my twist on a classic that the likes of Houdini have performed. It's gross and shocking—perfect for getting a great reaction from Ariel.

The only reason I was saving this for the hypothetical TV show is that the regular public (especially at my restaurant gig) wouldn't have been as appreciative as Ariel.

I take out what I need, replace the lockpick set in my tongue with a device for this effect, and configure everything as I earlier designed it.

Deciding a quick rehearsal is in order, I walk to the mirror.

During the actual performance, I'll have the needles examined for realness and have them counted, but for now, I just pantomime extending my hand.

Next, I open my mouth wide to show there isn't anything there—except for an innocent-looking tongue piercing, of course. On the TV show, I was going to ask a dentist to do this, but for Ariel, I'll just show her under my tongue, my gum line, and the roof of my mouth.

This is the point where my friends will realize something gross might happen and squeal—Ariel in excitement and Felix in horror.

Smiling in anticipation of all the reactions, I put the first needle into my mouth like a hungry masochist

Then I put another needle in, then another, and another, until the cushion looks like a bald porcupine.

And then comes the best part: I mime *swallowing it all*.

When I do this for real, I'll act it out more, with gagging and a pained expression on my face. If I remember to get water on the way to the rehab facility, I'll chug the needles down with that as though they were pills.

If I'm lucky, Felix will faint at that point. Ariel would get an extra kick out of seeing *that*.

Next, I unwrap a ball of thread, cut myself a long strand, "swallow" it, and do another set of pained expressions.

At this point of the effect, the classic route is to pull the thread out of the mouth—and reveal that all the needles have somehow threaded themselves on the thread. It never fully made sense to me what we're asking the spectator to believe when this happens, but it looks really cool.

This is also where some newer versions deviate from the classic. For example, Criss Angel pulled the thread out of his stomach on TV.

I begin with the classic approach and pull the thread out of my mouth with the needles already attached.

When it's out and I can speak, I'll have my mouth examined yet again and the needles counted—which is when we'll find one is missing for some reason.

I'll make a shocked face and act like I'm gagging for the last time and even have blood pour out of my mouth—another chance for Felix to faint.

Eventually, I will spit out a needle and have it fly right into my index finger, piercing it in the process.

For real.

It will hurt, but the realness of the finger injury will make everything that preceded it seem all the more genuine.

If Felix doesn't faint at that point, he will be considered officially cured of his weak stomach.

I practice spitting the last needle, but catch it in the cushion instead of my finger. I don't want too many puncture wounds when Ariel examines my hands.

The needle flies true, and it better: I've practiced needle spitting this way for enough hours to win a gold medal in it—assuming someone would make such an insane sport part of the Olympics.

Packing everything I need to repeat the effect in a short while, I join Felix and Rose for brunch.

As it sometimes happens when I have something new to perform, I'm only partially there as we eat and Rose tells us the PG version of her trip. Most of my brain cycles are busy fantasizing about the upcoming performance and the expression on Ariel's face when she sees it.

I soon realize I'm actually nervous about the performance. I guess I *really* want to make Ariel happy, at least for a few seconds, after everything she's been through.

When we finally leave, I'm not surprised to find Kevin and the fancy limo waiting for us downstairs.

At this point, I wouldn't be that shocked to learn that Kevin sleeps here. I'm beginning to think Nero is using him to make sure I don't get into more trouble. It's his way of ensuring that his goose keeps laying golden eggs—even when she gives him stocks as a joke, apparently.

The trip to the rehab facility is similar to the brunch: my mind is on the upcoming needle-swallowing, with everything secondary, even the majestically futuristic streets of Gomorrah.

"Wait here. I'll go get Ariel," Felix tells me when we enter the *Star Wars* cantina-like lobby of the facility.

"Sure," I say, the sight of elves, dwarfs, orcs, and a slew of other exotic creatures finally dragging me out of my performance musings.

"Sasha," says Ariel's voice next to my ear.

I turn around.

Ariel is grinning at me, and she looks good—supermodel good.

Or more to the point—the *cured* kind of good.

"Hey, you," I say, unsure how one talks to a friend in rehab.

"Don't you 'hey you' me," Ariel says, her grin widening. "Come give me a hug."

I gladly comply, and hugging her makes some deep-seated anxiety in my chest melt away.

"You smell so good," Ariel murmurs, her lips brushing sensually against my ear as she gives it a nibble. "I've missed you."

"What?" Startled, I extricate myself from the hug. "I what?"

She cocks her head.

My thoughts spin at a thousand miles per hour. Is she still under mind control—but by a horny teenage boy who can see through her eyes and speak through her mouth, Baba Yaga style? Or is the vampire-blood withdrawal messing with her libido and sexual preferences? Will she become a sex addict now, like Kit?

Wait a minute.

"Kit?" I say sternly, narrowing my eyes at "Ariel."

Sighing, the woman in front of me transforms into the mischievous Councilor.

"Ariel wasn't herself these last few days, so I didn't get a chance to interact with her and learn the proper behavior patterns," she says apologetically in her anime-character voice.

"You think *that's* the problem?"

"Sasha," Felix says breathlessly from behind me, and I turn around, alerted by some strange note in his voice.

Sucking in a breath, he rattles out, "Ariel isn't here."

A wave of dread hits me.

"Explain," Kit says imperiously, stepping toward Felix.

"They couldn't find her this morning," he says. "They pulled up the security footage, and it shows Ariel waltzing out of this place a few hours before we arrived."

"They just let her leave?" I ask.

"This isn't a prison," Kit says. "Unless we explicitly agreed to be held here, we can leave whenever we want."

"They should've had her under mind control longer." Felix looks around the place with narrowed eyes.

"There's a protocol for that too," Kit says. "They have to let you exercise your will when they think you can handle it."

"But she clearly couldn't yet," I say sharply.

Kit looks uncomfortable—an expression that seems foreign on her face. "I'm sorry about my unfortunate impersonation earlier," she mutters. "I didn't know she'd be missing and—"

I wave off her apologies, trying to analyze the implications of this development.

"She's an addict," I say to Felix. "So it's logical to assume she'd go seeking a fix."

"Gaius," Felix says, his face twisting in very un-Felix-like hatred. "She's probably looking for that asshat."

"Gaius?" Kit's left eyebrow rises impossibly high on

her forehead—no doubt a trick of her shapeshifting abilities.

"He got Ariel hooked," I explain.

"Or at least imbibing his blood is how Ariel got to this place," Felix says.

I'm about to yell at Felix for defending Gaius, if that's what he meant, but something about Kit's expression stops me.

"He was here earlier today," she says, her eyebrows furrowed so closely together they almost form a cross. "I thought he was here for me, but now I don't feel so special anymore." Her heart-shaped lips form into a pout.

"Gaius was *here*?" Felix and I say in unison.

"A few hours ago," Kit says. "He told me he recently got back from Russia, and we flirted for a bit. I then reminded him that I'm planning to check myself out today, and we agreed to meet in Brooklyn."

"Excuse me?" Felix manages to look even more confused than I feel.

"I had a whole week of celibacy," Kit says defensively. "Vampires make voracious lovers, so when one as old as Gaius offers a dalliance—"

"We don't care about your sex life," I interrupt, then take a breath. "We want to locate Ariel, and they have a history."

"Do you think Gaius could've gone to see Ariel after he saw you?" Felix asks Kit.

"Easily," she says. "He could've gone either before talking to me or after."

"What would it have been like for Ariel to see him?" I ask, frowning.

"Difficult." Felix puts a hand on my shoulder. "Like seeing a lake of vodka would've been for an alcoholic."

"More like walking, talking uncut heroin," Kit says, her face exaggeratedly serious. "Her willpower would've been severely tested."

I take a calming breath. "We need to find her. She probably left with Gaius, so we can start by locating *him*." I pointedly stare at Kit.

She stares back, her expression turning sneaky.

"Where exactly is your date with him?" Felix asks. "When is it?"

"I *could* let you tag along when I go meet him later today." Kit twirls her bleached hair around her finger. "We can all have an orgy, if you'd like."

"No, thanks, but can you please take us there anyway?" I ask, though a sinking feeling that isn't psychic tells me a "please" isn't going to cut it.

Sure enough, she says, "I'm going to need a favor in return."

"I don't make deals for generic favors," I say firmly, and Felix nods in approval. "Learning from my mistakes and all that."

"So sad." Kit lets go of her hair. "I'm not sure how you'll locate Gaius without me." She transforms into an old lady and in a raspy voice adds, "And if you're thinking of following me when I leave this place, I hope you remember that I can look like anyone."

The idea of following her did cross my mind, but

she has a point. She can get lost in a crowd better than a trained spy.

"You can still get a favor," I say. "We just need to agree upfront what it is."

"That's not as fun." The old-lady Kit pouts.

"How about a seer vision at some point?" I suggest. "I can glean ten minutes of the future for you."

She raises one silver eyebrow, and her forehead crisscrosses with deep lines.

"Or something computer related," Felix graciously chimes in, and she crinkles her nose in disgust.

"Fine." Kit turns back into her younger self. "A vision would work, plus another triviality. I need a place to crash for a few days."

"You do?" Felix looks her up and down incredulously. "You're a Councilor. Don't you have a mansion somewhere?"

"It's complicated." Kit examines the futuristic tiles of the rehab floor. "Someone—let's call them 'the enabler'—is there, which would not be good for the addiction I'm trying to curb."

"What about the dalliance with Gaius—isn't that also bad for your addiction?" is what I *don't* say. Nor do I ask her how she managed to find someone with a stronger sex drive than hers—assuming that's what makes "the enabler" an enabler. Though, he/she could just be a succubus or something like that. Having met one, I can see how a person could become a sex addict if there's a succubus around.

And speaking of Cognizant who might turn one

into a sex addict... How come I still don't know what Nero is?

"You can stay on the couch in our living room," Felix tells Kit. "I think you'll fit."

"You won't even know I'm there," Kit says and shrinks her height by a foot—I guess to show us what she'd do if she didn't fit on the couch.

"Right," I say, unable to shake the feeling that we just got outmaneuvered in this negotiation. "When are you checking out?"

"How about now?" She grows back to her normal size. "I'm craving brick-oven pizza, and there's the best place right next to our destination."

Without waiting for our opinions, she heads for the door.

"I guess she doesn't need to formally check out," I whisper to Felix as we follow.

He just shrugs.

When we get outside, Kit already has a ride waiting for us, so we all get in and drive off.

Felix asks Kit about the rehab, and she raves about the place like an infomercial. After a minute, I tune her out because something occurs to me.

I have my own way of tracking Ariel—my power.

Evening out my breathing, I slip into the needed focus—and find myself in Headspace.

FLOATING AMONG THE SHAPES, I debate summoning Darian again, but decide that Ariel takes priority.

So how do I get a vision about Ariel?

I think about her, but nothing changes.

Crap. This seemed to work before.

Unless I have to think about her deeper than just her name?

I picture her flawless beauty. I recall her tenderness toward me and Felix, and the mama-bear fierceness when someone tries to harm us. I can almost relive the child-like excitement on her face when I finish one of my magic effects. A smile touches my nonexistent lips as I think about her Batman obsession. At the core, Ariel is decisive, spontaneous, and adventurous, but there's a darker side to her too, like the addiction—

A new set of shapes appears in front of me.

Does that mean what I just did worked?

I zoom in to make sure the vision is short, then touch the nearest shape.

Spiraling into it, I get ready to figure out what kind of trouble Ariel got herself into this time.

CHAPTER SIXTEEN

I'M BODILESS, which means I'm having a vision of a moment in time when I'm not at the scene.

The room is small and plain—just four windowless cement walls and a white door.

Her expression meditation placid, Ariel is sitting on a metal chair with her eyes closed, all by herself.

And that's it.

She just keeps sitting there.

———

I SNAP BACK into the reality of the futuristic car ride, with Kit and Felix still chatting in the background.

They didn't notice when I slipped into the vision— proof that the lightning from my hands is getting too fast to spot.

What did this vision mean?

Why was Ariel sitting like that?

Was she meditating?

If so, why do so in such a boring room?

My chest squeezes. Is it possible that Baba Yaga has kidnapped her again? Would Ariel's eyes have been all-black if she'd opened them in that vision? That would've been a tell-tale sign of Baba Yaga's control.

Or Ariel could've just been meditating.

Also, I have no idea *when* that vision is going to take place. Though I usually foresee the near future, it's feasible I just glimpsed something from next year, or later.

"Hey, Kit," I say, interrupting Felix mid-sentence. "Are there meditation rooms in the rehab?"

"Sure," Kit says. "Tons."

"What do they look like?" I ask, hopeful.

She describes something spa-like, and I frown.

Felix gives me a puzzled look. "Why are you asking this?"

Sighing, I tell them both about my vision.

"Have another one," Kit says. "See if she opens her eyes in that one."

"Or save your power in case you need it in an emergency," Felix says. "If you saw the far future, it means Ariel is okay and we have a ton of time to help her. If it's the near future, finding Gaius could help. It can't be a coincidence that she disappeared just when he turned up."

Damn it. They both have good points.

"I'm going to try another short vision," I say, "This

way, I can attempt to see her eyes *and* leave myself some juice for later."

Matching actions to words, I get into Headspace and dwell on Ariel again.

Shapes nearly identical to the ones from before turn up.

Great. So having a vision about a specific person is similar to summoning another seer—I just think about their "essence." But how do I zero in on a specific time and place?

I'll have to ask Darian when I reach him again.

For now, I just touch the nearest shape—and get the same exact vision of Ariel sitting there, eyes still closed for the duration.

As soon as I'm out of the vision, I share my frustration with Felix and Kit.

"For all we know, Ariel has a secret meditation retreat," Felix says reassuringly.

"Yeah," Kit says. "Your seemingly identical vision might be her relaxing in peace a month from now."

"Maybe," I say. "I just wish I could see her eyes."

Our ride stops and we exit, heading for the huge building with the hub at the top.

As we walk, Kit and Felix talk me out of attempting more visions until we get some answers from Gaius.

Instead, Kit demands to hear my whole story from the beginning, and I give in. By the time we reach the gate leading to Earth, I get to the point where I was in front of the Council.

"You were there for the proceedings," I say as we enter the labyrinthian corridors at JFK airport.

"Yeah, and just so you know, I voted to get Chester off the Council," she says matter-of-factly. "And I voted against giving Baba Yaga the newly opened slot. I've gathered she's also not your friend?"

"Thanks," I say. "The last thing anyone needs is Baba Yaga on the Council."

"Unfortunately, it's only a matter of time before that woman gets what she wants," Kit says. "She's persistent and powerful, so the only hope is that she won't live long enough for another seat to open up. That happens extremely rarely. But if it does happen, she'd be the strongest contender."

"Not good," I mutter.

"Yeah," Kit says. "You better take it slow when it comes to Nero's Mentorship. As long as you're under his wing, you have nothing to worry about."

Great.

Nero's slave forever.

Exactly what I need.

"So who got the spot, then?" Felix asks sheepishly.

"Hekima," Kit says. "With him being an illusionist and running Orientation for so many years, he deserved the honor."

Interesting. No wonder my fellow students seem afraid of Dr. Hekima—and I equate teenage fear with respect.

The man is now on the Council.

"So what happened next?" Kit demands. "After the

Jubilee?" She winks—I guess to remind me of when she tricked me into a kiss.

I openly tell her the rest of the story as we walk through the secret passages, but when we come out into human crowds, I switch to a version with Cognizant business edited out.

We walk up to the limo.

"Where are we going?" I ask Kit loudly enough for Kevin to overhear.

"One Hotel," she says. "Right next to the Brooklyn Bridge."

Kevin nods and herds us into the car, where over snacks and drinks, I finish telling Kit my story.

We park next to a swanky hotel and leave Kevin waiting as we go up the granite stairs.

While Kit speaks to the concierge, I carefully examine the industrial-themed, plant-covered lobby. The only people in the lobby are a pair of bouncer types sitting at a table that looks like it came from a barn.

Could this place have a room such as the one I saw in my vision?

The rustic chic décor around us suggests it's feasible.

"Gaius isn't here yet," Kit tells us with a large dose of irritation. "I get that I'm here early, but—"

"We can wait," Felix says, looking up from his phone. "According to their website, there's a pool on the roof, with views of Manhattan and the Brooklyn Bridge."

"I'd rather get that pizza." Kit looks around. "After I use the little girl's room, that is."

"The bathroom is downstairs," the concierge says. "Just take the elevator down."

We follow the directions, and the downstairs bathroom surprises us by being unisex.

"Smart," Kit says and enters the place.

Felix looks at the entrance suspiciously. Feeling momentarily mischievous, I grab him by the elbow and drag him in.

His eyes widen as though he's seeing inside a strip club's locker room, but to me, this unisex bathroom looks a lot like a regular ladies' room. It must be the tall, thick walls of the individual stalls that make this place "gender neutral."

"See you in a second," I say and go into the stall closest to the door.

Felix grumbles something unintelligible, but I hear another stall door slam shut, so I figure he's also making use of the facilities.

I finish my business and get up—but then the mother of all psychic dreads catches me with my pants down.

Literally.

I pull my pants up and get ready to leave, which makes the dread skyrocket.

Okay. Not going to leave yet. Not before I figure out what is causing this.

If I've learned anything from my adventures thus far, it's to trust and respect such feelings.

Then it hits me. Unlike the other times when I was in this type of situation, I now have a huge advantage.

I can generate visions right here in this cozy bathroom stall.

Evening out my breathing, I close my eyes and attempt exactly that.

The prerequisite focus arrives with record speed, and I find myself in Headspace—surrounded by terrifying-sounding shapes.

CHAPTER SEVENTEEN

DO I just touch one of these, or do I attempt to focus my vision on the present moment in the bathroom?

I could think of Felix's essence. He's in the bathroom with us, and if I see a vision of his future, I'll also see a vision of my immediate future.

Of course, I could also end up learning what Felix does when he takes longer showers—and get scarred for life.

The good news is that I have time to think now, since for all intents and purposes, I've stopped the time flow on the outside—meaning whatever the danger is, it will only be a problem when I exit Headspace and not before.

I opt for the more active solution and summon Felix's essence. I bring to mind his gentle and affectionate nature, his analytical mind, the efficient way he tackles any problem that comes his way, his gossipy side...

No matter how much I do this, though, the shapes around me don't budge.

Either I didn't properly capture Felix's essence or the shapes here are already the ones I need—which would imply my subconscious mind has already done something similar to what I just did consciously.

If I had a body, it would be trembling in anticipation as I reach out to the nearest shape with my ethereal wisp.

———

I EXIT THE STALL.

The bouncer-looking dudes enter the bathroom and stop next to the stall I just vacated.

Something about the situation strikes me as extremely odd—something that goes beyond seeing men in the same bathroom as me.

Like me, they also look somewhat confused. Perhaps they don't feel completely at ease seeing a female in the bathroom?

Wait a second.

If they are bouncers at this hotel, they should be used to this bathroom situation.

In fact, I have no evidence that these guys are bouncers at all. With their bulging muscles and mugshot faces, they could just as easily be Russian mobsters working for Baba Yaga.

Crap. Would I find their eyes all-black if I ripped

off their sunglasses, or does Baba Yaga not need to mind-control most of her mobsters?

The fourth bathroom stall opens, and Kit waltzes out.

Seeing her seems to bring the goons out of their momentary stupor.

In the time it takes me to think, "I'm dead," the pair reach into their suit pockets with their meaty hands and produce guns larger than my head.

Before Kit or I can blink, they fire.

CHAPTER EIGHTEEN

I SPIRAL out of the vision, and my already-elevated heart rate spikes as a desperate plan forms in my head.

I unlock my stall door and open it by a tiny sliver.

A couple of anxiety-laden seconds later, the two men walk in.

They stop next to my stall—just as they did in my vision.

Every muscle in my body tenses in anticipation. If I get this wrong, Kit is toast.

Kit's stall opens—just as I've foreseen it.

The guys reach into their pockets.

I inhale a deep breath, then kick at the stall door with as much force as I can muster.

There's a sound of metal hitting tile, and I see the two goons groaning next to the sinks.

Kit disappears back into her stall.

I channel all my practice with Nero and Thalia and execute the martial arts move I've been learning.

My knuckles smash into the nearest guy's massive jaw.

Something audibly cracks.

Ignoring the pain in my hand, I hit my opponent once more—and he doubles over.

A fifteen-foot alligator scurries out of Kit's stall and leaps for the second guy with a speed one wouldn't expect of such a huge monstrosity.

I fight the urge to rub my eyes, and knee my doubled-over opponent in the face.

The gator's jaws crunch on the other guy's torso, the giant teeth entering the man's body like eighty sharpened daggers.

The guy I just kneed rolls to the side.

"He's going for the gun!" I shout at Kit/the alligator.

The gator lets go of her dead opponent, and leaps for the guy.

The goon grabs the gun and shoots without aiming.

The gunfire is muffled. No wonder the weapon looks so big—must have a silencer.

The bullet hits the wall above the middle stall, and shards of tile fly everywhere.

The guy points the gun at the gator, but the monstrous creature chomps at his shoulder before he gets the chance to fire again.

His scream of pain is cut short by another snap of the massive jaws.

Felix's stall opens.

My friend looks whiter than the toilet behind me.

Grisly work done, the gator turns toward me, stands on hind legs, and seamlessly morphs into Kit.

"What?" Felix looks at the two dead guys with wild eyes, then at me, and finally at Kit. "A crocodile?"

"An alligator." Kit calmly shakes a piece of lint from her sleeve. "A crocodile wouldn't make sense under the circumstances."

"Right." Felix walks to the sink and splashes cold water on his face. "That explains it all, thanks."

"Sure," Kit says, clearly missing Felix's sarcasm. "My choices were limited due to the Mandate."

"Huh?" I mumble, happy that I finally found my voice.

"They had no aura." Kit looks at the dead men. "I couldn't have them see me turn, which is why I backed into the stall. I also couldn't turn myself into an orc, or something else that doesn't belong here."

"But an alligator is perfectly reasonable?" I ask.

"But of course," Kit says. "Everyone knows there are giant alligators in the New York sewers." She looks around. "This being a bathroom, the sewer connection is rather plausible, in my opinion."

Her logic must've been convincing to the Mandate as she's not bleeding from any orifices, so I just shake my head, walk over to the sink, and follow Felix's example by splashing my face with cold water.

Kit checks the dead guy's pockets and shakes her head. "They don't have any ID."

"Check their bodies for tattoos," Felix says without looking at the dead men.

"There are stars on their shoulders," Kit says to Felix's back.

"As I suspected," he says, still without turning. "Those indicate a stint in the Russian prison system."

"Which means these are Baba Yaga's men," I say.

"We better get out of here," Felix says and walks to the bathroom exit in such a way that the mangled bodies do not enter his field of vision.

I walk over to pick up the gun off the floor, then pry the other one from the death grip of one of the goons. Up close, these guns don't look like anything I've seen at the shooting range, which, combined with how silently they fire, makes me wonder if someone smuggled these from an Otherland with more advanced technology. From what I've read about guns with regular silencers, the resulting sound should still be plenty loud, yet this gun was so muffled no one outside this bathroom would be the wiser.

Then again, maybe Earth silencer technology improved recently? Could this be the product of some secret government research?

Shrugging, I stash one gun in the front and the other in the back of my pants.

"We should call Pada to clean this up," I say, looking at the bodies.

"I can do anything he can do, but better." Kit turns into Pada and gives me one of the old man's grumpy smiles. "If you have as weak of a stomach as your friend, I suggest you wait outside."

I don't have as weak of a stomach, but I gladly seize

the excuse to rush out of the bathroom. Closing the door behind me, I cover my ears for good measure.

Felix does the same, and we stand there like that until Kit walks out of the bathroom.

"All good," she says and loudly burps. "Let's take a raincheck on that pizza."

Felix whitens so much he turns translucent.

I can't help but peek into the bathroom.

It's completely clean.

Did she turn into something that ate the bodies and licked up all the blood? If so, does that mean Pada uses the same methodology for his cleaning? Then what are those cleaning products he brings for?

On second thought, I don't think I want to know.

"We should head to the limo," I say. "There might be more where these guys came from."

"I'm not afraid of some humans," Kit says derisively.

"You nearly got shot," I counter. "I saw it in my vision."

Kit puts her hands on her hips. "I'm not leaving until I get what I need from Gaius. Unless one of you wants to take care of that itch?" she adds with a smirk.

I roll my eyes and face Felix.

"If we go sit by the pool, it would be too public for anyone to attack us," he says uncertainly. "And if Ariel is somewhere at this hotel—"

"Right," I say, feeling guilty that I forgot about Ariel in all this madness. "We wait for Gaius." I hand Felix one of my newfound guns and ask, "Can you tap into this hotel's surveillance system to make sure no one can sneak up on us?"

Felix hides the gun, and some color returns to his cheeks as he pulls out his phone and starts to excitedly swipe through screens.

I wave for Kit to follow, grab Felix's shoulder, and shepherd him to the waiting elevator.

"I summoned that," Felix says as we enter the elevator car. "Watch this."

The elevator doors slide shut, and we go up without anyone pressing any buttons.

"There's a security camera by the pool," Felix says without looking up from his phone. "I also commandeered a drone to cover the areas where the camera doesn't reach."

"Great job," I say as Kit sighs and mumbles something along the lines of "boys and their toys."

We exit onto the gorgeous pool deck, and the views of the city take my breath away.

When I recover, we grab lounge chairs, and after a brief minute of relaxation, I take out my phone and video-call Nero, figuring if I have to put up with his crap, I might as well enjoy his Mentor protection.

He picks up on the twentieth ring, and I see a golden cross with colorful frescos behind him, along with a familiar-looking man dressed in spotless white robes, a white yarmulke-like hat, and red leather shoes.

"I'm busy," Nero says to me and nods his head toward his companion.

"This is extremely urgent," I manage to say without blinking.

"I must take this, Your Holiness," Nero says to the man and swiftly walks away, nearly knocking down a bunch of red-gowned clergymen.

Finally, he stops in a corner. "This better be a real emergency, Sasha. The P—"

"Baba Yaga just tried to kill me again," I blurt out.

The black of Nero's limbal ring spreads through his eyes as he stares intently into the camera. "Are you sure about this?"

I tell him about what happened as quickly as I can and watch his features contort into an ever-darker expression.

"Kit should be able to keep you safe," he says when I finish. "I will reach out to Baba Yaga to make sure everything is crystal clear regarding our arrangement."

"And bear in mind that you and I also have an arrangement that is dependent on you protecting me from Baba Yaga," I can't help but say.

"Leave this with me," he growls, and squeezes his phone so hard he cracks the camera—which makes his image almost ghoulishly frightening.

"Thanks," I say and hang up, heart pounding.

"I don't think Baba Yaga will bother you again," Kit tells me. "She must've gone senile to dare mess with Nero in the first place."

I shrug, then lean back in the lounge chair. Closing my eyes, I do my best to relax.

Soon after, the sun warms me, and the gentle breeze lulls me into a nap.

———

"SASHA," Kit says, shaking my shoulder. "Wake up. Gaius will be in his room by now."

The reminder about Gaius—and by extension, Ariel —wipes all remnants of sleep from my brain, and I leap to my feet.

We make our way to the elevators, and Felix uses his mojo to get us to the eighth floor.

When we get to the room, Kit knocks.

No one replies.

She frowns and knocks again.

Same lack of result.

Frowning deeper, Kit makes Felix unlock the door.

We enter.

The room is empty.

Kit looks at her watch, then at us. "Where is he?"

"Running behind?" I suggest.

"I'm coquettishly late as it is," Kit says. "How dare he?"

Felix and I shrug uncomfortably.

Kit snags a phone from her pocket and angrily swipes at the screen. Tapping her small foot, she waits for the call to connect and frowns again.

"Voicemail?" she shouts. "Really? You stand me up— *me*—and now you don't pick up?" She tightens her grip on the phone, then inhales a comically deep breath and starts to spew the most creative combination of profanities. She finishes her rant with a lengthy discussion of the apparent "shrivelness" of Gaius's testicles and a treatise on poor blood circulation to his manhood. Instead of farewell, she suggests he drink the blood of a human who took Viagra and perform an impossible sexual feat on himself.

Felix clears his throat. "Wow."

"Yeah," I mutter. "Hell hath no fury like a horny woman scorned."

Kit gives us both a seething glare, then looks at the bed, then at us and then back at the bed, mischief replacing anger in her expression.

"We have to locate Ariel," I say preemptively. Kit was clearly about to ask us to "scratch her itch" again.

"Yeah," Felix says. "Could Gaius's absence have something to do with Ariel?"

"Maybe he was also kidnapped?" I look at Kit and then pointedly at the bed. "That would explain why he'd turn down such an amazing opportunity."

"That could explain it," she grumbles. "But who could kidnap a vampire as powerful as Gaius?"

"Ariel isn't a wimp either, but this would be her second time getting kidnapped," I say.

"Hmm," Kit says. "So what now?"

"We go to our apartment," Felix says. "Maybe Ariel simply checked out of rehab and went home."

"It's worth checking on," I say. "Plus, home is a good place to be if Baba Yaga is trying to kill me again."

"Assuming it *is* Baba Yaga," Kit says. "I overheard

your conversation with Nero, and I agree with him: if they made a deal, she wouldn't break it."

She exits the room, and Felix and I follow.

"Who else could it be?" I ask when we reach the elevator.

"Chester?" Felix summons the elevator. "Maybe he's purposefully made it look like someone else's work?"

"Chester wouldn't mess with *me*." Kit enters the elevator that's just arrived. "Besides, I don't think he cares about Sasha anymore—not since she ended up under Nero's wing instead of Darian's."

"Chester might not have known you'd be around when his goons attacked me." I press the ground floor button. "I did kind of beat his daughter in a fight... twice. Could that have put me on his radar again?"

"That I don't know," Kit says. "Though I think it doubtful the little pup would tattletale to Daddy. Werewolves are a prideful lot."

Felix nods in agreement as we exit the elevator. "Plus you didn't *really* beat her in any of those fights."

"Depends how you define 'really,'" I reply defensively.

"He means she didn't submit to you," Kit says, her eyes gleaming excitedly. "She didn't, did she?"

Is there anything Kit doesn't turn sexual? The way she says the word "submit" makes it sound like she's talking about BDSM—not something I would want to even think about in the context of an underage girl like Roxy.

"She ran away the one time, and was chastised by

Rose the other," I explain. "Not sure if that counts as submission."

"It doesn't," Kit says with an air of disappointment. "Werewolf submission is pretty elaborate and formal." Wistfully, she adds, "You'd know it if it happened. Trust me."

"Riiight," I say and exchange a furtive glance with beet-red Felix before jumping into the limo. "Kevin, take us home."

———

"ARIEL?" I shout when we enter our apartment. "Are you here?"

"She's not home," Fluffster mentally tells me as he walks out to greet us.

"Fluffster, meet Councilor Kit," I say. "Kit, this is Fluffster."

Kit's excited squeal is so high-pitched it must make Fluffster worry about the expensive wine glasses in the kitchen. "You're the cutest thing I've ever seen." She grabs him from the floor and ecstatically rubs his fur on her cheek. Reverently, she whispers, "Softest thing I've ever touched."

"He's a domovoi," I say pointedly.

"I know." She grins almost literally from ear to ear as she gently puts him back on the ground.

"He's extremely powerful in the house," Felix adds.

"I know." Kit reluctantly pulls her hands away from the chinchilla and looks around. "So, where do I sleep?"

"Here." I lead her into the living room.

She looks at the couch and wrinkles her nose. Then I can practically see the lightbulb appear above her head as she says, "If Ariel is missing, can I stay in her room?"

"No," Felix and I say in unison.

"Ariel would have to decide if you can use her room," I say. "Help us find her, though, and you can stay in mine." Seeing a glimmer in her eye, I add, "While I stay on the couch."

Kit looks thoughtful. "If you're sure Gaius had something to do with this, perhaps Vlad—"

"That's a great idea," I say and sprint for the front door.

Rushing over to Rose's apartment, I ring the doorbell and cross my fingers.

"Sasha." Rose opens the door, smiling. "What a treat."

"I'm actually looking for Vlad," I say. "Ariel is missing, and I think she might be with Gaius, so—"

"Vlad isn't here." The smile evaporates from Rose's face. "A lot of Enforcer business accumulated when we were on vacation. He's only going to be back tomorrow evening."

"Do you think you could call him and ask about Gaius for me?"

"Of course." Rose waves me into the apartment. Walking over to her circa-nineties landline, she dials a number.

I do my best to follow the movement of her fingers,

storing the digits in my memory—just in case.

Vlad must pick up on the second ring, because Rose immediately asks if he knows where Gaius is.

Then she frowns, covers the mouthpiece, and informs me that he doesn't.

"Sorry," she mouths. "Vlad said he'll try to find him, but he's still on leave."

She then makes kissing noises into the phone and hangs up as I try not to blush.

"He'll let me know if he hears anything," she says, walking over to her couch. "Now please tell me about Ariel."

I do as she requests, then return to my apartment and tell Kit and Felix what happened.

"Interesting that Vlad didn't pick up when *I* called him a moment ago," Kit says archly.

"We have to do something," I say and start pacing the living room.

"Like what?" Felix asks.

"I don't know." I stop and look at him, then at Kit.

"If she isn't kidnapped, there isn't much we can do." Felix rubs his chin. "She's a big girl. If she wants to drink—"

"No." My hands curl into fists. "You saw how she was when we rescued her."

"I'm afraid he's right, though," Kit says. "One has to want to get help. I speak from personal experience."

"We'll see," I say and storm into my room.

As I pace next to my bed, crazy ideas swirl through my head. Would Nero be willing to lock up Ariel for me? There's already a food-stocked cage at the fund that doubles as my office. We can put her there—

What am I saying?

I can't lock Ariel up.

If she isn't kidnapped, I'll have to use words, not force, to get her to go clean.

Though knowing how headstrong Ariel can be, it might be easier if she *were* kidnapped—

My phone rings.

It's a video call from Nero.

Great.

Maybe *he* has some answers.

CHAPTER NINETEEN

NERO IS RUNNING ON A TREADMILL. His sweat-dampened, broad-shouldered frame bobs up and down as he makes Olympic leaps forward with every stride. Vatican City is visible in the large window behind him.

"Baba Yaga said she isn't trying to kill you," he says without wasting time on pleasantries.

"She's not?" I ask, taken aback by the confidence in his voice.

"No. I asked her point blank. She can't lie to me about that or anything else," Nero says, his voice unaffected by the brisk jog. "No one can."

"But someone just tried to kill me." I walk up to my table, smack the phone into a stand, and plop into the chair. "That's a fact."

"Which is why I want you to keep your head down until I get back," Nero says. "Stay home under the protection of your domovoi and—"

"You can't tell me what to do on the weekends." I narrow my eyes.

"Actually, as your Mentor, I can and have told you exactly that," Nero says. "Remember Orientation?"

"Exactly," I say. "That's tomorrow, and I'm not missing it."

"You can miss one session." He waves a hand dismissively.

"No, I can't. Besides, Orientation isn't the only reason I can't stay home. Ariel is—"

"How about we make a deal?" Nero's running pace speeds up. "You stay home, and I prove to you Ariel isn't kidnapped."

"Do you know something?" I lean toward the screen.

"Does that mean we have a deal?" he asks, not hiding his smug expression from the camera.

"If you can prove to me Ariel isn't kidnapped, I'll stay home—with the exception of Orientation."

"Fine," he says. "But Kevin takes you there and back."

"Deal." Why would I say no to a limo ride?

"Your inbox," Nero says. "Check it."

Instead of interrupting our call, I open my laptop.

There's an email from Nero with a video attachment.

An email that arrived five minutes ago.

"You bluffed me?" I say into the phone incredulously. "You emailed me something, then made a bargain for it after the fact?"

Nero shrugs, his expression turning even smugger.

"If I weren't mad, I'd be impressed," I mutter as I launch the video.

It's security camera footage from a crowded place. I instantly recognize it as Earth Club, Nero's property in Gomorrah. The camera zooms in on one of the VIP tables, and I see Gaius sitting there, drinking a dubious red liquid from a large goblet. Next to Gaius is Ariel, her face placid.

"It looks like they went there straight from rehab," Nero says gently. "And then left together afterward."

"But why would my vision show her sitting alone in an empty room?" I ask stubbornly. "All this does is show me the culprit."

"She might simply be waiting for something," Nero says. "To what end would Gaius kidnap her?"

"I don't know," I say. "But I'm going to ask him when I find him—oh, and our deal is off."

"No, it isn't." The limbal ring in Nero's eyes takes over a chunk of the whiteness. "Stay home and I'll talk to Gaius to see if he can find himself another toy." The white in his eyes is nearly gone, and even the blue-gray of the iris shrinks. "Break your word to me, and there will be consequences."

"Fine," I say, fighting the urge to cringe or look away. "When you ask me nicely like that, how can I refuse?"

"Smart," he says in a calmer tone, and disconnects.

Great. I'm a prisoner in my apartment again. The

more things in my life change, the more they stay the same.

Then again, maybe this bargain was worth it. If Ariel isn't kidnapped, then this is just Gaius being her enabler—so if Nero convinces him to stop providing Ariel with his blood, she might be forced to seek help on a longer-term basis... that or find another vampire.

In any case, Nero didn't forbid me from exploring the outside world with my powers, so that's what I'll do. In fact, this is a good chance to practice entering Headspace while angry.

I stand up and try to focus.

I fail. My racing thoughts make concentration nearly impossible.

I take in a calming breath, and just like that, the focus slots into place, and I find myself floating in Headspace, surrounded by eerie cuboid shapes.

Instead of thinking of Ariel's essence, I decide to see if the shapes I first encounter are the ones something—perhaps my subconscious mind—is making available to me for a reason. Before proceeding, though, I zoom in on the nearest shape a few times to make sure the duration of the vision is fairly short.

I don't want to waste too much power on this theory.

The eerie sensation worsens when I reach for the looming cuboid, but I suppress the hesitation and make contact—activating the vision.

AN INTRICATE COFFIN made of polished redwood sits in front of me.

MOISTURE BLURS my vision and anguish squeezes my chest as I contemplate the bitter finality of this moment.

INSIDE THAT BOX is the dead body of—

———

I'M BACK in my room, still standing.

My knees feel weak, so I preemptively collapse on the bed and try to make sense of what happened. It doesn't take long because there's little room for misinterpretation.

I just saw a vision of a funeral, and the anguish I felt during it can only mean one thing.

Someone I care deeply about is going to die.

CHAPTER TWENTY

MY THOUGHTS SWIRL LIKE A TORNADO.

Who was in that coffin? My vision self was about to think the name before the vision halted.

Whoever it is, how will he or she die? And when?

More importantly, what can I do to prevent it?

The vision was too short for me to get any of the answers. I just know that the deceased was someone I would cry over, which rules out everyone I wouldn't mind seeing dead, like Baba Yaga.

Could it be one of my parents?

They're too young and in too good of health to suddenly die, but what if that vision is from years in the future?

No. I've never gotten one from so far ahead before. Why start now? It's more likely a near-term unnatural death that has something to do with me and the various enemies I've made since discovering my nature. If so, the easiest way to safeguard my parents is twofold: keep them away from me and change whatever near-future plans they may have.

Thus determined, I grab my phone and video-call Mom.

"Bonjour," Mom says with a smile as soon as she picks up. "How are you doing?"

I look her over carefully. She appears healthy. Her jewelry is as impeccable as always, and she's wearing what look like expensive new glasses—meaning she's being her usual extravagant self.

"I'm okay," I lie. "Just wanted to check how you're feeling."

"I'm feeling great." Mom moves the phone closer to her face. "Finally relaxing. Too bad I have to go back soon."

"I have good news in that regard," I say, moving on to the "mess with plans" stage of my idea. "I got my job back, so if you still need me to help you stay in France, I can do so."

Mom literally jumps up and down in excitement, so I use my laptop to wire her some money and then extricate myself from the conversation as quickly as etiquette allows.

I then call Dad the same way.

"Hey, kiddo," he says, his Boston accent stronger than usual. "Is this urgent?"

Though he doesn't look as healthy as Mom, nothing particularly worrying stands out, so I smile. "Not urgent at all," I say. "Just wanted to say hello."

"Things are crazy with the business this weekend,

but I'm glad you got in touch." Dad's eyes radiate pure joy, making me feel guilty that it took such dire circumstances for me to reach out to him. "Can I call you back in a few days?"

"Sure," I say. "But you've got to take it easy. Stress isn't good for you."

"I agree." He runs his hand through his gray hair. "This is why I have a Bahamas vacation planned."

"You don't want to do Bahamas," I say, getting into magician-level lying mode. "Didn't you hear about the virus on the news?"

"I was too busy," Dad says. "But I didn't book anything yet, so—"

"I think you should go to the Cayman Islands instead," I say, frantically searching the internet for an excuse as to why. "They don't have any outbreaks of disease and"—I find a useful tidbit on the web—"the Miss Universe pageant is happening there next week. I bet there's going to be lots of tourists down there for the event—a chance for you to meet some people."

Did I just tempt Dad with scantily clad women?

"That sounds like a wonderful idea," he says. "But I really ought to run."

"No problem," I say. "Don't forget to send me some pictures from the Cayman Islands. I want to live vicariously through you."

"I will, I promise," Dad says. "Talk soon."

I hang up and step out of my room to share my vision with Felix, Fluffster, and Kit.

"Do you think it was me?" Kit asks and instantly

makes her skin look pale and parchment-like, à la an embalmed corpse.

"My intuition says no," I say tactfully, and what I don't add is, "I don't even know you well enough to cry at your funeral."

"What about me?" Felix turns almost as pale as Kit.

"It could've been you." I place a calming hand on his shoulder. "This is why I want you to carry the gun I gave you everywhere you go. And if you can, work from home over the next couple of weeks."

He nods. "I like your idea of changing up the usual routine. I'll do that as much as I can."

"Smart," I say. "On my end, I'm going to try to have more visions and zero in on the cause of this funeral."

"Could it have been your funeral?" Fluffster nervously stuffs his tail under his butt. "Someone is after you again, after all. Is it feasible that you saw a warning of what happens if they succeed?"

"I would not have had a body in the vision if I were dead." I strengthen my grip on Felix's shoulder. "Since I had tear ducts, I know I was alive."

Felix's shoulder tenses under my hand. "Could it have been Ariel?"

"I doubt it," Kit says and turns herself into Ariel. "Out of all of you, she's the hardest to kill. On top of that, if she is indeed hanging out with Gaius"—she makes herself look like Gaius—"she would be extra hard to dispatch."

"But could it be her addiction that does her in?" I let go of Felix to rub the bridge of my nose.

"No." Kit turns back into herself. "Blood addiction mainly interferes with one's ability to function in non-vampire society. If anything, the addicts heal faster and don't get sick as often."

"Okay," I say. "Let me go get more visions. Don't disturb me unless you have something pertaining to this new development."

Everyone nods as I leave.

Once in my room, I learn that having a funeral-sized sword of Damocles hanging over my head isn't Headspace conducive.

It takes me what feels like hours of meditative breathing to get my mind clear enough. But finally, I end up back in Headspace.

Unfortunately, the shapes that surround me look nothing like the cuboids of the funeral vision. They are closer to cones and don't even play scary music. I bet the vision would be of me going to my accountant, or something even more mundane.

I make sure the vision is super short and touch one of the cones anyway.

———

"TODAY WE CONTINUE the subject of the Otherlands," Dr. Hekima says. "Let's begin by—"

———

I'M BACK in my chair.

That was clearly a vision of tomorrow's Orientation —and it wasn't as useless as I feared. If someone I cared about had died before the lesson, I wouldn't have gone to class. That means either the funeral future isn't a threat anymore, or the death that prompts it will happen after tomorrow's lesson.

I go into Headspace once more.

Again, the initial shapes are not the same. This time around, I ignore them and seek out funeral-related visions.

I dwell on the time when Grandma Ballard passed away. I was eight years old, and my parents took me to the funeral. Not surprisingly, the experience was a blend of confusing and scary. Mom was devastated, and even my dad cried. The funeral parlor smelled like rotten cabbage. Strange people I'd never met before (or seen since) took turns pinching and slobbering on my cheeks...

New shapes show up in front of me.

Though they're not the cuboid shapes I sought, something about these is similar somehow, though I can't put my ethereal wisp on how. Extending the length of the vision in case I've found something useful, I proceed to touch the shape.

———

I DON'T HAVE A BODY.

Around me is a funeral home, a ton of gloomy people, and a prominently displayed corpse. The deceased is an ancient woman who looks completely unfamiliar to me. Same goes for all of the mourners. As I keep watching the funeral for what feels like a few hours, I don't recognize a single person.

———

WHEN THE VISION TERMINATES, I start pacing around my bedroom in frustration.

I managed to see a random funeral instead of the funeral I targeted. My powers are clearly not up to snuff.

Oh well.

Without much ado, I go into Headspace again.

This time, I see a funeral of an old man, but otherwise the vision is just as useless—not a single person involved looks familiar.

I repeat the feat a few more times with similar results.

Sounds like merely thinking of a funeral's essence isn't a workable strategy. I heard that at least one person dies every ten to sixty seconds, which is too many random funerals for me to sift through.

So, I return to Headspace with another strategy: see the futures of the people I care about—starting with the parental units.

I think of Mom. In my resulting vision, she's walking inside the Louvre, happy as a clam on Prozac. Thanks to Mom's serendipitous phone check, I even know this happens a week from now.

Next, I get a vision of Dad snorkeling on Seven Mile Beach in Grand Cayman, though I don't get a chance to figure out *when*. However, given what Dad said about his busy schedule, I can assume it will be a while from now, so he must be okay as well.

Next, I think of Ariel, ready for a vision I've been dreading the most.

To my huge relief, she isn't in the empty room this time. Instead, she's walking the tourist-packed streets of Midtown, with Gaius at her side.

So, the good news is that Ariel doesn't seem kidnapped in this future and is alive. The bad news is that I don't know *when* she will be walking where she did. I didn't get a chance to sleuth that out.

Suppressing a yawn, I try to focus again, so I can look into Felix's future next.

But I can't get back into Headspace. Not even after multiple tries.

I must've tapped myself out with too many visions.

I'll have to resume this tomorrow—and keep a close eye on Felix and the rest of the possibilities in the meanwhile.

I check my phone and learn why I feel so sleepy.

It's already three a.m.

Exhausted, I trudge through my evening routine, then crawl under the blanket and pass out.

CHAPTER TWENTY-ONE

"SASHA!" Felix screams from somewhere. "Are you going to Orientation today or not?"

I jolt upright and grab my phone.

Wow.

How could I have almost missed something as important as Orientation?

Stumbling out of bed, I yank on some clothes and open the door.

"Finally," Felix grumbles. "I assume it's okay if Maya rides in Nero's limo with you?"

"Of course." My voice is sleep-roughened. "Let me freshen up, and we'll go."

Teeth brushed and other bathroom business concluded, I let Felix rush me out of the building.

Maya is waiting by the limo.

"Dude," I whisper to Felix. "Did she walk here alone?"

"Yeah," Felix says. "I doubt Roxy would have—" He stops, suddenly pale.

Like me, he just realized that it could've been Maya's funeral that I foresaw. Though we've just met, I like Maya enough to shed a tear or two if she died— particularly if her passing was particularly tragic and/or I saw Felix cry at her funeral.

Which he would, I'm sure.

Shaking away the unpleasant thought, I greet Maya and tell Kevin we're late. Then I viciously attack the snack bar while Felix gives Maya an abridged version of the recent events.

Kevin gets us to Queens so fast that it interferes with my digestion. But his speed pays off. Maya and I take our seats in class just as Dr. Hekima walks in.

"Today we continue the subject of the Otherlands," he says in exactly the same tone as in my vision. "Let's begin with a quick review of last week."

He then goes over what I already know—that other universes exist and are called the Otherlands in Cognizant parlance. These worlds/universes each have different stars and galaxies, and even the flow of time can vary among them. There is an infinite number of them as far as anyone knows, but the gates lead to an insignificant portion of that totality.

"I alluded to the dangers of the Otherlands the last time we met," Dr. Hekima says when he's done with the recap. "Today I really want to drive home that point."

He raises his arms and pulsing red energy streams

from his fingers into everyone's heads, indicating that he's about to use his illusionist powers on us all.

The room goes away, replaced with what looks like a radioactive wasteland.

As soon as my eyes register the landscape, we all start gasping for nonexistent air. Illusion or not, it feels like my lungs are about to burst.

Dr. Hekima snaps his fingers once again, causing the world around us to change to that of a lush forest.

"There are Otherlands where the environment itself will kill you," he says when everyone recovers their breathing. "But even seemingly friendly ones like this world can have creatures so dangerous no Cognizant dares live or even travel here."

A cute deer-like creature runs out of the forest.

This Bambi is dangerous? Is he kidding?

Then I see what the Bambi is running away from, and my eyes threaten to jump out and run away in horror.

If the xenomorph creatures from the *Alien* franchise impregnated one of those wraith-like dementor beings from *Harry Potter*, the result would look like this—especially if someone then genetically engineered that already horrific offspring to have a plethora of tentacles and teeth.

"That's a drekavac," Dr. Hekima whispers, but what he says next is lost on everyone because in that moment the drekavac catches up with Bambi and touches it with one of its pustule-infested limbs.

The poor creature produces an apocalyptically

loud, gut-wrenching scream that makes it sound as though it's losing its soul—an illusion that is enhanced a second later, when the Bambi collapses on the ground like a sack of very dead potatoes.

The monster looms over its victim, but thankfully, Dr. Hekima snaps his fingers again, and we find ourselves back in the classroom.

"Getting killed by a drekavac is the worst fate that can befall anyone," he says to the shocked classroom. "Their mere touch brings about such debilitating pain that weaker victims die from it."

He meaningfully looks everyone over.

We're all mute in horror.

I don't know about the teens, but *I* will certainly explore the Otherlands very, very carefully going forward.

"The environment, the flora, and the fauna are just a few of the many ways you can perish in the Otherlands," Dr. Hekima says. "Some gates are one way only—so no one knows what happens there—and other gates lead to worlds that we, the Cognizant, turned into deathtraps."

He snaps his fingers, and we find ourselves in a deserted landscape that he seems to have pulled straight from *Mad Max* movies—right down to a couple of scary-looking hobos chasing some dude.

"This is what's left of the world where Tartarus last ruled," Dr. Hekima says just as the two men catch their prey.

The name Tartarus sounds familiar. I think we

covered it in Greek mythology class. If I recall correctly, it's both a figure and a place. The figure was the son of Chaos, and the place was the underworld where souls got tormented in the afterlife.

"The humans on this world know about the Cognizant and rightfully blame us for the desolation," Dr. Hekima continues, pointing at the endless dunes. "They wait by the gates to catch one of our kind, and if they succeed, they do horrific things to them."

As though to punctuate his words, the two men start to cannibalize their catch alive.

Before the scene gets even gorier, Dr. Hekima snaps his fingers, bringing us back to the classroom.

Everyone is vampire pale, even Roxy, and I wonder if Felix had fainted at this point of his Orientation.

"In some cases, the gates lead to worlds that a particularly powerful Cognizant took over to gain power." Dr. Hekima snaps his fingers, and we find ourselves in a dirty dungeon that brings to mind the Inquisition.

"For example, Lilith—a powerful Cognizant who once lived here on Earth—now has a prison world where she forces the human populace to worship her as their one and only god." He snaps his fingers once more, and we end up back in class. "She's a capricious and jealous deity," he continues, "and will imprison or kill any Cognizant who dares to arrive on her world."

Like Tartarus, Lilith is a name I've heard before—in the prior Orientation, when we talked about the super-rare Cognizant with multiple powers. Also, like Tartarus, she's part of Earth mythology—

"The point I'm trying to make is really simple," Dr. Hekima says, distracting me from my musings. "Be very careful when traveling to the Otherlands, and do not enter any gates unless you're absolutely sure where they lead." To highlight his words, he shows us a glimpse of all the scenes from today in quick succession. "Even if you think you know the gate is safe, I strongly advise you think twice before entering, and definitely wait until you're done with all of Orientation before you even try. And, it goes without saying that you should bring your Mentor with you every time."

Oops.

I've already ventured out a bunch of times without having finished the course and without dragging Nero with me.

Then again, I bet the point of today is to scare the youngsters, not me. Being older and wiser, I will hopefully *not* get myself eaten by a drekavac just for thrills—or waltz into a world without oxygen.

"We're almost out of time." Dr. Hekima looks at his watch. "Does anyone have any questions?"

My teen classmates still look overwhelmed, but I raise my hand, nearly jumping out of my seat in excitement.

"Yes, Sasha." Dr. Hekima gives me a warm smile.

I hear Roxy whisper something like "teacher's pet," but I ignore her as I rattle out, "Who made the gates?

Who discovered the Otherlands? When? How? Could—"

"I had a feeling this might come up." Dr. Hekima clicks his fingers, and we find ourselves surrounded by a gate hub that looks identical to the one in JFK. "The gate makers are the answer to most of your questions, but before I talk about them, I should talk about teleportation—a rare Cognizant power that creates a rift in reality that allows them to instantly go from place A to place B."

Everyone nods. They must've heard of teleporters before. On my end, I'm shocked at how calmly I accept news of real teleportation power—or drekavacs and Tartarus for that matter.

Is this how it's going to be going forward? Or would I do a double take on, say, acid vomiting—a power of that Zeitgeist mutant from *Deadpool 2*? At the very least, I hope I will draw the line at something as strange as Karakasa-Obake—the walking-and-talking umbrella from Japanese mythology that also happens to be a cyclops and wears a sandal—

"Though teleportation usually happens within the confines of a single Otherland," Dr. Hekima says, "the more powerful of the teleporters can take this to the next level." He points at the nearest gate. "They can take themselves from world to world."

He snaps his fingers again, and we end up in another hub. I recognize it as the top of the skyscraper in Gomorrah.

"It is said that the most powerful teleporters would be able to bring another Cognizant with them when they traveled." He glances at his watch again. "My own conjecture is that the most rare and powerful of them could make gates such as these." He looks around. "The truth is that no one has met a gate maker in centuries. Some think they have found a paradise world and settled there without providing the rest of us with a gate."

He changes the scene again, and we're suddenly in the middle of Times Square—only something about it is unusual.

"I want to leave you with this," Dr. Hekima says. "If the number of Otherlands is truly infinite, there must be worlds without gates and without us, the Cognizant." He spreads his hands, and I finally understand what's slightly different about this Times Square.

There should be occasional Cognizant auras in such a crowded place, but they're completely missing in this version of New York.

When he sees the recognition on my face, he smiles and says, "I believe the gate makers left some human worlds as sanctuaries without our kind." He dispels his illusion, and the smell of stale coffee prevalent in the dingy Orientation room hits my nostrils. "Some other worlds might contain exiled Cognizant who can't join the rest of our kind without a gate maker's help. Alas, there's no way to prove these theories of mine, and besides, I'm really out of time now." He gets up and walks to the door without waiting for any follow-up questions.

I raise my hand anyway but put it down when Dr. Hekima leaves the class.

As soon as he's gone, my classmates come out of their stupor and start to loudly gather their stuff.

Maya and I finish first and head for the door just as Roxy gives me a dirty look.

Given dreams about funerals and all that, I grab Maya's elbow and quickly drag her down to the limo, where Felix is waiting for us.

The b-hive stalk after us, but we jump into our ride before they can catch up.

As we pull away, I check on our pursuers through the tinted glass and catch Roxy staring at the limo like a hungry wolf might stare at a delicious lamb.

Deciding to switch attention from one bully to another, I pull out my phone, call Nero, and tell him about the funeral vision.

"You should've told me about this yesterday," he growls when I finish. "I'm heading back to New York right now. Do not leave your apartment until I get back."

"Yes, sir," I say, saluting the phone. "I'll stay home like a good—"

I stare at the phone in outrage. He hung up before I could finish my sarcastic reply.

"I still say yours can be the most dangerous power of them all," I overhear Maya say to Felix, and when I look at her, her expression is completely serious.

"You really think so?" Felix asks, not helping his case by blushing.

"Let's take the United States as an example." She grabs a Coke from the bar. "Computers are now everywhere in this country, which means that a powerful cyberattack can cripple everything from commerce to clean drinking water and beyond." She takes a sip of her Coke. "So yeah, I'm confident if you put your mind to it, you could be the world's worst supervillain."

Felix scratches his head. "There's the small matter of the Council killing me afterward or during. And"—he shoots me a guilty look—"obviously, I wouldn't do something like that on moral grounds."

"All I'm saying is that you don't give yourself enough credit," Maya says sagely. "You're powerful."

He puffs up, and I suppress a smile. I never thought someone could use "you can cause an apocalypse" as a self-esteem boost, but it seems to have actually worked on Felix.

"Cyberattacks are just one option," he says. "If I build a whole army of Golems, I could take over the world *that* way." As though to punctuate his words, his unibrow dances the robot on his forehead.

"Speaking of your project." Maya pushes her glasses higher up her nose. "Can I finally see it?"

Felix reddens, and it takes me a moment to figure out why: Maya has just invited herself into his bedroom. And given the mischievous look on Maya's small face, I bet she did it on purpose.

"I think it's finished." Felix looks at me for help, but I feign ignorance. "I didn't test it out as much as I'd wish, but—"

"This is so exciting." Maya beams at him. "I can't wait to see it."

"I really hope the 'it' in question is still the robot," I mutter under my breath, but Felix must've heard me, because he turns a deeper shade of red.

Maya moves on to another topic, but I only listen with half an ear. It's time for me to resume my research into the funeral vision since I don't have any evidence that I've thwarted it.

Closing my eyes, I get into Headspace and attempt to see the funeral once again.

Just like last night, all I accomplish is a glimpse into a random family tragedy instead of my target.

A few more futile attempts later, Kevin pulls up next to our building, and Felix, Maya and I head upstairs.

"Do you want to see Golem with us?" Felix asks when we enter.

"Can I take a raincheck on that?" I take off my shoes and sneak a peek at Maya's face. She looks relieved I refused. "I'm going to change and chillax for a bit," I continue. "Maya, will you stay with us for dinner this time? I still owe you a pseudo demonstration of your own powers."

"My parents are waiting for me at home again," she says with a pout. "But maybe another day?" She looks meaningfully at Felix.

"Do you want to have brunch with us next weekend?" Felix asks.

"I do," Maya says solemnly.

"Great," Felix says. "It's this way."

He beelines for his room.

Ignoring my wink, Maya rushes to follow him, and soon after they walk into his bedroom, I hear an excited squeal.

"I hope she's impressed with his robot and not something else," I say to no one in particular.

Shaking my head, I walk into the kitchen to get some water and stop dead in my tracks.

What's happening under the kitchen table makes no sense at all. Instead of the one chinchilla that I'm used to, I'm seeing two—and that isn't the weirdest part.

That would be what the two chinchillas are doing. One—the male, I presume—has mounted the other, his little front paws near her ears. To call this humping would be an understatement; he's shaking as though he's having a seizure. There's also loud chirping.

Somehow the whole thing is more cute than disturbing—and that in itself is disturbing, isn't it?

"Fluffster," I say when I recover my speech. "What are you doing? *Who* are you doing?"

They go at it for a few more seconds, then separate. The chinchilla that was on bottom runs out from under the table and instantly turns into Kit.

A completely naked Kit.

"I'm going to take a shower," she says. Looking down at Fluffster, she adds, "Thank you."

She leaves, but I keep standing there, unsure what to say or do.

"Can I have some oatmeal?" Fluffster says in my head.

I rush to help him out, grateful for something to do.

When he starts munching, I blurt out, "Do you want me to get you a girl chinchilla?"

"What?" He looks up. "No. Of course not. An animal cannot give consent." He grabs another piece of oatmeal with his tiny paws. "You might as well ask me if I want to get it on with the cat." He looks thoughtful for a moment, then adds, "You probably should keep Kit away from the cat."

"Good thinking," I reply and barely restrain myself from adding that I hope he didn't catch any supernatural herpes today.

He finishes the oats and looks up. "Can I use my dust bath now?"

"Sure," I say, and we go to my room.

I pour fresh dust into the bath and let Fluffster use it. Then I change the dust right away, even though it's usually good for several sessions. Because—sex cooties.

"Let me check on her," Fluffster says and scurries out of the room.

"Right," I say. Only after he leaves do I add under my breath, "Who knew the domovoi were such considerate lovers."

Fluffster doesn't reply in my head, so I sit down on the bed—which is when a wave of inexplicable emotional agony slams into me.

If this were *Star Wars*, I'd label it "a great disturbance in the Force," but as is, it can only be one thing.

This has to do with the funeral vision.

Someone I love is in mortal danger.

CHAPTER TWENTY-TWO

EVERY CELL in my body is screaming for me to leap to my feet and do something, but that would be pointless. I have no idea where the danger is, and who the target is.

I take in a deep breath, then another, and hope all my practice in Nero's cell pays off.

Headspace eludes me, so I try again, using all my willpower to reach the prerequisite focus.

I fail once. Twice.

I take in another deep breath, and another.

Finally, something clicks into place, and I spiral into Headspace.

———

THERE ARE ANTARCTICA-COLD, maroon-colored, coppery-tasting triangular prisms all around me, and they exude a whole opera of fear and grief.

Is this the vision my subconscious wants me to see?

I have to assume the answer is yes. But what if it's not? How long should I let the vision run for?

Felix once guessed the initial shapes might be optimal length—but how much am I willing to bet on *that* theory? There's a good chance I might have to run many visions over and over again, the way I did yesterday, and I don't want to repeat yesterday's mistake and run out of juice before I get any answers.

I zoom in on the nearest shape just once. Hopefully, this will be a good compromise.

When I proceed to touch my target, I feel resistance of the kind I came across when I had trouble with scary visions in the beginning of my Headspace journeys.

Whatever this is, it must be another level of terrible.

Clenching my metaphysical jaws, I keep focusing on the shape and willing my wisp to make the connection —over and over.

On the tenth attempt, the vision violently sucks me in.

———

I DON'T HAVE A BODY, and my perspective is floating just outside Felix's room when he and Maya exit.

"I'm sorry to cut this short." Maya waves her phone next to where my face would be if I had one. "Mom just told me we'll have Grandpa over, so I have to get there early."

Besides a text from Maya's mother, the phone

shows a background that is a selfie with Felix cheek to cheek. The time on the screen is 5:34 p.m.

"That's not a problem," Felix says. Wistfully, he adds, "I've never met any of my grandfathers in person."

They walk to the front door, and I float after them, like a ghost.

Felix unlocks the door and holds it open for Maya in that exaggeratedly gentlemanly way of his.

Maya pushes the glasses up her nose with her tiny index finger, then saunters out.

Felix follows her in a daze—as though hypnotized by the sway of her narrow hips.

They stop next to the elevator and reach for the button together. Their fingers touch, and they both giggle like teenage girls.

The elevator opens.

If I had eyes right now, I'd blink. Repeatedly.

A familiar slender, dark-haired, young-looking man is inside the elevator. His marble-green eyes dart from Felix to Maya, then back to Felix.

"You," Felix says. He must've also recognized the man as Koschei, Baba Yaga's right-hand man.

"Me," Koschei says in that crypt keeper voice of his.

Felix steps in front of Maya protectively, herding her away from the elevator.

With barely perceptible movements, Koschei reaches into his blazer, pulls out an intricate knife, and leaps forward.

Before Felix or Maya can react, Koschei is already slicing Felix's throat.

"Sorry, kid," Koschei says when my roommate falls into an ever-growing pool of blood. "Can't leave witnesses."

Maya opens her mouth to scream, but Koschei stabs her chest at the same time as his thin palm covers her mouth—

———

I'M BACK on my bed, my whole body shaking as if I drank a cistern of espresso.

Staggering to my feet, I grab my phone.

It's 5:34 p.m. already.

The horrific vision I just saw is only seconds away.

Grabbing the gun that I confiscated earlier, I run out of the room so fast my socks skid on the parquet floor.

Felix's back disappears as he closes the front door behind himself.

Channeling all my recent practice at running, I sprint after him.

If Kit opens that bathroom door in the wrong moment, Maya and Felix are toast.

Or if I trip.

Or if I'm too slow.

When I'm at the door, I nearly drop the gun as I unlock it and leap out.

Felix and Maya are halfway to the elevator.

"Stop!" I point my gun at the elevator door. "Back here, now!"

They either think I'm threatening them with the gun, or they don't like my tone because they whiten. But the important thing is they rush back.

Maya is within reach first, so I grab her by her hoodie and shove her into the apartment, then repeat the same rough treatment with Felix.

Panting, I drop the chain on the door but leave it open a crack so I can hear what's going on outside. If my vision looks to be coming true, I'll have a moment to lock up—not that a lock is going to stop Koschei.

"Fluffster!" I yell. "I think Koschei is about to attack me. Get ready to kick some ass."

I'm not sure if Fluffster was already by the door or if he appears so fast I don't register his movements, but he's suddenly next to me, his cute rodent face looking determined and very un-chinchilla-like.

Felix and Maya are still staring at me wide-eyed, recovering their wits.

The elevator dings outside.

I hear soft footsteps and can almost picture Koschei walking out of that elevator.

This is when I realize that my theory of him wanting to kill me has gaps.

He works for Baba Yaga, and she told Nero that she's not after me.

And you can't lie to Nero.

Or can you?

Is Nero so dumb as not to include Baba Yaga's minions in the "don't kill Sasha" deal?

No.

If anyone can make an airtight deal, it's Nero.

But then that leaves another possibility, one too frightening to even contemplate.

What if Nero is the one lying… to me?

Did Baba Yaga get to him somehow? Did she pay him to tell me not to worry?

No.

As much as he can be a pain in my butt, that's just not something I can picture Nero doing.

Baba Yaga figuring out some sneaky way to lie to Nero seems way more plausible.

Then I realize something weird is happening.

Koschei's footsteps sound wrong.

Instead of getting closer, they sound farther away.

When I hear knocking on someone else's door, the realization about the real danger smacks into my brain —and as it does, I get hit with the mother of all seer dreads.

CHAPTER TWENTY-THREE

I'M RIPPING at the chain when I hear Rose's voice say, "Koschei? What are you doing here?"

"Baba Yaga sent me," he says just as I yank open my door. "She wanted me to tell you this isn't personal, just business."

I raise my gun as I run.

Koschei is clutching the front of Rose's gown with one fist, the intricate knife I saw in my vision clutched in his other fist and poised for a strike.

I shoot, praying I don't hit Rose.

A red spot blooms in Koschei's shoulder, but the knife flashes down.

Rose screams.

I fire again—and though the bullet hits him in the torso, he doesn't even look my way. The knife flashes in the air again, and Rose lets out another horrid scream.

I aim for his head and pull the trigger.

The bullet grazes his skull.

He staggers slightly, but the knife is rising in the air again, like in a scene from *Psycho*.

I close the distance and press the gun to his temple. Stomach roiling, I squeeze the trigger.

His head explodes, and he and Rose drop to the floor.

Panting, I shoot him in the chest, over and over, until the gun clicks empty.

His Cognizant aura flickers out, but I know it's only temporary.

They call him Koschei the Immortal for a reason.

Fighting a bout of nausea, I pick up the knife from the floor and turn to face Rose.

She's lying on the doorstep of her apartment, bleeding profusely.

I start to bend over her, but a flash of purple energy surrounds Koschei's body.

His Cognizant aura comes back, and all the bullets pop out of him, clinking on the floor.

I take a dragging step back and clutch the knife in front of me.

Koschei's body rises, Nosferatu style.

I realize I'm standing in the martial arts pose I've been practicing—props to Nero's training.

Koschei's green eyes lock on me, then cut toward Rose's prone body.

I squeeze the handle tighter and wish either Nero or Thalia had taught me how to use a knife.

Koschei looks back at me. "She won't make it," he informs me calmly. "My work here is done."

Turning, he walks back to the elevator.

I stare at him, struggling to breathe as he presses the button.

"You're not going to kill me?" I ask numbly as the doors open and he steps in.

He cocks his head. "Did you want me to?"

Before I can reply, the elevator doors slide shut, like the curtains in some macabre theater.

Still numb, I glance at my apartment door.

Felix's head is peeking out, so I shout, "Call an ambulance. Now!" and kneel next to the puddle of blood spreading out from Rose's body.

Her breath is coming out in pained gurgles, and her Cognizant aura is faint.

"The stone Nero gave you for the Jubilee," she chokes out. "Bring it to me."

Can she use it to heal herself?

Hope adds strength to my legs as I sprint to my apartment, almost trampling Felix, Maya, and Fluffster in the doorway.

"Stay inside!" I bark at them as I zoom into my room.

For all I know, Koschei is trying to draw them out.

Yanking open a drawer, I locate the necklace and sprint back—this time nearly knocking down Kit, who just came out of the bathroom wrapped in a towel.

As I whoosh out of the apartment, I hear Felix giving the 911 operator our address over the phone.

Reaching Rose, I kneel next to her and put the stone into her bloody palm. "Here it is, what you asked for."

In the short time I was gone, the dark red puddle on the floor has grown, and Rose's pale skin has taken on a translucent tint.

A lump forms in the back of my throat as the gurgling sounds of her strained breathing intensify, and her gaze struggles to focus on me.

An agonizing second later, recognition glimmers in her eyes. "I think I know what this was about," she rasps out, bloody spittle accompanying her words. "If I'm right, this should help." Her fingers spasmodically tighten on the stone.

"What are you talking about?" I ask frantically, then shake my head. "Never mind that. Don't talk. Save your strength for healing."

"No." Her gaze sharpens on my face. "You have to take care of Vlad."

"You'll take care of him yourself," I say through the growing obstruction in my throat. "Stop talking crazy."

A gurgling cough shakes her frame, and blood dribbles out of the corner of her mouth. "You have to promise me," she whispers, her eyes locked on me with the same odd intensity.

I squeeze her empty hand. "Of course. I promise."

She looks at the stone in her palm, as though trying to hypnotize it. A breath later, a flood of blush-pink energy streams from her whole body into the stone.

The rock shines, and her Cognizant aura disappears.

No.

This is not happening.

I press my fingers to her neck.

No heartbeat.

Hands shaking, I take out my phone and press the glass screen to her lips.

No sign of breath.

On autopilot, I swipe across the phone's screen with ice-cold fingers, dialing Nero.

The phone rings a few times before his voicemail comes on.

"Rose is dead," I say, my voice like a stranger's in my ears. "I need you."

Hanging up, I stare numbly at the phone before I remember something important.

Vlad.

He has to know.

My brain feels like a sieve, but I somehow recall the numbers I saw Rose put into her phone.

I punch them in.

Vlad's phone rings once. Twice. On the third ring, the call connects.

"Hello?" he says, sounding worried.

I swallow the rock in my throat. "Vlad, it's Sasha. About Rose…"

"Where are you?" His voice is terrifying.

"Her apartment. I think she—"

The phone line is already dead.

Dead.

The word presses on my chest like an iceberg,

breaking something deep inside. Spots flashing in my vision, I sit there for an indeterminate amount of time.

"Rose," Felix exclaims from somewhere near me. "What happened?"

I jump to my feet and spin around so fast I nearly puke.

Felix, Maya, and Kit are behind me, horrified expressions on their faces.

Sudden fury lashes at me. "I told you to stay inside. Do you want Koschei to kill you too?"

Felix looks as though I smacked him as he backs away.

"Koschei did this?" Kit's usually mischievous expression is grave. "The Council will have to dispatch the Enforcers right away—though probably not Vlad."

"Vlad is on the way," I hear myself saying as though from afar.

"Take Sasha inside," Kit says imperiously to Felix and Maya. "I'll get the nearest Enforcer to deal with any errant humans arriving at the scene. We want this place empty when Vlad appears."

I clear my sandpaper-like throat. "I should be here when he arrives. I promised to look after him."

Ignoring my words, Maya and Felix grab me by the shoulders.

A part of me wants to fight, but I let them drag me into my room since my submission has a bonus effect: it gets those two inside the apartment, where I want them.

Time moves in discrete jumps, as if I'm stoned. One moment I'm by the door, the next I'm by my bed.

Since my legs are trembling, I find it easiest to collapse onto it.

"What happened?" Fluffster says inside my mind.

"Koschei killed Rose," Felix whispers. "Sasha saw it happen. I'm worried about her."

Fluffster jumps onto the bed and cuddles up next to me. Either Felix or Maya cover me with a blanket and soothingly stroke my back.

None of it works.

I just lie there, my thoughts circling like a fidget spinner.

This can't be true.

Rose can't be dead.

Maybe someone in the Cognizant community has a power akin to what Koschei does to himself—the power to bring Rose back?

No.

Kit or someone would've mentioned it.

My chin quivers, and there's a pressure in the back of my eyes, but the tears don't come—as though my tear ducts are clogged. When I was little, no matter how awful I felt, a good bout of weeping would always make me feel better—a bit like a proper puking can sometimes make even the worst nausea recede.

I bet the tears don't come because I deep down believe I don't deserve to feel better. After all, *this* was what the vision of the funeral was about—and I didn't figure it out in time. I failed to save Rose. She wasn't even on the list of people I was worried about—and she should've been.

Once I start down the guilt road, more and more self-flagellating thoughts arrive. If I'd let my last vision have a longer duration, I would've seen Koschei walk toward Rose's apartment after he killed Felix and Maya—and there would have been a chance to do something. Maybe. Also, the very reason he killed her might be me, as I'm beginning to think Baba Yaga's plan is to torment me by killing people I care about.

The back stroking stops, and Maya and Felix tiptoe out of the room.

Do they think I fell asleep?

More than anything I wish I *were* asleep, and this were all a nightmare.

Then again, how do I know that it's not?

For that matter, how do I know I'm not having a vision right now? I've seen people I care about die in my visions.

The problem with that theory is I don't remember entering Headspace before all this happened. But then would I? If I hadn't gained conscious control over my visions, I'd think I'm in one of those unsolicited awake visions, or even a dream like the ones I'd started with. But I do have conscious control now, so it can't be one of those.

Hold on. Can you go into Headspace from inside a vision? No one explicitly told me this, but it seems like it should be an impossibility. Else you'd get visions inside visions inside visions ad infinitum, which seems kind of crazy.

Okay then.

I need to reach Headspace.

Having something to do without leaving my fetal pose and releasing Fluffster's fur is good, so I try it.

And fail.

Over and over.

Am I sabotaging myself because I *want* this to be a vision?

Pushing that and other thoughts away, I drag in a breath through the lump in my throat and slowly let it out. Then I do it again and again.

The Headspace focus seems to be within my grasp when I hear the horrific noise.

Someone roars in pain; then there's ripping and crashing.

Fluffster extricates himself from my tense grasp. "I'm going to go find out what's happening."

The noises continue, but I can't bring myself to move.

Finally, the clamor stops, and Fluffster runs back into the room.

"That was Vlad," he explains to me mentally. "He did not take the news well."

"Vlad?" I look at the domovoi.

"He went berserk, then stormed off somewhere." Fluffster paces the room. "Kit is concerned. She thinks he should let his Enforcers handle this and recuse himself on the account of having a personal relationship with the victim. She thinks that Vlad is going to get revenge without due process, which can have dire consequences for him with the Council."

It figures the Council would take such a stupid position. How could anyone blame Vlad for seeking revenge? If I could will my muscles to move, I'd probably be out there myself, doing my best to test how immortal Koschei really is.

My promise to Rose swims up through the turbulent swamp of my thoughts.

I'm supposed to take care of Vlad, yet I've been doing a horrible job thus far. I wasn't there for him when he discovered his lover's dead body. Now I'm letting him become persona non grata with the Council.

But then what *can* I do?

Headspace is the answer again.

If I can reach it, I can both prove to myself that this isn't a vision and check on Vlad's future.

So, I repeat my earlier breathing efforts for a while, until eventually, the prerequisite mental focus arrives.

———

I FLOAT in Headspace for some time without forming thoughts or noticing the surrounding shapes.

Lacking a body, I enjoy the lack of nausea, as well as the absence of the weight on my chest and the painful knot in my throat.

But I didn't get here to spare myself pain.

I wanted to be sure I wasn't having a vision, and it seems like I wasn't. That hope, thin as it was, was my version of denial.

That, or it *is* possible to have a vision inside a vision and so on.

No.

That's denial talking again.

Rose is gone, and whether my reality is a vision or not, the only logical way to behave is to pretend like it isn't and keep living my life.

Somehow.

My thoughts turn to Vlad since the least I can do for Rose is try to keep my promise.

I bring to mind the imposing brow on his extremely symmetrical, carved-out-of-ivory face.

Nothing changes.

I guess I need to dig deeper. Vlad was violent and volatile on the best of days, but given how protective he was of Rose, the rage he must now be feeling is—

The shapes around me change.

Without much ado, I shorten the vision duration and reach for the one in the middle of the swarm.

———

THE GRISLY ROOM looks like a slaughterhouse.

"*Gdye on?*" Vlad barks at the remnants of the mobster-looking dude on the metal table.

The guy squeals out something incoherent in Russian.

Vlad indiscriminately rips a tattooed chunk of flesh from the man's body, tosses it into a large, mostly filled-up bucket, and yells in rapid-fire Russian—

———

I'M BACK on the bed, my neck corded like a climbing rope.

If I'm to help Vlad, I need to know where he will be, and my gruesome vision held no hint of his location.

That means I have to try this again.

Suppressing a pained moan, I resume my earlier Headspace-friendly breathwork.

Inhale. Exhale.

Inhale.

Exhale.

Something in my head shifts, and I find myself in Headspace once more. As I float among the unfamiliar shapes, I consider my options.

I can get another vision of Vlad—and probably see him torturing more of Baba Yaga's people to get to Koschei.

For many reasons, I'm not a fan of that idea.

What if I seek out Koschei instead?

Could I get lucky and catch Vlad as he's getting his revenge? Given his last encounter with Koschei, he might need looking after at that moment in the future above all others.

Though everything in me revolts at the idea, I try to think of the essence of Koschei.

I start with his physical attributes, and soon I have his distinct voice and skinny good looks firmly in my mind's eye.

Nope.

Not enough.

I do my best to guess Koschei's vile personality next.

I must be good at this distasteful exercise because the shapes around me change once again.

Keeping the length of the vision unchanged, I reach out with my wisp and reluctantly spiral into the vision.

———

KOSCHEI IS STANDING on the corner of West 57th Street and 12th Avenue, staring at his smartphone.

It's 6:57 p.m. and the address in his GPS matches the number etched into the modern-artsy building looming above.

Koschei heads for the door, and I ghost-float after him.

The elevator stops on the fourteenth floor.

He makes his way to apartment 14N and knocks.

"Who is it?" a familiar female voice asks from behind the door.

"This is Keanu, your superintendent," Koschei says, his gravelly voice barely disguised.

"Please come back in a few hours," the woman says, "I'm not dressed."

Koschei frowns, then steps back from the door and gives it a powerful kick.

The door creaks but remains in place.

He kicks it again.

The door flies in, and Koschei enters.

A very dressed Lucretia is standing next to a throne like chair in the middle of a living room furnished almost identically to her office at Nero's land.

"Baba Yaga sent me." Koschei pulls out a knife. "She wanted me to tell you this isn't personal, just business."

"Don't make this about someone else." Lucretia puts the huge chair between them. "I can sense that you don't want to be doing this."

"This isn't personal for me either." He takes a step forward and raises the knife. "When you came to the banya, I always admired you... from afar."

"Then don't do this," she says, her usually in-control tone sounding more desperate by the second. "I know she's not using her mind control power on *you*, so you have a choice."

"I do," Koschei says, almost apologetically. "But I'm also a few kills away from being rid of my obligations to her. As much as I wish someone else could take your place, you're a part of her plan."

Instead of a reply, Lucretia grabs something from the intricate design of the throne.

Metal shines in the air.

Koschei blinks and stares at the rapier in Lucretia's hands with a mixture of awe and regret.

She kicks the large chair toward him and assumes the en garde position.

He dodges the chair and closes the distance between them.

Lucretia's rapier strikes with the speed of a scorpion stinger.

Though skewered like a kebab by her blade, Koschei keeps moving forward until the rapier sticks out of his back.

Lucretia strains to pull her weapon out—

CHAPTER TWENTY-FOUR

THE VISION IS OVER, and I'm back in the fetal position.

As I process what I just foresaw, a surge of stress hormones drowns my still-budding grief, lessening the constant pressure on my tear ducts.

Lucretia is in danger.

My breathing speeds up, and I can feel my sympathetic nervous system shifting into the fight-or-flight response.

Good.

It should help me fly to Lucretia's place and fight Koschei with her.

I leap to my feet.

The room spins for a few seconds, but then the adrenaline clears my vision and reinvigorates my muscles.

I grab the phone.

It's 6:21 p.m.

Koschei was outside Lucretia's home at 6:57, which doesn't leave me much time. If there's traffic (and there's always traffic in Manhattan), it can take longer than a half hour to get to Midtown from here.

I use an app to check if public transportation would be faster, but it tells me the shortest trip would be forty minutes and change.

Grabbing my gun, I rush out of the room—but then recall that I've unloaded the thing at Koschei.

Ariel might have bullets stashed somewhere in her room, but I don't have time to search for them.

Hopefully, Kevin, Nero's bodyguard/driver, has some spare bullets in the limo.

"How are you?" Fluffster asks me when I whoosh by him in the hallway. "Are you going to the bathroom?"

"Koschei is about to kill Lucretia," I say over my shoulder. "She's my shrink. I have to save her."

"What? No, don't go." Fluffster's tiny feet struggle to keep up with my crazy pace. "Koschei will then kill two people instead of one."

"He didn't kill me when he had the chance." I spin around to face him as I pull on my shoes by the door. "I think Baba Yaga is now pretending to honor her agreement with Nero when it comes to me. That or she wants me to suffer the loss of some people before she finally puts me out of my misery."

"But I can't protect you out there." Fluffster's mental message sounds miserable.

"I'm sorry, I don't have time to discuss this," I

unlock the door. "Just keep Felix and Maya safe until—"

"They already left," he interrupts. "You people are insane."

"You let them leave?"

"Maya had to get home," he replies as something furry scurries across my peripheral vision. "Kit volunteered to take her—and she commanded a couple of Enforcers to go with them. Felix tagged along."

"And no one deigned to run any of this by me?" I look behind the shoe rack and realize the ball of fur that just streaked across the room is Lucifur.

Fluffster follows my gaze. "Rose's cat is going to stay with us. We tried to tell you all this, but you looked catatonic."

"Fine." Staring at the cat, I realize she looks sadder than the time she swallowed a key and nearly died. "I really don't have time for this. If there's any way you can comfort the cat, please do so."

"I tried." Fluffster hangs his head. "She must know what happened."

"I'll make them pay for what they did," I promise the cat and yank open the front door.

The hallway looks like a tornado chased a herd of bison through it.

"Vlad was very upset," Fluffster explains before I can even ask. "He was quite inconsolable."

I run to the dented elevator doors and press the button.

The doors screech open—it looks like Nero will have more building repairs to do.

I see them as soon as the elevator doors open.

"You've got to be kidding me," I mutter.

Clenching my hands, I step out to face Roxy and her two minions.

CHAPTER TWENTY-FIVE

THE LIMO that is my destination is just a sprint away, but the three literal bitches have expertly placed themselves between me and the entrance door. Their lupine grins look sinister on their Dior-painted faces.

"I told you she'd come out eventually," says Ashley—or Maddie—in a voice of a sixty-year-old smoker.

"It was my idea to follow the limo," says the other—the one who'd helped Roxy chase me through Battery Park the other day, when it took Rose and Vlad to save me from a mauling. "Why do you always take credit for everything I do?"

"Kevin!" I shout as loudly as I can.

Kevin—who was standing outside the car, fiddling with his phone—looks our way.

"Maddie," Roxy commands the smoker-sounding one. "Get the door."

Maddie sprints for the door at the same time as Kevin launches for the building.

Maddie makes it there first, grabbing the door with both hands.

Kevin—who's a big guy—looks at Maddie without much concern as he pulls the door toward him.

The door doesn't budge.

He puts some effort into it.

Still no luck.

Is Maddie super strong, or is this the physics of the door?

The latter must be the case—the Mandate would prevent Maddie from displaying supernatural strength in front of someone without an aura, like Kevin.

"I didn't realize your driver doubles as a bodyguard," Roxy says, ignoring the struggle. "But looks like he can't save you anyway."

"She's scared." Ashley takes in an exaggerated breath. "I can smell it."

"I'm not scared of you," I say. "Whatever this is, I don't have time for it. Can we do this later?"

"You're not leaving." Roxy puts her exquisitely manicured hands on her hips.

"Think about it." I nod toward Kevin. "You might have a bigger advantage if he isn't around."

"We don't need to shift to deal with you," Ashley says, pitching her voice low. "There are three of us and one of you."

Actually, it's just two of them, unless Maddie lets go of the door and lets Kevin in, but two against one are still not good odds—especially since I'm more worried about getting delayed than getting into a fight.

"Enough of this," I grit through my teeth and reach for my gun.

It's empty, but I can still bluff my way out.

Roxy leaps at me, knocking the gun out of my hand before I can point it at her.

The weapon clatters on the floor.

"Grab that!" Roxy yells at Ashley. At me, she hisses, "You're going to pay for what that senile witch did to me."

My nostrils flare, and I glare at Roxy's grinning face. "What did you just say?" I plant my legs wide—instinctively falling into the stance I've practiced so much.

"Your geriatric retard of a girlfriend took my powers for a week," Roxy snarls, her perfect chin held high. "Now you'll—"

"You mean Rose?"

"Who else?" she sneers. "How many other decrepit—"

My vision reddens, and I execute the punch Nero and Thalia had me drill.

My fist smashes into Roxy's chin.

She seems to fly up, then crashes onto the granite floor.

I soccer-kick her in the ribs.

She gasps, struggling to get up while her minions gape at me in stunned fascination.

"Say something else about Rose now, bitch." I kick her again. "I dare you." I kick another time.

"Stop!" Ashley screams through the pounding in

my ears.

I spare her a glance.

She has my gun aimed at my head.

I show her my teeth and kick Roxy in the head this time.

Ashley's weapon clicks futilely.

Roxy covers her head just in time to take a kick into her forearms.

My boot scrapes her arm, resulting in a very satisfying smear of blood.

"Freeze!" Kevin orders.

I look back.

Kevin is now inside the lobby holding two guns—one pointed at Maddie, one at Ashley.

Maddie and Ashley have their hands raised, and my/Ashley's gun is on the floor.

Through the haze of rage, I realize that Kevin must've resorted to this once he saw my gun come into play.

I wish he'd done it sooner. I have somewhere to be.

To my shock, Kevin doesn't lower his weapons.

If anything, he looks like he's about to shoot.

Roxy notices this new danger and rolls onto her back with a pained grunt.

Worried she's about to try something, I raise my boot, ready to stomp her face with my heel.

"Don't," she says through a split lip. "I submit." Her Mandate aura dims, then gets back to normal intensity.

Maddie and Ashley look at her with eyes the size of gourmet pizzas.

I feel strange—as though someone's dripped some caffeine directly into my brain.

The feeling dissipates quickly, though. Maybe it's just the shock of seeing some of the damage I've done to Roxy?

"I also submit," Ashley says ceremonially, then plops on the floor and stretches out to match Roxy's posture. This time, it's her aura that flickers, and I again feel that same rush of strange energy.

This must be some kind of werewolf ritual.

In fact, didn't Kit talk about "submission" in the context of Roxy?

"I submit too." Maddie gets on the floor, and her aura does the flickering deal as well. I receive another boost of energy—or whatever this is.

Shaking my head, I decide to figure out all this werewolf weirdness later. "We have to get to Midtown," I tell Kevin. "I need to be there as soon as physically possible."

"You exit first," he says, keeping his guns aimed at the teens on the floor.

I pick up my gun and sprint for the limo, taking a seat in the front so I can be more aware of the road.

Kevin gets in a few moments later, starts the car, and looks at me expectantly.

"West 57th Street and 12th Avenue. The modern-artsy building there. 14N. Hurry."

The car's tires screech as we launch into motion.

"Do you have any bullets for this kind of gun?" I

wave my weapon. I don't want to distract him, given our speed, but I need to be armed.

"Glovebox," he says without looking at me. "Box with the golden lettering."

I locate the bullets and reload my gun.

When I look up, I cringe at the density of the West Side Highway traffic.

Taking out my phone, I call Nero again.

I get his voicemail, so I blurt out everything that has happened today—only editing out the supernatural bits so that the Mandate doesn't punish me for Kevin overhearing.

Next, I try Vlad's phone. He doesn't pick up, so I leave a voicemail to call me—then text him the same message.

No reply.

Maybe he doesn't want to get his phone bloody, or is in general too busy torturing Baba Yaga's goons.

A spot opens up in the left lane, and Kevin swerves there, just barely missing a yellow cab. That only buys us a few feet, though, and I get more and more worried that we won't make it in time.

The traffic picks up from a crawl, and Kevin resumes his kamikaze maneuvers as I bounce up and down in my seat. Lucretia is about to fight for her life, and there's nothing I can do about it.

Stupid traffic.

Stupid Roxy.

Thinking of the teen werewolf, I feel a slight pang of remorse. I kicked her so hard that my foot is now aching. Unless werewolves heal faster than normal, which is feasible, she must be in pain.

Not that she deserves my pity. The stuff she said about Rose—

I stop that line of thought, not wanting to fall apart. I need to focus on Lucretia now.

My mind refuses to obey logic. *Rose is dead. Rose is dead.* The insidious whisper brings with it a crushing pressure to my chest and tear ducts, but the tears refuse to come out, no matter how much I crave the relief of a good cry.

We come to a screeching halt on the corner of 57th and 12th, and Kevin unbuckles his seatbelt.

"Where are you going?" I ask him.

"With you, to deal with the dangerous Russian thug," he says—repeating the euphemism that I used for Koschei when I left Nero the voicemail.

"No, don't. It will be very dangerous." I unbuckle my own seatbelt and open the door.

"That's my job." Kevin exits the car. "Whatever happens in 14N is nothing compared to what the boss will do to me if I let you get hurt."

There's no time to argue and no way I can describe the unique nature of this danger without the Mandate making me bleed from all orifices. So I let him tag along.

"This is my husband." I nod at Kevin when we get to the security guard. "He and I are here for marriage counseling. Our therapist's name is Lucretia Rossi. 14N."

"Husband?" Kevin gives me a look when the elevator doors close.

I shrug. "I'm usually much better at lying."

He nods and pulls out his gun.

I do the same.

The elevator stops, and Kevin takes the lead.

I sprint after him.

We find 14N's door broken in.

Kevin does a TV cop imitation as he carefully rushes in with his gun raised. I do my best to mimic his actions and follow.

There are signs of struggle all over, but Koschei is missing.

"I'll check the perimeter," Kevin whispers into my ear. "You see if you can help her."

He nods at the couch blocking my view and hurries into another room.

Heart sinking, I walk around the couch, already knowing what I'll see.

Lucretia is lying sprawled on the floor, her knife wounds identical to Rose's and her Mandate aura missing.

As if controlling my body remotely from some bunker, I dazedly step over the bloody rapier and kneel next to her to check what is already obvious.

No pulse.

No breathing.

No Mandate aura.

Numb, I collapse over Lucretia, embracing her dead body in a hug.

CHAPTER TWENTY-SIX

I DON'T KNOW how long I stay down there, draped over Lucretia's still body.

My thoughts are like squirrels on Red Bull, and the pressure on my eyes is beyond unbearable.

Then one rational question crawls through the haze and confusion: how can Lucretia be dead? She's a prevamp—a type of Cognizant who turn into vampires when they die. But then I recall something Ariel had mentioned once: if a prevamp isn't powerful enough, they will not turn.

Not unless they preemptively drank the blood of a vampire.

It could easily be the case that Lucretia didn't drink such blood—as a therapist, she knows how addictive that can be. Plus, Ariel also mentioned such a choice has an annoying side effect: the donor vampire becomes the new vampire's sire and can control him or her for a decade.

Koschei and Baba Yaga must've known about Lucretia's vulnerability. Else why would they bother committing a crime that would only transform Lucretia into a potentially more powerful enemy?

But hold on.

At our recent session Lucretia mentioned that she drank blood from Gaius after some injury. She said she didn't get addicted from it, that it was like getting a shot of morphine when you need it.

So maybe she turned, but Koschei killed her twice, once as a regular Cognizant, then as a vampire?

How *does* one kill a vampire?

Suddenly, ice-cold hands grip my shoulders.

Then there's a sharp pain as Lucretia's fangs penetrate my neck.

CHAPTER TWENTY-SEVEN

"LUCRETIA." I do my best to break her iron-like hold. "It's me, Sasha."

She doesn't let go, just sucks at the wound on my neck.

I go for my gun, but she slaps it out of my hand, launching it across the room.

"Snap out of it," I hiss, kicking at my newly animated friend. "You don't want to eat me."

"Let her go," Kevin says from somewhere. "Or I *will* shoot."

"You will not shoot anyone," says a familiar hypnotic voice.

"I will not shoot anyone," Kevin repeats, sounding glamoured.

"Throw that gun away," the voice says.

Kevin tosses his gun in the same direction where mine disappeared.

"Lucretia, dear, let Sasha go this instant." The voice is dripping with honey-laced malice, and despite my shock and panic, I realize who this is.

Lucretia releases my shoulders, and I struggle to my feet.

"Where is Ariel?" I demand as I turn around to verify my suspicion, my hand unwillingly nursing the bite on my neck.

Yep.

The pretty face of the newcomer belongs to Gaius—the bane of Ariel's existence.

"Where is she?" I repeat, stepping toward him.

"I heard you the first time." Gaius's eyes go from mirror-like to normal.

Kevin stands rod-still.

Lucretia rises on her elbow and looks around the room, her eyes wilder than drunk college coeds on spring break. Focusing on me, she takes in the wound on my neck and pales—a difficult feat since un-death has already made her paler than her usual bleached china-doll complexion.

Speaking of un-death, she still has no aura—yet Gaius and other vampires do.

Maybe it needs to be reapplied?

I push the mystery away as she says to me, "I can feel how scared you are. I'm so sorry."

"You're still an empath after turning?" I blurt out, then realize there are any number of better questions I should ask, the majority of them a variation on what I already asked Gaius.

"Indeed," Gaius says with an almost fatherly pride. "She's going to be invaluable to me." He looks at my neck and adds, "You're both lucky I came when I did—the newly turned have trouble controlling themselves."

"I wouldn't have hurt Sasha," Lucretia says, sitting up.

"False," Gaius says teasingly. "You could've easily killed her—which neither Nero nor the Council would've appreciated. Such things often happen to newbies."

"No way," Lucretia says, but scoots away from me—as though she needs the distance to stave off the temptation.

"You must feed," Gaius tells her, nodding toward Kevin—who, due to glamour, shows no reaction to this horrific suggestion.

"Wait a minute." I take another step forward.

"Can't I just get a bag of blood?" Lucretia leaps into a standing position with the effortlessness of an Olympic athlete. "Drinking from a human is—"

"My apologies for the misunderstanding," Gaius says, the honey evaporating from his voice to leave behind pure malice. "As your *sire*, I *command* you to drink from that human."

Lucretia looks like he just rammed a truck into her brain. With a zombie-like determination, she comes toward Kevin.

"Hold on." I step in front of her. "Don't do this."

"That's right," Gaius croons, ignoring me. "You will

find it harder and harder to fight me with every command I give."

Lucretia shoves me aside with Ariel-like strength, and as I catch myself on the couch, a realization hits me.

Of course. Lucretia is now Gaius's virtual slave—and will be for a whole decade.

"Gaius, please." I rush forward as Lucretia bites Kevin.

"Would you rather it be you?" Gaius steps into my path, his large body forming an impenetrable barrier.

Behind him, Lucretia is feeding. Her throat moves reluctantly at first, but after she takes a few gulps, she starts sucking more and more enthusiastically.

"Lucretia!" I shout, futilely trying to go around Gaius. "Kevin isn't a Happy Meal. You're going to kill him."

With great reluctance, Lucretia pulls herself away from Kevin's neck.

The driver looks pale but otherwise normal—assuming you ignore the emptiness in his glamour-affected eyes.

"I didn't say you could stop," Gaius says to Lucretia over his shoulder. "Drink from him, and stop only if I say stop."

Though it's clear Lucretia tries to fight the command, she obeys quicker this time.

Once she resumes drinking, she does it faster and faster, like she's getting thirstier with every gulp.

Kevin's paleness begins to match that of the two vampires in the room—which can't be a good sign.

"Stop this!" I punch Gaius in the jaw, then shove at him, but he just lifts a perfect eyebrow.

"Is violence really the answer?"

If I could, I'd rip Gaius's throat out right now. As is, I have to use misdirection.

Feinting to the right, I pretend to go around him, then suddenly leap to the left.

He chuckles behind me, clearly amused as I grab Lucretia and do my best to pry her head away from Kevin's neck.

I might as well try to break a cement block in half.

Kevin's body slumps in her arms.

"No." I tug harder. "Lucretia, stop it!"

Odd slurping noises escape from her mouth as she keeps on sucking like a gluttonous leech.

"There's no more blood remaining in that body." Gaius walks up to the bloody rapier on the floor, picks it up, and examines it appreciatively. "Let's go."

Lucretia lets Kevin collapse on the floor and sprints after Gaius—who's left the room so fast he must've used vampire powers.

I dash across the room and get my gun, then run out into the hallway, unsure if I'm going to shoot them both or only Gaius.

The hallway is already empty.

Maybe it's for the best. I don't have enough energy to chase them.

Closing the front door, I circle back to Kevin.

Dropping to my knees next to his unmoving body, I check the vitals.

Nothing.

He's dead.

Just like Rose.

I want to shout obscenities, but the scream is stuck in my throat.

It was my fault. Again.

A second person died today because of me.

There will be two funerals.

The pressure behind my eyes now feels like boiling acid.

Facing away from the corpse, I cup my eyes with my palms.

Dead.

Did he have a family? Children?

Did some poor woman become a widow tonight?

The remnants of adrenaline that I was running on evaporate, leaving me utterly drained.

Rose and Kevin.

Ariel missing.

Lucretia as a vampire bound to Gaius.

It's hard to breathe, impossible to think.

There's just that awful burning pressure and crushing emptiness.

I don't know how long I stay there, kneeling next to Kevin's body, before I hear faint footsteps outside the door.

I find it difficult to care.

The door hinges squeak.

I should stand up or at least ask who it is, but my legs and lips refuse to move.

And then it's too late anyway.

The new arrival rushes toward me too fast for my eyes to follow.

CHAPTER TWENTY-EIGHT

HE STOPS in front of me, and I recognize the prominent cheekbones on his face—a face contorted into a mask of fury.

It's Nero.

He found me. Must've learned where I'd be from my voicemail. But he's too late. If only—

"Are you hurt?" he demands. "What happened?"

Unable to form words, I shake my head.

Nero doesn't seem satisfied with my laconic answer. Crouching next to me, he pats me down, as if looking for damage.

His gaze zeroes in on the puncture wounds on my neck.

"Who did this?" He sounds like a T-Rex defending his turf.

My adrenal glands come back to life, giving me the strength to croak out, "Lucretia. She was dead. Then she wasn't. Gaius made her do that." I nod toward Kevin's body and feel a rush of dizziness.

"I'm taking you home," Nero states as though from afar.

If I could speak, I'd warn him about being near me.

I'd tell him that everyone who gets close to me is in danger.

That everyone I care about is a target—and that I wouldn't want him to die.

That I would not be able to survive it if he were next.

Strong hands lift me into the air, clasping me against a broad chest, and a clean, woodsy, masculine scent envelops me like a fluffy blanket.

He carries me out of the building, and as he walks, the heat of his body leaches a tiny portion of my pain away.

It doesn't help much, though. There's an ocean of pain where that came from.

Distantly, I hear him bark orders into his phone. He wants someone to arrange a proper burial for Kevin, as well as make sure Kevin's family is secure financially.

He then places me into the front seat of the limo, and I lose sight of him as he closes the door.

Without his proximity, the horrible emptiness inside me grows to the size of Jupiter, the pressure behind my eyes impossibly intensifying.

Could it eventually cause blindness?

Could my eyes pop out of their sockets, like—

Nero opens the driver's side door, gets in, and starts driving.

"Can you tell me what happened in more detail?" he asks as we stop at a red light. "It might be important."

I sit, staring straight ahead as I hug myself.

I feel as if I might fly apart if I start speaking.

Eventually, I find the strength to mumble a delirious retelling of events under my breath.

I must make *some* sense because Nero's face is a kaleidoscope of frightening reactions.

"So maybe the vision was that of Rose's funeral," I say unsteadily in conclusion. "Or maybe of Felix's or Maya's if I hadn't saved them. Or maybe Kevin's. Or maybe someone else will die next. Maybe—"

I fall silent as we stop.

I didn't recognize the surroundings at first, but I do now.

This is Nero's swanky building.

He took me to *his* home, not mine.

Before I can process this development, I'm in Nero's arms again, feeling the soothing effects of his touch.

It's especially nice when we get into the elevator, and Nero strokes my back as if I were a cat.

I shouldn't think of cats, though, particularly cats that look as miserable as I do.

Too late.

I curve into a tighter ball in his arms, my breathing ragged as my mind replays the sight of the poor cat who seemed to understand what had happened to her owner.

We exit the elevator, and Nero carries me toward his penthouse.

Once inside, he takes me to the kitchen, sets me on my feet, and cleans the wound on my neck. Next, he unpacks a small Band-Aid and gently applies it to the marks.

Putting the medical kit away, he frames my face with his large palms, staring into my eyes.

I can't help but stare back.

His limbal rings are record thick today, making the blue-gray of his irises that much more mesmerizing.

It's purely an illusion, but I feel like his gaze physically assaults the floodgates blocking my tear ducts.

I sway forward, as if drawn to him.

He lowers his hands to my shoulders and pulls me into an embrace, pressing my cheek against his muscular chest as he wraps his arms around me.

I clutch at his sides, trembling all over as a lump in my throat cuts off my breathing and the pressure behind my eyes grows unbearable.

"Shhh," he murmurs. "It'll be all right. Everything will be all right."

And as if it were waiting for him to say that, a sob breaks through my knotted throat, and the floodgates burst open.

CHAPTER TWENTY-NINE

AT FIRST, I cry uncontrollably.

Nero gently strokes my back and rocks me with every wail, sob, and sniffle—which makes me feel a fraction of a percent better.

When my voice goes, the sobs turn into hoarse gasps, and I squeeze Nero's shirt with my last remaining strength.

He massages my shoulders and whispers reassuring nothings into my ear.

I don't know how long we stand there like that, but when I eventually pull away, there's a large wet spot on his chest.

Oblivious to it, Nero strides to the chair nearest me, pulls it away from the table, and gestures for me to sit with all the grace of a maître d' at a fancy restaurant.

I plop my butt down and wipe my face with my sleeve.

As if in one of my illusions, a glass of water appears

in Nero's hand. He places it in front of me, and I gulp it down.

Seems like crying and drooling on my boss is quite dehydrating.

Nero walks up to the gigantic kitchen counter and fusses with the state-of-the-art teakettle sitting there.

"Drink this too." He puts a steaming cup in front of me. "It's lemon balm and chamomile."

I gratefully pick up the cup with my icy hands, blow on the top, and take a careful sip.

"It's nice," I say hoarsely. "Thank you."

Nodding, Nero heads for the industrial-sized refrigerator and takes out a couple of perfect-looking avocados, a bag of berries, and some leafy greens

My phone rings.

I take it out and catch Nero frowning.

It's Felix.

I pick up to yell at him for leaving the house.

When I'm done, he yells back at me for going on another rescue mission by myself.

We make peace quickly, though: he's home and safe now, and I explain the strict deadline that I was working under.

"I think you should stay with Nero until we figure out what's happening," Felix says. "I can't think of a safer place for you to be."

And before I can express my thoughts on the matter, he hangs up.

I sip my tea and ponder the reality of my situation.

I am at Nero's place.

Which is a confusing situation, to say the least.

As though in an effort to befuddle me further, Nero places a bowl of freshly made salad in front of me and goes back to the fridge.

"I'm not hungry," I say but examine the gorgeous-looking dish.

"Just eat as much as you can," Nero suggests, opening the fridge.

I spear some salad with a fork and gingerly put it into my mouth.

Wow.

Either I'm hungrier than I realized, or this is the best salad I've ever tasted.

I wolf down my bowl to the sound of something sizzling on the stove.

"Potatoes with mushrooms," Nero explains when he spots me glancing furtively in his direction.

"Smells delicious," I mumble, swallowing the last of my salad.

Nero brings over the whole skillet, puts down two plates, and ladles a huge serving onto mine.

Despite the salad, my stomach angrily growls at the sight.

How unladylike.

And he heard it.

How else can I explain the smile that's touching the corners of Nero's eyes?

Stabbing a few bits of potato and mushroom, I jam the forkful into my mouth.

A moan of pleasure accidentally escapes my lips.

The smile is gone from his eyes, but their limbal rings thicken. To his credit, Nero doesn't say or do anything to indicate that he heard me.

"You eat, I'll be right back," he says, and before I can argue, he walks out of the kitchen.

By the time he's back, I've finished half my plate.

He plates some food for himself and attacks it with the gusto of a hungry street dog.

"Some music?" He points at the smart speaker nearby.

Since my mouth is full, I just nod.

"Alexa," Nero says in his deep voice. "Play 'Gangnam Style.'"

I'm so surprised by his choice that I nearly choke on a mushroom.

The beats of the most-watched YouTube video ever made begin too loudly, so Nero asks the speaker to lower the volume.

I swallow and say, "I thought you'd put on Johnny Cash or Leonard Cohen or something. Not—"

"Because if my voice is deep, I must like singers with deep voices?" The smile is back in the corners of Nero's eyes.

"Well, no, but I didn't exactly think you'd like K-Pop." I pointedly spear more potatoes with my fork. "Unless you just like this one song?"

"K-Pop seamlessly mixes some of my favorite genres," Nero says and puts on another, less familiar-to-me song. "The lyrics for this are—"

"Wait, you speak Korean?" I know I shouldn't be

surprised by anything when it comes to Nero, but the words of the current song are so incomprehensible that—

"I work closely with Lee Kun-Hee," Nero says. Then, perhaps mistaking why my eyes widen, he adds, "He's the chairman of Samsung Group."

"I know that," I say. "I'm just shocked you learned Korean to speak to a client, no matter how rich."

"I know the language of everyone I interact with." He forks the last remnants of potato into his mouth. "When someone speaks to me with an interpreter, they can lie."

"Hmm. I didn't know that."

The topic of lying to Nero is a sensitive one. It reminds me about his assertion that Baba Yaga isn't trying to kill me. Allegedly, she didn't trigger his lie detection alert when she made that claim, even though her goons came to kill me in the hotel bathroom.

Then again, Koschei very pointedly left me alone after he—

No. Better not go down that path; else I'll start crying again.

Though it now lacks any flavor, I finish the rest of the food on my plate.

When I look up, I catch Nero staring at me with what can only be sympathy in his gaze.

That's a first. Is the Pope about to become a Buddhist?

"It will get better one day." Nero reassuringly places his palm on my wrist.

I shake my head, not trusting myself to speak.

"I promise you it will," he murmurs. "You learn to live with it, over time."

I blink away the errant tears and stare at him.

The way he said it makes it seem like he's speaking from personal experience.

Lucretia *did* mention something about Nero's fear of losing someone he cares about. It must've happened to him in the past.

But who?

And when?

I'm not suicidal enough to ask, so I just put my other palm on top of his.

We sit like that for a few long seconds; then he pulls away and asks if I want dessert.

"No, thank you," I say, unsure what to do with my hands now that they're not touching his. "I'm stuffed."

"In that case, follow me." He gets up. "I set something up for you earlier. It should be ready now."

I stand up, and he leads me through a multitude of rooms until we enter a giant bathroom that looks like a showroom for extravagant spa equipment. Lit candles are everywhere, and an enormous tub stands in the middle of it all, with water cascading into it like a waterfall into a canyon.

Nero eyes the water level and checks the temperature with his hand. "Perfect." He turns to me. "This is for you."

My heartbeat speeds up.

He presses a button, and the water bubbles up as the Jacuzzi jets come to life.

Does Nero expect me to get naked and get into a hot tub in front of him? Is that what the romantic candlelight is about?

A part of me wants to do exactly that for some reason. But another part knows I might not be in the best state of mind to make any choices right now—especially when those choices include getting naked in front of my boss, full-time Mentor, and part-time tormentor.

Unsure what to do, I walk up to the water and let my fingers trail through it.

The temperature *is* perfect, and nothing has looked so inviting in a long time.

"There are fresh towels over there." Nero points at a huge rack. "Enjoy."

With that, he solves all my dilemmas by striding out of the room and leaving me to stand there, confused by the disappointment I feel at his departure.

Oh well.

I strip and get into the tub.

The jets hit me from every direction—producing a relaxing, massage-like effect.

I sigh in pleasure.

There must be warm water in Heaven.

In fact, I feel so good that I'm starting to feel guilty. How can I be so relaxed after all that's happened?

The heavy pressure on my chest returns, but before

long, the food coma conspires with the bubbling water to soothe me again.

After a few minutes, I get so chilled-out I feel loopy.

Who needs Xanax when there are carbs and hot tubs around?

My eyelids get heavy, and I give in to the strong temptation to close my eyes.

CHAPTER THIRTY

I WAKE up on the softest sheets I've ever felt.

Did I splurge on a five-star hotel?

Nope.

I remember now.

I'm at Nero's penthouse.

The last thing I recall was closing my eyes in a hot tub.

Did I fall asleep in it? If so, how did I end up here?

Rubbing my sleepy eyes, I look around.

This must be Nero's master bedroom. Or at least I hope so—it's the size of my whole apartment.

Nero himself is nowhere in sight.

Am I relieved or disappointed? It's always hard to think first thing in the morning.

I look under the three-thousand-thread-count sheets.

Yep.

As I suspected, I'm as naked as a stripper at a nudist colony.

Reluctantly, I get up.

My clothes from yesterday are on the nightstand next to my phone, as is an unfamiliar pair of lacy panties, brand-new yoga pants, and a sporty-looking T-shirt.

Hmm. What's worse: the idea of Nero stopping by La Perla first thing in the morning to get those panties, or that he might've kept them handy just in case I pop in for a sleepover?

Or some other woman, come to think of it.

I push the thought away, not liking it at all.

Feeling too clean to put on yesterday's clothes, I opt for the new stuff.

Of course, it all fits and is as comfortable as those sheets.

Must be for me after all.

As I reach for my phone, I realize yesterday's clothes smell freshly laundered as well.

What the hell? Does Nero have invisible servants, or am I just hoping he does because it would sort of make me Beauty and him the Beast?

According to my phone, it's 9:30 a.m. On a Monday. Wow.

Nero didn't wake me up to go to work. Hopefully, it means I officially get the day off. Just in case, I look for any work-related emails or texts.

Nope. Complete radio silence.

Nice.

And, given that it's Monday and after sunrise, Nero must be at the office. His work ethic is a Wall Street urban legend.

Which means I might be able to snoop around.

I walk into the ginormous master bath and find a still-sealed toothbrush that's an exact replica of mine. The toothpaste is also my favorite, as is every other toiletry on display.

I guess staying with your lifelong stalker has its perks.

I take care of all my bathroom needs and stroll out of the master bedroom—which is when the yummy smells reach my nostrils.

Letting my nose lead me, I make my way to the kitchen.

Nero is dressed in very flattering workout clothes and is cooking something on his futuristic-looking stove.

He's not at work?

Is today some national holiday I forgot about?

I sneak a glance at my phone.

Nope. It's not.

"Morning," he says without turning. "How did you sleep?"

Do I confront him about waking up naked? I can almost picture him saying, "Would you rather have drowned in the hot tub?"

"What's cooking?" I say instead, and the add-on "good looking" is on my lips but fortunately doesn't come out.

He turns around and puts a plate in front of me with a flourish.

It's Eggs Benedict, one of my favorite foods, and I bet he knows that.

The side is grilled asparagus—another favorite—with tomatoes, and mashed potatoes shaped like a mini sand castle.

Fancy.

He puts an identical meal in front of himself, then pours us some tea and splashes some orange juice into champagne glasses. Next, he opens a bottle of Cristal in one smooth movement and turns our juices into mimosas.

Brunch à la *Sex and the City*.

With my boss.

Totally normal.

Riiight.

"You're not at work." I cut up the eggs and do my best to keep my drooling to a minimum. "Did someone finally go overboard with the air-conditioning in hell?"

Nero smiles with his eyes again. "Even *I* can take a day off on a rare occasion."

I taste the eggs. They are divine. Nero is a much better cook than Felix. And maybe most chefs in Tribeca.

"Of course. You *can* take a day off." I sip the mimosa. "It's just that you never do." I chase the fizzy drink with some tea—it's the same soothing combo of chamomile and lemon balm from last night. "When was the last time you just took a day off like this?"

"The summer of 1825," Nero says without a trace of levity.

"You're kidding, right?" I attack a spear of asparagus with my fork.

"It was right before the world's first public railway opened," he says, still with no hint at a joke. "I knew I had some busy time ahead, so I took a day off."

"Well," I say. "There's being a workaholic, and then there's taking a vacation every 192 years. For your sake, I *hope* you're kidding." I salute him with my drink.

"And if I'm not?" Staring at me intently, he clinks his glass against mine.

"Then I hope you enjoy your day off." I nervously lick the remnants of Hollandaise sauce from my lips.

"I'm beginning to." He stares at my mouth with a hunger that doesn't seem to be breakfast-related.

My cheeks redden. I'm clearly a lightweight when it comes to alcohol, no matter how diluted. Feeling a sudden need to purify myself, I wipe my lips with a napkin.

He's still staring at my mouth, so I decide to change the topic. "Doesn't it cost the fund a gazillion dollars when you're off?"

"About forty-nine million," he says, again with a straight face. "But we had outstanding performance last week, thanks to your work."

Is he being sarcastic right now? It's the second time he's implied that my random stock picks have made him money—but that can't be.

"Let me guess." He lifts his gaze to meet mine.

"Despite your clever way with language, you didn't actually use your visions to provide me with any of the stock tips last week, right?"

Luckily, my mouth is currently stuffed with bacon, egg, and English muffin, so I mumble something unintelligible. I should've known better than to use all those funny stock names. He was bound to catch on.

"I thought so," he says. "But do you think your choices were *actually* random?"

I swallow the food in my mouth. "They weren't random."

"Another misleading true statement." He looks impressed. "Let me rephrase. Do you think you only chose those stocks because they had mildly amusing abbreviations?"

"Mildly amusing?" I take a gulp of my mimosa for bravery. "It's not my fault if some people don't have a sense of humor."

"Be that as it may, every choice you made was spot on." He salutes me with his drink without a hint of mockery.

"Seriously?" I mindlessly clink his glass.

"Do you want me to send you our P&L?"

"No, that's okay." I take another sip of my drink, though I probably shouldn't. "I believe you."

"Good." He leans toward me. "I never lie to you."

Instead of calling him out on that lie, I get a sudden urge to kiss him.

As though in a vision, I can picture how the kiss

would unfold, from the pressure of his firm yet soft lips to the—

Wait, what?

What is wrong with me?

The alcohol has clearly hit me hard.

Instead of following the insane urge, I push my mimosa away and say, "In that case, here are two more tips for free: Southwest Airlines and the National Beverage Company."

He lifts his bubbly drink and gives me a full-blown grin. "Your choices are LUV and FIZZ?"

"I also contemplated giving you the parent company of KFC and Pizza Hut." I smile back at him. "Their ticker is YUM, and so is your food."

"Thank you." Nero takes out his phone and writes something on it.

I stare at him incredulously. "Are you about to email someone to invest in LUV, FIZZ, and YUM?"

"Just the first two." He looks up from his message. "You said you only *contemplated* YUM. Are you saying you've upgraded it to a recommendation?"

"Why not?" I say. "Invest in YUM while you're at it. I have as much confidence in *it* as I have in all the others."

"Thanks," he says, unfazed. "Just a second."

I cram the rest of the food into my mouth as he types.

How could my random picks have made money? Am I *that* good at stock market prediction? If so, I'd much rather become that skilled at keeping myself and my loved ones safe—the stock market be damned.

The tasty morsels turn to sand in my mouth as the image of Rose lying on the floor plays in front of my eyes.

The ache in my chest returns with a vengeance, and the room starts to spin around me, the walls closing in.

"Sasha." A strong hand covers my palm, massaging it gently. "Don't go there. Stay here with me."

I blink, startled out of the dark memories by his warm touch. Or maybe by the surge of hormones that said touch generates.

I look up at him.

His gaze is hypnotic, pulling me toward him, as though his powers can break the laws of gravity.

He leans toward me. The preternatural gravity must be multidirectional.

I feel his warm breath.

Butterflies set up a sweatshop in my stomach as I recall what happened the last time our faces were *this* close.

Time slows, and a perilous question swirls through my mind.

Why *can't* I kiss him again?

He's comforted me, cooked for me, has taken a day off for the first time in centuries to be there for me.

But no.

I've been over this before.

He's my boss and Mentor.

Then again, I don't really care about my job, and the

Mentorship is a temporary situation. And it's not like he's teaching me much anyway. Perhaps if I kiss him, it can lead to more interesting lessons in—

I stop that thought in its tracks. For all I know, all this unusual niceness might be a trick, a way to make sure his little pet seer behaves herself. Once my usefulness to Nero is over, he could easily find himself another seer and abandon me.

Just like my biological parents and Rose did.

Reluctantly, Nero pulls away. And though I was just about to pull away myself, knowing he decided not to kiss me stings.

I jerk my hand away from his soothing touch.

Something like hurt flashes in his gaze, and he jackknifes to his feet. Grabbing his dirty plate, he strides to the dishwasher.

"Let me help you clean up." I stand and pick up my own plate with treacherously shaky fingers.

"I got it," he says but moves out of my way when I put the plate next to his.

Within moments, the table is spotless, and I stare at it uncomfortably, unsure what to do next.

"I'm going to the gym," Nero says with no hint of emotion in his voice.

"Bully for you," I say and hope I sound just as emotionless.

"I think you should join me," he says in a tone that's a touch too bossy for my taste.

"I'm not in the mood." I look down at my perfect-for-workout outfit and curse myself for choosing it—

and him for being clever enough to leave it by the bed.

"You can use the endorphins that physical exercise will provide," Nero says in a more reasonable tone. "You should—"

"Are you claiming this as your Mentor time again?" I lift my chin.

"No." He holds my gaze. "You can come with me or not. It's your choice."

"Fine," I surprise myself by saying. "Since you're asking so nicely, I guess I could use a workout after this huge breakfast."

"Good," he says and turns around. "This way."

He walks so fast that keeping up is already a workout.

After a few turns, we find ourselves in his private gym—a room the size of a basketball court filled with top-of-the-line equipment.

"Warm up here." He gestures to an elliptical, and I get on.

He steps on the treadmill next to me, starts it up, and takes off his shirt, tossing it on the machine next to him.

My cardio shape takes a sudden dive as my heart rate speeds up out of proportion with my movements.

My boss is an impressive specimen of maleness, and running really highlights that fact.

A few drooling minutes later, he informs me that we're sufficiently warmed up.

Very true in my case.

In fact, I may be in the middle of a hot flash.

We move to the free weight area, and he shows me how to do a few exercises while I fight off the urge to trace the grooves of muscles on his torso with my tongue.

To my relief, he then steps back, and I'm able to focus on actual weightlifting.

Before long, I'm glad he dragged me to the gym. Working out is the perfect activity when you're angry or otherwise in turmoil. Every time I lift a weight, I picture punching someone or something—and this helps me go extra heavy.

"Good job," Nero says as I drop the dumbbells with a grunt. "Now let's do the bench press."

I agree, but soon realize I've made a huge mistake. Watching his rippling muscles flex as beads of sweat form on his smooth, tan skin is chipping at my self-control like a river at the foot of a limestone mountain.

"I'm tired," I say when I can't take it anymore. "I'm going to hit the shower."

He stares at me intently, and I tense, worried that he'll offer to wash my back—and that I might accept.

"Will you find your way there?" he asks to my relief.

"Yeah, I'm sure."

Escaping the gym, I rush to the master bathroom and take a cold shower—something that's becoming a ritual with Nero.

It helps a little, though when I step out of the shower, my face still looks a bit too flushed.

Oh well. I quickly dry off and put on my freshly laundered clothes from yesterday.

Clearly, it's time to go home.

I navigate my way to the penthouse entrance—and find Nero standing there, still shirtless.

I try not to swallow my tongue as I notice the droplets of sweat on his chiseled chest.

"So… this has been fun. Thanks for everything." I take a step forward, but he doesn't get out of my way. I try again, more bluntly this time. "I think I'm going to head home now."

"No." Nero crosses his arms in front of his chest like a bouncer. "You're not."

CHAPTER THIRTY-ONE

"I AM TOO," I say, then realize how childish that must sound. In a more adult tone, I add, "You can't hold me prisoner."

At least I hope he can't, but then who knows what being a Mentor entitles him to. Or being a ruthless asshole, for that matter.

"You're not a prisoner," he says, almost grudgingly. "I just want to make sure you're safe." He comes closer. "When I find out what's going on, I will let you leave."

"Well then, that's simple." I take a step back. "Your partner, Baba Yaga, is trying to kill me."

"That's impossible," he says firmly. "She said she isn't, and she can't lie to me. We've been over this."

"Then she's making me wish I were dead," I say as my earlier suspicions about Nero being in cahoots with Baba Yaga resurface.

"I don't think that's an explanation for the moves

she's made," he says. "Lucretia works for me—and though she wasn't covered by the agreement, I doubt Baba Yaga would want to get on my bad side. Also, pissing off Vlad is foolish. She wouldn't do that just to get back at you."

"Uh-huh. So you're saying that if she did want to hurt me, she'd pick a softer target, like Ariel—who's still missing, by the way."

"Or Felix," he says. "Or your family."

I taste bile in the back of my throat.

"Don't worry. I'm keeping an eye on your adoptive parents," Nero says, taking another step toward me. "And I told Felix to stay home, where your domovoi and Councilor Kit should provide sufficient protection."

My nausea subsides, but I still step back, out of his reach.

His eyes narrow, but he doesn't move. "I don't think hurting you is what Baba Yaga ultimately wants—which is why I have someone on the case, trying to get to the bottom of it."

I blink. "You do?"

"Yes. They call her Freda Krueger," Nero says in the tone people use to name-drop a celebrity.

I lift my eyebrows. "I know of a very famous Freddy by that last name, from *A Nightmare on Elm Street*. Never heard of a female version, though. Please don't tell me Hollywood is making yet another remake with—"

"Her real name is Bailey Spade," Nero says and looks at me expectantly. When I don't show any recognition, he adds, "She went to school with Felix."

"Still doesn't ring a bell." I shuffle from foot to foot. "He's never mentioned her."

"Well, the name isn't important," Nero says. "She's agreed to look into this matter for me, and she possesses some unique skills that make her an ideal person to get to the bottom of this."

"You hired a Cognizant detective?" I rub my temples.

"You can think of it that way," he says. "What's key is that her report is due in a few hours, and I think you'll want to wait for it."

"Doesn't sound like I have a lot of choice." I cross my arms in front of my chest, mimicking his stance. "What do you expect me to do if I stay?"

"There was something I was hoping you could show me." He reaches into the pocket of his workout shorts.

A hand in the pocket? That's a surefire way to get a girl's attention. I can't help but stare at his crotch in fascination.

Is my boss about to go pervy on me? What would I do if he does?

His hand comes out of the pocket holding a deck of playing cards. He extends it toward me on the palm of his hand. "I'd like to see your card magic up close."

I let myself blink.

He's good. In fact, if they gave out medals for being master manipulators, Nero would get the gold.

He must've figured I'd be almost as excited about this prospect as I was when I contemplated another kiss.

"I guess I can show you a thing or two," I say, using all my acting skills to seem less eager. "I'd need a table if—"

"Follow me," Nero says and leads me into a wing of the house I haven't seen. On the way, he stops by a closet and pulls on a T-shirt.

My ovaries go into mourning, but the rest of me is grateful.

I was worried about my ability to focus on the cards.

We end up in a small for this penthouse, twenty two by twenty-eight-feet room.

I gape at the decor in jealous fascination.

"I host high-stakes poker games in here," Nero explains when he sees my open-mouthed expression. "I thought it might make a good setting for this."

No kidding. The place looks like a miniature casino.

If someone wanted to design the best set for my card effects, this would be it.

"Can I use this table?" I walk up to the green poker table and feel the perfect-for-card-spreads surface with my palm.

"Of course." Nero takes the chair opposite me. "That was the idea."

"Great." I sit up straighter and feel the surge of confidence that always accompanies my performances. "Shuffle those cards."

Nero surprises me yet again by giving the cards a professional riffle shuffle. He follows that with a set of flashy cuts that the best Monte Carlo croupier would be proud of, and as I watch his strong, sinuous hands perform all these delicate movements, I find myself needing another cold shower.

"Give me those," I say in a hoarse voice.

Nero moves the deck toward me, and I could swear there's a tiny smirk on his lips.

I spread the cards face up for Nero to see. "Are you happy with the way you mixed them?"

"Sure," he says without looking up from my hands.

"Good." I gather them up. "Now name your favorite poker hand and a number of players."

"The Royal Flush," Nero says, still staring at my hands. "And four players."

What he's doing is called "burning the hands"—and it's a real hazard when it comes to my art.

To perform the effect, I need him to look away—but how? On my home turf, I'd have a plan for a distraction, but here, I have to resort to something else.

Questions make great misdirection, so I blurt out, "I've been meaning to ask you this for ages. What kind of Cognizant are you?"

As I hoped, Nero looks up, allowing me to do sneaky business.

Though I don't expect him to answer, I still feel distracted by the mere possibility that he might tell me. It's a good thing I've put in all those hours of practice with cards; otherwise, I'd mess this up.

"It's not that I don't want *you* to know." Nero cocks his head. "It's just better if *no one* knows."

"I can keep a secret." I find it ironic that I'm saying that phrase as I'm doing something secret under Nero's very nose.

"I believe that you can," he says. "But there are beings like Bailey, who can still get the information from you without your willing participation."

"There are?" I nearly drop the cards. "Your pet detective sounds scary."

"She's not mine," he says, staring at me intently.

"Whatever." I grasp the cards. "Let's just get on with the demonstration."

With exaggerated fairness, I deal four poker hands on the table and ask, "Which player?"

"Which player what?" Nero asks, belatedly resuming burning my hands.

"Which player is to have the Royal Flush?" I can't help but allow myself a gloating grin.

"That one." He points at player number three.

"Please check," I say, feeling the usual rush of dopamine from an effect gone right.

Nero turns over the cards, revealing the Royal Flush in Hearts.

He stares at the cards, then at me, then back at the cards. "Remind me never to play cards with you," he finally says and smacks the Royal Flush on the table.

I've heard this a million times before, but having *Nero* say it fills me with a thousand kittens' worth of warm fuzzies.

I then show him some of my favorite classics with cards, and Nero eats it all up with genuine enthusiasm.

To finish the set, I invent an effect on the fly. I start by having Nero choose a random card and lose it in the deck. Then I tell him that we'll get back to the card in a little while.

Next, I perform the needle-swallowing effect as I practiced it at home—and Nero makes the appropriate grossed-out expressions at just the right moments, though the way he stares at my mouth throughout is distracting as hell.

For the grand finale, I spring the cards at the card table at the same time as I spit out the last needle—and it spears a single card in the air.

Nero's "lost" card.

He stands up and claps. "That was very impressive." He gives me an admiring look. "You're amazing."

I redden from the top of my head all the way down to my toes, and want to dance in glee.

If he's faking this, he's good.

Scary good.

First, he was trying to slither into my heart through my stomach with his cooking. Now he's using the type of flattery that could definitely get him into my pants.

But I can't let myself fall for it.

I must do something to break the evil spell.

There's only one thing I can think of—and it happens to kill a few birds with one stone.

"Tell me about my father," I blurt out.

The excitement instantly evaporates from Nero's face, and he sinks heavily back into the chair, his face turning serious.

"Please?" I say. "Anything you can."

"You're a lot like him," he growls quietly. "He also could never leave anything alone."

I suppress a surprised gasp and just sit there quietly, afraid to startle Nero out of this unnatural-for-him bout of sharing.

"Like you, he makes up his own rules on the fly. And you get your imagination from him too, as well as your resourcefulness." He gestures at the chaos of cards on the table. "You also got that almost pathological sense of loyalty from him." He stops talking and sits there, looking lost in thought.

I realize I haven't taken a breath since he started speaking, so I do so now.

I'm not sure if he realizes it, but Nero has just talked about Rasputin in present tense. This answers something I desperately wanted to know.

My biological father is *alive*.

I decide to really push my luck, so I soothingly ask, "How can I find him?"

The distant expression on Nero's face shifts into the familiar stony mask he often wears at the fund.

"I can't tell you that," he says. "I've already said too much."

Pushing was clearly a mistake. My hands ball into fists, and I leap to my feet. A part of me knows he's just adhering to the contract with my father, but another, very large part wants to slam a fist into his stubborn chin.

"I'd like to be alone for a bit," I say in as cordial a tone as I can manage under the circumstances.

"Let me take you to the living room." He gets up and leads the way, his back tense as he walks.

I follow him into yet another opulent room, which must be our destination. The south wall is covered by a TV large enough to hang in Times Square.

"I'll be in my office," Nero says and promptly disappears.

Did I upset him with this request for privacy?

Good.

I'm sure he could tell me more about my parents if he really wanted to.

He just doesn't.

I catch myself pacing the room and realize I need to calm down.

Eager for a distraction, I walk up to a wall of shelves featuring a huge Blu-ray collection.

How quaint. Does Nero have something against streaming?

I check out some movies at random. *The Wolf of Wall Street, The Big Short, Trading Places, Boiler Room, Margin Call, Wall Street*—there's a definite pattern to Nero's entertainment choices, and it's almost sad.

Even in his rare leisure time, he watches work-related movies.

Feeling a little calmer, I park my butt on an ultra-comfortable lounge chair and close my eyes.

This is when it hits me.

It's been hours since I've woken up, and I haven't used my powers to check on Vlad.

I'm not doing a very good job of "taking care of him" for Rose.

I bet Nero would be extra smug if he knew how distracting he has been.

Well, "better late than never" has always been my motto.

Without opening my eyes, I slip into the prerequisite state of focus, reaching Headspace in record time.

———

IGNORING MY SURROUNDINGS, I concentrate on Vlad, and my environment changes.

The shapes around me now have notes of fear and grief as strong as the ones that accompanied the fateful vision where Felix and Maya got killed.

These will show me something equally terrible.

Reluctantly, I proceed to touch the nearest shape without changing the vision duration—I do try to learn from my mistakes.

The resistance is there again—and it confirms my gloomy suspicions.

Biting my nonexistent tongue, I will my wisp to touch the shape.

It doesn't work at first, but on the twentieth attempt, the metaphorical maw of the vision opens up and I fall in.

CHAPTER THIRTY-TWO

I'M BODILESS, surrounded by water.

It's a pier. The sign in the distance says "St. George Staten Island Ferry Terminal."

There are only a handful of people standing on the pier, and all have their backs to me, with the exception of Vlad.

The expression on Vlad's face reminds me of the feral samurai masks no doubt designed to demoralize opponents.

These strangers should be afraid.

Vlad moves forward, and I find my point of view floating to perch over his shoulder.

The other people on the pier turn out to be Koschei, Ariel, Lucretia, and Gaius, plus three black-clad Enforcers whom I recognize from the aftermath of my disastrous TV performance.

Vlad's head tilts from side to side. He must be examining his opponents. His gaze doesn't linger on

Ariel, who's staring back at him with a glassy expression, nor Lucretia, who looks like she'd rather be anywhere else. His focus seems to be on Koschei—no doubt the knife in the man's hand caught his attention.

The very knife that killed Rose.

Koschei takes a step back, as if pushed by the force of Vlad's gaze.

Finally, Vlad turns his attention to Gaius—who takes out Lucretia's rapier.

"You and your fucking ambition," Vlad growls, his face twisting into a savage grimace.

"I merely evened out the playing field," Gaius says coolly. "Without the power boosts from your pet witch, you're no match for me, let alone all of us."

If Gaius wanted to subdue Vlad, mentioning Rose was a tactical error.

Like a CGI effect, Vlad blurs into motion.

The three vampire Enforcers leap forward, placing themselves between Vlad and Gaius.

Vlad's fist enters the chest of the first one with a nauseating crunch.

Pulling out the man's spine, he tosses it onto the pier.

The Enforcer is no more.

I guess that's one way to kill a vampire.

The other two attackers hesitate—which Vlad uses to his advantage by grabbing their heads and slamming them together.

They explode like watermelons under a hydraulic press.

That's a second way to kill a vampire.

"Attack him!" Gaius shouts at Lucretia and Ariel.

The two women approach Vlad from left and right as Koschei rushes at him from the front.

Gaius zooms around Lucretia—probably intending to stab Vlad in the back with the rapier.

Ariel gets to Vlad first, and for a moment, he hesitates—which allows her to grab his left arm in her super-strong grip.

Hesitation gone, Vlad punches Ariel in the chest, causing her to fly in a wide arc into the water—which is when Lucretia sinks her teeth into Vlad's neck, ripping out a large chunk.

Oblivious to the pain, Vlad grabs Lucretia by the shoulders, rips her away from his neck, and tosses her into the water on the other side of the pier—a distraction that costs Vlad greatly because it allows Koschei to bury his knife in Vlad's chest.

Vlad falters—which gives Gaius an opening to stab him in the back with the rapier.

Vlad grabs Koschei's wrist and rips off his knife-holding hand. He then throws both the hand and the knife over his shoulder, spearing Gaius in the eye.

Gaius yelps in pain, but keeps his composure. Ripping the rapier out, he stabs Vlad again.

And again.

Vlad falls to his knees.

Koschei looks down at him almost pityingly.

Gaius swings the rapier in a slicing motion, chopping at the wound Lucretia left on Vlad's neck.

The flimsy rapier is not equal to the task, so Gaius rips the knife from his eye and uses it to finish his grizzly job of cutting off Vlad's head.

Koschei cringes as the head rolls away and Vlad's headless body drops to the ground, his Cognizant aura disappearing.

"It's done," Koschei says to Gaius. "Now we—"

CHAPTER THIRTY-THREE

I'M BACK in Nero's lounge chair, adrenaline pulsing through my veins so fast it's difficult to think.

Grabbing my phone from my pocket, I dial Vlad but get his voicemail—only instead of a beep, his service provider's automated voice states, "The mailbox is full and cannot accept messages at this time. Goodbye."

He must not have checked his voicemail for a while.

I contemplate texting him not to go to Staten Island, but stop myself. What if my text is what gives him the idea to go there?

Instead, I type out, *Do not engage Koschei. Call me immediately. It's a matter of life and death.*

I wait a couple of seconds for a reply.

None comes.

Either he ditched his phone or isn't paying attention to it.

Or maybe he's so overcome with grief that he doesn't care about the danger? Sadly, this would fit the facts all too well. He saw the overwhelming odds on the dock and attacked anyway.

Well, I won't let him do that.

Except I'm missing basic details—like when is the attack happening?

It was daytime in the vision, and it's daytime now. But which day? Do I have minutes or hours?

My intuition tells me there isn't a lot of time—and I'm beginning to trust my intuition.

Leaping to my feet, I run to find Nero. He said he would be in his office. Where is that? Is it that room where I picked his safe—also known as the room we kissed in?

Almost hyperventilating, I do my best not to trip over the expensive furniture. If I fall, it'll delay things by a few critical moments.

Thoughts buzz in my head like angry bees.

This can't be happening to me again.

If I don't prevent it, Vlad is going to die. And though Ariel's fate wasn't definitive in the vision, she might drown—same for Lucretia.

Speaking of Ariel—why is she following Gaius's orders?

And why is Gaius working with Koschei?

Vlad mentioning Gaius's ambition was a clue. Could it be that he wants Vlad's job? He made it sound like Rose was in the way of that with her power-boosting ability—

I burst into Nero's office like a human missile.

He's chatting with someone on Skype and doesn't seem to notice me.

I skid to a stop in front of him. "I need your help."

"I'll call you back," he says to the screen and looks up at me.

I rattle out the situation in as coherent of a narrative as I can manage.

As I talk, Nero's frown deepens. When I get to the end, though, his face turns unreadable.

"We can drive to Staten Island through New Jersey," I say in one breath. "But it might be a little faster through Brooklyn, depending on the traffic. Going over the water is also—"

"Who says we're going anywhere?" Nero rises from his chair with menacing grace.

"Didn't you hear a word of what I just said?" I step toward him, my hands balling into fists. "Vlad will die. Ariel might—"

"Ariel is a soldier with super strength," Nero says dismissively. "She knows how to swim."

"But Lucretia—"

"Has turned into a vampire, so she's going to be very hard to kill now." He crosses his arms over his chest. "She won't drown either."

"But Vlad—"

"Is being reckless," Nero says. "Attacking a suspect in his lover's murder without due process? Attacking fellow Enforcers—including the guy who runs the investigation? This won't look good to the Council—"

"Screw the Council." I glare up at him. "Are you saying you're not going to help me?"

"I'm saying you might want to respect Vlad's wish to commit suicide by revenge," Nero says. "I'm also saying he can get what he wants posthumously. By killing him, Gaius and Koschei will cross a line. With you as a witness, they—"

"You can't be serious."

"You don't think this might be Vlad's actual plan?" His limbal rings overtake most of the eye surface. "He can't kill the unkillable Koschei on his own, but with the resources of the Council..." He shrugs.

My hands tighten at my sides. "I promised Rose I'd take care of him."

"*Take care of him*," Nero repeats, and I can almost hear the air quotes he puts around the phrase—giving it a dirty connotation.

Is he jealous of Vlad? If so, how little does he think of me? Rose isn't even in the ground yet. To even consider Vlad in a romantic capacity...

Taking in a deep breath, I calmly say, "Vlad's fate aside, I will never take a risk when it comes to Ariel's life. She's not acting like herself, so there's no guarantee she'll swim once Vlad tosses her into the water."

Nero looks thoughtful for a second. "It sounds like Gaius glamoured her," he says. "She *should* still act on her instincts, though."

"You don't sound too sure."

Nero grunts something unintelligible and walks up

to his safe. Blocking my view, he types in a password, and the metal door opens.

He takes out a piece of paper and stares at it for a few heartbeats. "I'm contract-bound not to show up on Brighton Beach," he says without looking up from the paper. "That's been established as Baba Yaga's territory."

"The pier is in Staten Island, so you're good on that score," I say, and allow myself a glimmer of hope.

"Baba Yaga's people are off limits." Nero is still studying what I assume is the contract.

"How is that defined?" I strain to see the paper for myself, but he jerks it out of my sight.

"A few people, like Koschei, are listed by name," he says. "The rest are defined as anyone guarding her—"

"Gaius isn't officially working for her," I say triumphantly. "Same goes for the Enforcers and Lucretia. Ariel can be said to be her enemy. If we were to make sure they wouldn't all gang up on Vlad, he and I could take care of Koschei—meaning you don't have to lay a finger on the only official minion of Baba Yaga."

"Maybe I'd be following the literal interpretation of the contract, but not the spirit of it." His grip tightens on the paper as he looks up at me.

"Russian goons tried to kill me," I remind him.

"We already established that Baba Yaga wasn't trying to kill you. She can't lie to me."

"Fine. But the main purpose of the contract was so that Baba Yaga doesn't hurt me, right?"

Nero nods.

"Then she was the first to break the *spirit* of it," I say. "When she killed Rose, she hurt me. Perhaps it was not a physical attack, but I'd rather have gotten a million bruises."

Just saying the words makes my eyes water—and I let it happen since that helps my cause. I also realize I just doubled down on below-the-belt tactics by reminding Nero of the other day, when an orc he hired gave me a bruise. Given how savagely Nero slaughtered the whole orc crew as a result, there might be some guilt there still.

And it looks like something I said got through—at least I hope that's what the tumult of emotions on Nero's face is about. With him you never know, though. A lot depends on something Nero may not possess.

A conscience.

"Damn you," he growls and angrily tosses the paper back into his safe. "I will help you." He takes out a gun from the safe. "Just know this: if Gaius or the others announce themselves to be working for Baba Yaga, my hands will be tied."

"I understand. Either way, I would still have a chance to warn Vlad about my vision. Plus, if they say they work for Baba Yaga, they will be bound by your contract and thus be unable to harm me. That might give me an edge."

"The contract covers self-defense." He hands me the gun, and I realize it's mine—or rather, the one I stole from the goon the other day. "If you attack Baba Yaga or her people," Nero continues, "they gain the right to harm you—which is why you will *not*."

I want to ask him what the gun is for in that case, but decide not to go there.

"Come." He grabs my wrist and drags me out of the office at a running pace.

We sprint through the penthouse until we reach a section I haven't seen—a glass staircase leading to the roof.

Before I can question him, we're staring at the sprawling view of the city below.

But the view is not what takes my breath away.

Our mode of transportation is standing there.

A shiny helicopter.

I've got to hand it to Nero. When he offers to help, he does it in style.

CHAPTER THIRTY-FOUR

NERO PUTS a headset over my ears and starts the impressive machine. I watch the building grow small underneath us with opened-mouthed fascination.

The view below is every tourist's wet dream.

"Press that button by your ear if you want to talk," Nero says in my headset.

I press the button. "I didn't know you could fly a helicopter."

He just grunts something as we turn toward the Empire State Building.

"Wow," I say without pressing the button. "If this weren't a rescue mission, I'd probably really enjoy this."

Then again, if this weren't a rescue mission, I'd suspect Nero of trying to seduce me, Christian Grey style.

"I need to resume my earlier conversation," Nero says. "Please keep your headset muted. She's very private about her skills."

She?

I don't get a chance to ask because Nero must hook something up to the headset system, and I hear dial tone.

Someone picks up right away, and a pleasant female voice says, "If it isn't Mr. Bowser." She chuckles. "It's not like you to hang up just as things were about to get juicy."

Bowser?

Does she mean the videogame character who happens to be the archenemy of Mario? I could sort of see it. Though Nero looks nothing like the turtle-dinosaur hybrid from the game, Bowser's voice *is* very deep.

I already like this person and her sense of humor.

"Ms. Spade," Nero says. "Proceed with your update."

Ah. This is the mysterious Bailey Spade, a.k.a. Freda Krueger.

Ignoring the to-die-for views of the city skyline, I lean forward in my seat and prepare to listen carefully —something the roar of the blades makes difficult.

"You were right," Bailey says, sounding more serious now. "Baba Yaga *is* dreaming about a seat on the Council. She seems sure one is about to open up, and that she's going to get it. Unfortunately, I don't have more details than this. The woman rarely sleeps. Probably because of her lack of melatonin. The older we get, the less we produce."

Melatonin production? Rarely sleeps? What does that have to do with anything?

"What about Koschei?" Nero angles the helicopter toward my neighborhood downtown. "We agreed you'd—"

"He's a few favors away from getting free of Baba Yaga—which is *his* biggest dream," she says. "Afterward, he plans to escape into the Otherlands. I'm still not sure if he has access to a private gate or not. I'm pretty confident he can't be bought or reasoned with as you'd hoped."

I deeply regret agreeing to pretend not to be on the call. I have so many questions I feel like I'll burst.

"Any surprise discoveries?" Nero asks as we approach the harbor.

"Yes. A huge one." Bailey sounds either giddy with excitement or amused by the double entendre of what she just said. "Baba Yaga has an ally. You'd never guess who it is."

"Gaius?" Nero growls.

"How did you know?" Bailey sounds like a five-year-old who found a pair of socks in her Christmas box.

"I have my sources," Nero says. "Tell me every detail."

"He proved his loyalty to her when he traveled to Russia and killed an enemy she's been dreaming about," Bailey says. "He's also looking to get a Council seat, and wants to take over Vlad's role as the Leader of the Enforcers."

I pry my gaze from the Statue of Liberty and force my overwhelmed brain to process what I just heard.

My earlier guess was right. It was Gaius who asked Baba Yaga to kill Rose. As I saw during Ariel's rescue, Rose had a way of making Vlad more powerful, and thus was an obstacle for Gaius—who wants to topple Vlad.

Then something occurs to me.

Right around the time Gaius was heading to Russia, Ariel talked to me from his phone—and then Baba Yaga mysteriously acquired my number.

"What about Ariel?" Nero asks. "How does she fit into this?"

"Wait, how did you know that I know her?" Bailey sounds confused.

"She and Gaius are intertwined," Nero says. "I didn't know that you knew her."

"Oh. Well, I do." Bailey sounds relieved at his simple explanation. She must know about his tendency to spy on people. "I know Ariel from my rehab gig, which means talking about her would violate the therapist-patient privilege."

She knows Ariel from rehab?

Wait a second.

Felix *did* mention her.

He said he had a friend at the rehab facility who could enter people's dreams and heal them that way.

She must be that friend.

Except it sounds like she does more than heal with her powers.

She can use it to get information from people's dreams—something I discovered in Darian's memories.

283

And now that comment about Baba Yaga's sleeping habits makes sense. She invaded the witch's dreams.

What a repugnant place *that* must have been.

"What can you tell me without breaking the privilege?" Nero asks. "Ariel's safety is at stake. Gaius is going to use her to attack Vlad—and you can imagine how dangerous that will be for her."

"She's making good progress," Bailey says. "She now does want to be rid of her addiction. She was on the verge of—"

"Hanging out with a vampire doesn't seem to support your theory." Nero fiddles with the controls as we approach Staten Island.

"He probably glamoured her into compliance," Bailey says. "A week into rehab is when the patient is most vulnerable to that."

"So you don't think she's back on his blood?" Nero asks, and I want to kiss him for doing so.

It's the question that's been worrying me the most.

"I doubt it," Bailey says. "Giving her blood at this stage of withdrawal would make her less susceptible to glamour."

"I have to go," Nero says as we approach a large baseball stadium. "You did good."

"Thank you. Now about my compensation—"

"We'll discuss that shortly." Nero starts our descent. "Now I really have to go."

"Later," she says.

Nero hangs up and lands the helicopter.

"Home of the Staten Island Yankees," he says when we take our headgear off. "We're a jog away."

"Let's make it a sprint," I say when we come out, and without waiting for a reply, I start running.

Nero effortlessly catches up, then runs ahead—probably to explain his landing to stadium security. That, or to buy the place, assuming he doesn't happen to already own it.

He's right, though.

It takes us no time at all before we burst onto the pier that looks exactly like the one in my vision—right down to Vlad and the rest of the gang.

Only we're too late.

CHAPTER THIRTY-FIVE

JUST AS FAST AS in my vision, Vlad blurs into motion.

The three vampire Enforcers place themselves between Vlad and Gaius again.

"Vlad, no!" I scream.

It doesn't work.

Following the vision script, Vlad's hand rips into the chest of an Enforcer and pulls out the spine.

Damn it.

After what Nero said, I wanted to prevent Vlad from crossing that line. Killing another Cognizant, especially an Enforcer, is going to get him into trouble with the Council.

At least, assuming they find out.

Speaking of Nero, he whooshes down the pier even faster than Vlad.

Following their fatal script, the two other vampires in front of Vlad hesitate.

Since I can't hope to match Nero's speed, I take out my gun instead.

Vlad grabs their heads again.

The two vampire noggins explode.

I take careful aim at Koschei's head, and praying I don't accidentally hit Ariel, I squeeze the trigger.

Koschei's forehead shatters into bloody pieces, and he falls on the pier, temporarily dead.

In the vision, this was when Gaius asked Lucretia and Ariel to attack, but he doesn't seem to be doing that now.

Everyone, including the now-resurrected Koschei, looks at the source of the shot—which is when they see Nero, a mere leap away from them.

"Dive," Gaius orders Lucretia and Ariel, and jumps into the water himself.

"Nero, grab Ariel!" I shout.

Nero leaps for her, but Ariel jumps into the water before he gets a chance to grab her.

At the same time, Koschei sprints for the edge of the pier.

Vlad races after him, but Koschei manages to dive in—and Vlad jumps in right behind him.

Nero watches the surface of the water intently, but not a single head reappears.

Then I see Ariel climbing up the adjacent pier.

"We need to catch her," I tell Nero and sprint back.

Nero passes me on his way out, but when I exit to the street, I find him looking around, frustrated.

"Where is she?" I demand.

"She was gone by the time I came out," he says grimly. "Must've managed to hitch a ride from a passing car."

"She was soaking wet," I say. "What man in his right mind would—"

I stop, realizing what I'm saying.

Even in wet clothes, Ariel is so gorgeous few men would refuse to help her.

In fact, the wet clothes might've helped.

Covering my eyes with my palms, I curse under my breath.

Nero puts a reassuring hand on my shoulder. "Vlad is alive," he murmurs. "So is Ariel. You know how much worse this could've gone."

"You're right, of course." I lower my hands, resisting the urge to ask why I feel like a failure if I did so well. "So what now?"

"I summoned a cab for you already," Nero says. "I'm going to stay behind and do my best to cover up Vlad's mess."

A car pulls up to the curb next to us.

Nero mimes for the woman driver to roll down her window, hands her a hundred-dollar bill, and without letting it go asks, "Do you mean Sasha any harm?" He points at me.

"What?" The woman looks like she's contemplating driving away, but the sight of the money must be too tempting.

"I know I sound like an overprotective boyfriend but humor me." Nero gives her a shockingly charming smile. "Do you have any bad intentions toward this woman?"

"I don't know her," the driver says, snatching the hundred. "And no, I don't mean her any harm."

"Thank you." Nero opens the door for me in a gentlemanly gesture. Leaning in so close that he almost kisses my cheek, he whispers, "Ride safe."

My skin burning where his lips brushed against it, I scramble into the car.

The driver pulls away, then examines me in the rearview mirror.

"I know." I meet her eyes. "Overprotective is an understatement."

"I can see why you'd put up with it, though." She winks at me. "I meet a lot of people, but rarely men like that."

I sigh, and we ride in silence for a while.

"Where are you taking me?" I ask when we get on the highway.

She tilts her navigation app toward me and clicks on the screen.

As I suspected, Nero's penthouse is the destination.

That's a no go. I want to talk to Felix face to face, sleep in my own bed, and pet Fluffster.

"Can you please change the destination?" I say. "I want you to drop me downtown—which means a shorter drive for the same money for you."

"No problem," she says. "What's your address, sweetie?"

I tell her.

We drive onto the Verrazano Bridge and hit traffic.

Oh well, at least the view is spectacular.

Staring at the water in the distance helps me calm down enough to realize I should let Nero know about my decision to go home. Taking out my phone, I text him with the news.

Nero replies almost instantly: *You'd be safer in my place.*

Thank you, I text back. *When we talked about Felix's safety, you yourself outlined how well my apartment is set up.*

Fine, Nero texts back. *I will see you at work tomorrow, the usual time. I'll have a limo waiting for you.*

I don't write something snarky back, even though my fingers are itching to do so.

Was he implying I could've played hooky if I'd stayed with him?

Nah. There's no way he was going to take a second day off to keep me company. It would take an extinction-level catastrophe to bring *that* about.

Then again, maybe he had a candle-lit dinner planned for us tonight.

Yeah, sure.

While we're at it, we'd hold hands and eat the liver of a pink invisible unicorn. Maybe with some fava beans and a nice Chianti.

The car in front of us moves an inch forward.

This will be a long ride, but there is something I can do to kill the time.

I can get a vision to make sure Vlad and Ariel are okay.

Thus determined, I gather the mental effort and quickly reach Headspace.

I FLOAT AMONG THE SHAPES, wondering how to best do this.

Who should I start with: Vlad or Ariel?

Ladies first, I guess.

I focus on Ariel's essence until a new set of shapes show up.

They play safe music, so I have a good feeling about this—assuming the vision is going to be about Ariel.

I touch the shape.

ARIEL IS SITTING in a car with her eyes glazed over.

The view outside her window looks like New Jersey, but might be Staten Island as well.

She rides.

And rides.

And rides.

I COME BACK to my own stuck-in-traffic car.

The vision I just saw proves Ariel is fine for now. In

fact, if her ride is long enough, maybe she will snap out of Gaius's glamour and come home?

That would be awesome, but I'm not going to hold my breath.

In any case, it's Vlad's turn.

I come back to Headspace and think of Vlad.

A horde of shapes shows up when I succeed.

I examine them in surprise.

That's a lot of shapes—many more than usual.

What's more interesting is that some of the shapes far apart from each other are very different in color, temperature, and geometry.

I wonder if the only thing they have in common is Vlad, but are otherwise of different locations, times, and events.

The music they all play is equally eerie, though—which means I need to see them to make sure Vlad isn't in danger.

But how?

If I touch one, I'll see one vision and that's it.

There's no guarantee I'd get this batch of visions on my next trip to Headspace.

What I need is to somehow see them all, not just one.

Except I have no way of doing that.

If I had lungs, I'd sigh, but as is, I try to summon Darian for the umpteenth time.

He might know a way to do the thing I just thought of—and if I'm lucky, have advice on this whole Baba Yaga debacle.

Oh, and if the call connects, I need to ask him how to "hang up" on these conversations without exiting Headspace. I don't want to lose all these vision-shapes.

Unfortunately, Darian is still not accepting psychic calls.

Or can't accept them.

I float in quiet thought, surrounded by the varied Vlad-related shapes.

Then an idea occurs to me.

Darian isn't the only seer I know.

I've now met another one—Yaroslav the bannik.

As soon as the realization comes, I want to smack myself with my ethereal wisp for not thinking of this sooner.

There are actually two ways to speak to the bannik I should have thought about: Headspace and the real world.

After all, Baba Yaga has the other side of Nero's contract—and isn't supposed to harm me. Doesn't that mean I can waltz into the banya unimpeded and talk to whomever I want?

Theoretically, yes, but I wouldn't trust these contracts with my life.

So Headspace it is.

I start with his impressive stranded-on-a-deserted-island hotness and then do my best to get to the essence of the man by recalling his deeds. He let me escape Baba Yaga's clutches despite the fact that he would be left at her mercy. He helped me with his intricate plan. I can almost picture his deep, sad eyes. His—

I must be getting better at this summoning stuff because a moving shape appears next to me—to the side of the Vlad-related shapes.

It's clearly of the same species as that of Darian the other day, yet this version of the man is as different from Darian as any two people are from one another.

Well, here goes nothing.

I reach out to what I hope is Yaroslav.

He pulses in excitement, and I get the impression he's reaching for me at the same time.

The connection is made.

For lack of a better term, we fall into each other.

CHAPTER THIRTY-SIX

A PALE WOMAN is lying face down on a towel in front of me, the surrounding steam condensing into large droplets on her naked flesh.

I'm way too close to her, so I try to step away—and find that I can't.

Of course.

I'm in Yaroslav's memories. It figures. With my luck and given the circumstances, something X-rated is about to go down.

That better not be me he's staring at in some vision of the future.

"So beautiful," Yaroslav's voice says in my head as he smacks the woman with the birch tree branches in his hand.

The thought was in Russian, but because I'm in his memory, I still understood it as though it originated in my own head.

"This is the weirdest client session I've ever had," says the woman in a familiar voice.

"Does that mean you wish me to stop?" I say with Yaroslav's melodious Russian accent.

"Are you blackmailing your therapist?" The woman looks over her shoulder, confirming my suspicion.

It *is* Lucretia.

———

IN THE MIDDLE of absolute blackness of emptiness glows a synapse-hologram I recognize as Yaroslav.

Just like Darian had been, the bannik is translucent and attached to the uncanny shape-entity that is his Headspace representation.

Also like before, I'm a hologram myself—connected to the entity that is me, that in turn is interwoven with him on the Headspace level—or however this works.

"I was wondering if you had enough power to do this." Yaroslav looks me up and down admiringly. "I shouldn't have doubted you."

"Thanks." I float down an inch. "I'm here because I'm in desperate need of seer training. Can you help me?"

"Of course," he says. "But we better make this quick —conversations like this cost a lot of power."

Sounds like Darian didn't lie about that. That's a first. Let's see if he did lie about something else, though. "Quick question: did you see any memories of mine when we connected?"

"I didn't have the pleasure," Yaroslav says disappointedly. "How about you? Did you see any memories of mine?"

"Just a glimpse of you using the banya," I say. "A very brief glimpse."

He looks relieved, so I feel okay about my deception by omission.

And surprise, surprise. Darian did lie when he claimed those were hallucinations. The seer Headspace conversations *do* allow each seer to glimpse the other's memories.

Good to be sure.

"So what did you want to learn?" Yaroslav asks hurriedly. "Time isn't our friend right now."

Right. The power-related deadline.

I quickly explain to him what I'm trying to do with the horde of Vlad-related visions.

"That's easy," he says. "You just initiate them all, the way you would a single vision."

"Do I just touch them all at once somehow?" I float up a little from excitement. "I thought I could only touch one."

"If you're willing to expend your power, and if you have enough of it, you can initiate many, many visions at once in a way very similar to when you initiate just one."

I float even higher. I can't wait to go back into Headspace and try this out.

"Is there also a way to zone in on a specific time and

place in someone's future?" I ask, figuring I'd use this opportunity fully.

"There might be a way to do that, but I haven't discovered it myself. Instead, I do what you say by instinct." He reaches to stroke his holographic beard, but his hand goes through it.

Wait.

Something is odd about that hand.

I study it closer and realize what that something is.

Yaroslav's index finger is missing.

Odd.

The finger was there when I last saw him.

Noticing where I'm staring, he frowns. "Actions have consequences." He flies forward so I get a better look at the damage.

Close up, it looks really bad.

Like something or someone chewed the finger off.

Recently.

"Did Baba Yaga do that?" I drop nearly a foot, then fly back up to be eye level with him.

"After your escape from the banya, she asked Koschei to choose my punishment." Yaroslav's hands turn into fists. "The bastard took his time." He floats down like an autumn leaf, and I inadvertently follow.

"I didn't think I could hate Koschei more than I already do," I say. "Sounds like I was wrong."

"You hate him?" Yaroslav locks eyes with me.

My holographic jaw tightens. "Him and Baba Yaga. They—"

"Listen, we're almost out of time, but I have to tell

you something about Koschei." The bannik bobs up and down. "He made a mistake turning me—a seer—into such a motivated enemy. Every piece of the finger he took drove me to use more of my power. I've looked into countless futures in search of Koschei's permanent death, and eventually, I found it."

"You have?" I float up. "He *can* be killed?"

"I don't know if it would work for *you*," he says. "In my vision, I was the one who did it. I found a future where I was free, you see, and—"

"I thought we were short on time. Just tell me the key parts."

"You're right," he says. "I saw myself travel to the Otherland called Buyan. I stayed at the Golden Hare Inn. For dinner, I ordered duck's eggs, and there was a nee—"

CHAPTER THIRTY-SEVEN

I'M BACK in the car.

Crap.

I never got a chance to ask him how to exit our conversation without leaving Headspace.

Now I just have to hope I can rediscover that large batch of Vlad-related visions again.

More importantly, he didn't finish telling me how to perma-kill Koschei.

Was Yaroslav about to say there was a neem—a type of evergreen tree—growing by the Inn?

Or was there a neep—a type of Scottish turnip—on his plate next to the duck eggs?

I had so much I wanted to ask him. Plus, I didn't even get a chance to tell him what happened to Lucretia—who's clearly his secret girlfriend.

It probably won't work, but I have to try to get in touch with Yaroslav again.

I calm my nerves and reenter Headspace.

Having the shapes surround me fills me with relief. I could've been the one who ran out of power and thus short-circuited the conversation, but it must've been Yaroslav.

I still try to summon him.

It doesn't work.

Fine. I guess I'll get back to what started this whole thing: visions of Vlad.

I think of Rose's beau in the same way as before.

A large cloud of shapes appears around me.

Like the earlier horde, these shapes are not homogeneous, but—and I'm just going by memory—I don't think they are the *same* group as before. It's almost as though I now have a brand-new set of visions about Vlad—all as sinister-feeling as the prior gang, but of different events.

Time to put the bannik's words to the test and activate a bunch of visions all at once.

He said it was easy, just a matter of doing what I'd usually do, but I normally just reach out with what I've been calling an ethereal wisp—something I kind of thought of as a singular thing.

Was I closer to the truth when I thought of the wisp as a nebulous appendage? Should I now envision my Headspace self as a Lovecraftian monster after all?

I zone in on a handful of Vlad visions, picking ones that are particularly different from one another.

Targets chosen, I attempt to touch them all, but nothing happens.

Okey dokey.

Let's approach this from another angle.

I picture myself as an octopus—multilimbed, lacking a spine, and with consciousness spread throughout my body.

That, or simple perseverance, does the trick.

As one, a set of wisps/appendages reach out to the shapes I've been aiming for.

As one, the shapes pull me in—and I worry I'll be ripped apart.

But no. For a moment, I simply feel as though I'm in multiple places at once—and then my consciousness spirals away.

———

VLAD APPROACHES a fellow Enforcer and raises his hand to the man's face.

"I'm sorry," the vampire shouts. "Gaius—"

Vlad rips the jaw from his face, turning the rest of the explanation into macabre gibberish.

He then methodically rips off other parts of the vampire—and by the time he's done, the room looks like the back of a butcher's shop on a busy weekend.

Not bothering to clean the blood from his clothes, Vlad heads for the door—

———

VLAD IS IN A DARK BASEMENT, surrounded by dismembered bodies.

Attaching a long hose to a huge water tank, he locates a bloody drain in the cement floor, deposits the hose there, then walks back and unscrews a large valve.

Water pours out into the drain, washing away the blood and gore—

———

I FLOAT NEXT to a giant room that looks like an armory for SWAT or Navy SEALs.

Vlad walks up to the counter, makes his eyes become mirrors, and stares at the clerk.

"Do your smoke grenades produce fire?" Vlad asks.

"No," the guy replies in a mesmerized tone.

"Bring a smoke grenade, a shotgun, a—"

———

BLOOD-COVERED Vlad stands in front of five armed Russian goons. His eyes seem to absorb the light in the already poorly lit basement.

One of the mobsters points his sausage-like finger at Vlad and says something in Russian, his voice shaking.

Vlad replies in Russian as well—but all I can make out is a mention of Baba Yaga and the promise of painful death in his tone.

The goons pull out their guns.

Vlad blurs into motion—

―――――

VLAD STANDS in a hospital-like room that looks like the one where Baba Yaga kept the Johnnies—the mobsters she uses like marionettes with her mind-control magic.

The Johnnies are lying comatose here as well, IVs and all. Vlad walks up to one big guy, and sinks his elongating fangs into the man's neck.

Thirst satisfied, he rips his snack's head off and looms over the next comatose body—

―――――

VLAD PARKS the giant fuel tanker in a dark alley, then attaches a long hose to the back and carries the other end into a familiar-looking basement.

He then hooks up the hose to an empty tank.

The smell of gasoline hits my nonexistent nostrils as Vlad fills the tank with viscous liquid—

―――――

VLAD IS STALKING the halls of the blood-splattered banya.

He viciously kills every guard. Every customer. Every member of staff—

―――――

VLAD STANDS in front of a gasoline-soaked man with a Zippo lighter.

"Yes, I supply that cursed restaurant with beef," the man shouts hysterically. "I do so at a loss." He strains to free himself from the ropes that bind him. "They're not the kind of people you say no to."

"That restaurant will have no more business." Vlad flicks on the lighter—

———

VLAD KILLS people with bare hands.

———

VLAD KILLS people with various weapons.

———

VLAD RIPS—

CHAPTER THIRTY-EIGHT

WHEN I FIND myself back in the real world of my car ride, I could swear I've just witnessed thousands of hours of violence.

Damn.

Vlad has clearly watched too many revenge movies and excessive amounts of torture porn. Some of the stuff in those visions could've easily come from *John Wick*, *The Punisher*, *Hostel*, *Kill Bill*, and *Saw*, just to name a few.

And what was the deal with all that gasoline? Also, why was he—

"Sweetie, are you okay?" the driver asks me. "You turned white all of a sudden."

"I dozed off and had a nightmare," I say, my voice hoarse. "I'll be fine."

The traffic in front of us is dissipating, so the driver speeds up, leaving me in peace.

Closing my eyes, I even out my breathing until I can brave Headspace again.

Do I dare get more visions of Vlad?

No.

Not unless I'm willing to puke inside this nice lady's car.

But Ariel could use my attention again. Hopefully, *she* isn't on a crazy killing spree.

I try to reach Headspace—but it doesn't work. After a few more tries, I give up.

Vlad's murder marathon must've drained me of my seer juice. I guess I have to be careful using the multivision skill.

Exhausted, I sink into a nap.

When I open my eyes again, we're pulling up to my building. The driver parks between a red Lamborghini and a limo that's an exact replica of the one Kevin drove.

A panda-like man opens the door for me with a huge grin.

"Hi, Bentley," I say to my former trainer. "What are you doing here?"

His grin widens. "Nero hired me and Thalia to look after you."

Nero hired not one but *two* martial arts experts to guard little old me? If that's his way of showing how much of a pain in the butt I am being, message received loud and clear.

"Didn't Nero fire you?" Thanking the driver, I climb out of the car.

"He said, and I quote, 'You're lucky I need muscle on short notice.'" Bentley's impersonation of Nero's voice sounds more like a bear.

I look around. "Where is Thalia?"

"In the car," he says. "If you ask me, she's too serious, even for a nun."

I walk up to the limo, smile, and wave at the emaciated woman inside.

Thalia waves back, but without a smile. It's not clear if this is her usual demeanor, or if she's extra grumpy at the indignity of having to drive my ass around.

Leave it to Nero to talk a nun into being a chauffeur.

"I'm going home," I tell Bentley. "I won't need you today."

"We'll be here until Nero personally calls to relieve us of duty," Bentley says. "You're not the boss here. Sorry."

"Whatever," I say. "See you later."

Before he gets a chance to chat me up some more, I run for the lobby.

Neither Bentley nor Thalia follow me.

I enter the elevator and ride up.

There's a construction crew on my floor repairing the damage Vlad had wrought.

Given what I just saw in those visions, there's going to be a lot of clean-up after Vlad in the near future.

I open the apartment door.

Fluffy paws pitter-patter across the floor, and then grumpy rodent eyes stare up at me.

"Nero insisted I do a sleepover at his house," I say preemptively. "I didn't have much choice."

"Oh, come on," Felix says, appearing from the kitchen with a sandwich in his hand. "You have free will."

I hungrily eye the sandwich.

Felix smirks as he hands it to me.

"Free will is why you *stay* with Nero," Kit says, approaching from the living room in a lacey pink nightie. "You would too, if you had the chance."

"I'm pretty sure *I* wouldn't," Felix mutters and returns to the kitchen.

"I was worried sick," Fluffster says in my head as I attack the sandwich.

"I need to sit down," I say between bites, and walk into the living room.

Lucifur is curled up on the loveseat, so I sit next to her.

She doesn't look up.

I examine her worriedly.

It might be wishful thinking, but she looks better today than when I saw her last.

"She ate today," Felix says as he walks in with a new sandwich. "I think she'll be fine."

Kit sits down on the couch. "Just let her get acclimated, and she'll rule the place."

"You better tell us everything," Felix says as I stuff more of the sandwich into my mouth. "And I do mean everything."

I swallow and bring them up to speed, starting with

the vision of Lucretia in trouble and the fight with my werewolf classmates.

"You got yourself pet werewolves?" Kit turns herself into Roxy, then Maddie, then Ashley. "You have no idea how jealous I am right now."

I nearly choke on my next bite. "What do you mean *pet werewolves?*"

"They're young, so I doubt they fully understand what submitting to you means," Kit says. "An adult werewolf would probably sooner die than submit to someone who isn't from their pack."

I look at Felix. "Can *you* explain it to me without making it sound so statutory rapey?"

He reddens. "It's a werewolf thing. Because they submitted, they will forever see you as dominant. So let's just say they will never cause you any trouble again."

Kit grins. "And you can make them do all sorts of juicy—"

"Moving on with the story," I say and proceed to tell them about Lucretia's turning, Gaius's involvement, and Nero's appearance on the scene.

I then gloss over my private time with Nero, and ignoring Kit's complaints, I steamroll ahead to the vision of Vlad and the helicopter ride conversation.

"Bailey Spade is Freda Krueger?" Felix's eyes are like saucers underneath his unibrow. "I can't believe she never mentioned it."

"I like her." Kit gets a dreamy look on her face. "So snarky. So sexy. So—"

"Bailey and Sasha do share a twisted sense of humor." Felix grins, recovering from shock. "Except Bailey is more—"

"Can I finish my story?" I say sternly.

Felix bites his sandwich, and Kit rolls her eyes. I proceed to explain the rest, finishing with my conversation with the bannik.

"I've been to Buyan." Kit turns herself into a large black cat for some reason, then back into her usual human shape. "It's a quaint place."

Felix swallows his food. "My family on my father's side is originally from Buyan."

"Does that mean you know how to get there?" I ask him excitedly.

"No. I've never been. I avoid Otherlands without technology when I can help it."

I look at Kit. "What about you? Can you tell me how to get there?"

She nods, then walks over to the coffee table and picks up a notepad and a pack of crayons. I keep them there, so I'm always ready to perform a classic of mentalism called the drawing duplication.

"From JFK hub, you take the south purple gate." Kit draws a purple circle in the leftmost part of the notepad. "From there, a western green one." She draws a green circle so that it intersects the purple one in its southern corner. "A red gate next." She draws the red circle to intersect the purple one in the western corner and then proceeds to explain the rest of the path, drawing more and more circles as she does.

When she finishes, the resulting map/diagram looks vaguely familiar.

Felix frowns at the notepad. "Is this some new way of mapping the Otherlands? It looks like something out of my computer science class and not at all how Hekima taught us."

"No. His method is newer and more precise," Kit says. "But this"—she gestures at the drawing—"is how the gate makers allegedly did it, back in the day."

"This is so great." I rip the paper from the notepad, put down what's left of my sandwich, and head for the door.

"Where are you going?" Felix steps in front of me, arms bent at his sides—which makes him look like an angry meerkat.

"Isn't it obvious?" I tap my pocket. "To Buyan. Vlad needs a way to kill an unkillable asshole, and I plan to help him do it before he gets himself killed."

"Do you speak Russian?" Kit asks. "Because they only speak a dialect of it on Buyan."

"No," I say. "I know a little Spanish, and that's about it."

"I can go with you." Fluffster stands on his hind legs. "I speak Russian, remember?"

"You don't have your powers outside this apartment," Felix says. "You'll be a liability. If anything, Sasha should take Nero. His Russian is fluent and—"

"Nero has a contract with Baba Yaga forbidding him from killing her people, and Koschei is listed in there by name," I say. "He won't participate in this."

"Then I'll go." Felix puts the remainder of his sandwich next to mine and stands up.

"Are you sure?" I look him up and down.

"I think so," he says, shifting from foot to foot.

"Is your robot ready?" I ask. "Maybe you can send it in your stead?"

"Golem *is* ready," Felix says proudly. "But I have to connect to him to make this work, and I can't do it across gates."

"Oh." I pinch the bridge of my nose. "That makes sense."

"Am I not invited then?" Kit pouts. "I speak adequate Russian, you know." She says something in what sounds like perfect Russian to me, and Felix and Fluffster roll their eyes—meaning they understood.

"I assumed you didn't want to go," I tell Kit.

"Why?"

"You drew a map on how to get there," I say. "I'd only do that if I couldn't lead the way."

"You asked how to get there, and I showed you how to get there." Kit's pout is reaching almost comical proportions. "I didn't want you to think I'm blackmailing you into taking me with you by hoarding knowledge. I wanted you to *want* to take me. But if you don't, I'll understand."

"I think Kit really needs a friend," Fluffster says inside my head. "Be kind to her."

I nod at the domovoi, and with a straight face and as much formality as I can muster, I say, "Kit, would you please do me the honor of tagging along?"

The pout disappears, and she pretends to consider my words.

"Extra please?" I say sweetly. "With a cherry on top?"

"How can I deny you?" Kit's face suddenly looks rounder and rosier-cheeked. Her outfit changes to a sarafan—a bright Russian jumper dress that reaches to the floor. A headscarf later, Kit looks like the Matryoshka doll Felix got me a few years back. All she's missing is a set of smaller Kits to jam inside herself—and I don't mean in a dirty way. "Are you also joining?" She bats her extra-long eyelashes at Felix.

"Of course," he says.

"You really don't have to," I say at the same time.

"I'm going." Lifting his chin, Felix marches out of the living room.

"He's so hot when he's acting confident," Kit whispers into my ear. Louder, she adds, "It's just too bad it doesn't happen very often."

Not dignifying Kit's comment with a reply, I follow Felix.

"Get the lights," Fluffster says in my head.

Hiding my eye roll, I do as the domovoi wants, then also turn off the lights in the hallway and the kitchen for good measure.

"Good luck," Fluffster tells us as we leave.

"They have me," Kit tells him. "I'm better than luck."

Felix and I exchange glances and shrug.

"I almost forgot." Felix looks at me guiltily. "I've been carrying this for you."

He takes out my Jubilee necklace from his pocket.

The necklace Rose used her powers on, right before she—

No.

Not going to think about that now.

Reverently, Felix slides the jewelry over my head, like the President issuing a medal of valor.

My breath quickening, I turn away from my friends—and come face to face with another reminder of earlier events: the construction people are still repairing the hallway.

Kit and Felix follow my gaze, and their faces also turn somber.

Kit recovers first, and by the time she marches out of the building, there's a spring in her step.

"Kit?" Bentley runs up to her and gives her an enthusiastic bear hug.

"Sasha told me you're her bodyguard," Kit says.

"Is that your Lamborghini?" Bentley asks, pointing at the red car I noticed earlier.

"It is." Kit takes out a set of fancy keys and dangles them in front of Bentley's nose. "Want to drive us to JFK?"

"Is Sasha coming?" he asks, his face turning surprisingly serious. It makes him look like a panda worried about his species' ability to reproduce.

"Of course I'm going," I say.

"We must take the limo then," he says, looking wistfully at the keys. "Nero's orders."

"Wouldn't want to disobey Nero," I say mockingly. "Limo it is."

"Thanks." Bentley looks back at Kit. "By the way, you can't park there. Your precious will get towed."

"I told her the same thing when we pulled in," Felix says. "She didn't believe me."

"Would you like to repark it?" Kit dangles the keys again.

"Oh, yes," Bentley says excitedly. "But please don't leave without me."

"No problem," Kit says.

"Please be quick about it," I add.

Bentley snatches Kit's keys and beelines for the Lamborghini.

The rest of us walk leisurely toward the limo.

As the roar of the Lamborghini's 750-horsepower engine reaches me, so does a wave of powerful dread.

"Wait!" I shout, spinning toward Kit's car.

The Lamborghini explodes.

CHAPTER THIRTY-NINE

MY RETINAS REGISTER the flash of fire first; then a deafening boom devastates my eardrums.

The blast wave throws me backward, straight into Kit. The Councilor grabs me, sparing us both a fall.

Felix isn't as lucky, however. His back slams into the pavement.

Thalia runs out of the limo clutching a fire extinguisher.

I extricate myself from Kit's hold and rush over to Felix.

"I'll be okay," he gasps. "Go help the nun."

I run around the pyre to check on Kit and Thalia.

Kit's arms look scaly as she rips the flaming remnants of the driver's door away. Reaching inside, she pulls out a burning body.

She places it on the asphalt a foot away from the car, and Thalia desperately aims a stream of foam at it.

The fire fizzles out, but Thalia keeps spraying.

Kit puts a hand on the nun's shoulder. "He's gone. There's no more aura."

She's right. The charred flesh lacks more than just its aura. It's barely recognizable as having once been a person—and will probably haunt my nightmares for the rest of my days.

Same for the barbecue smell.

"Why?" Thalia drops the now-empty fire extinguisher, her reedy voice hoarse and her thin face twisted by grief. "Why would someone do this?"

Does she realize she just broke her vow of silence?

I turn to face her. "To get to me," I answer grimly. "Baba Yaga doesn't care about collateral damage."

"Baba Yaga?" Thalia's hands bunch into fists. "Whoever that is, I'll make her pay."

"Get in line," I say. "A long line."

"We were actually going on an errand that could help us cripple that bitch," Kit says, her voice low and lethal. "You're welcome to join us."

Sirens blare in the distance.

Someone must've already called the emergency services.

"We have to go," Felix says. "We don't want to be stuck here trying to explain what happened to the human police."

Kit takes out her phone and types something, then puts it away. "Let's go. A couple of Enforcers will handle the cops."

No one moves, so Kit herds us to the limo like stunned sheep.

Thalia recovers her composure first, and jumps behind the wheel.

Kit and I help Felix into the limo, then climb in ourselves.

With a screech of tires, Thalia launches the ride forward.

I locate the first-aid kit and order Felix to show me where he's hurt.

"It's just a few scratches." He exposes his back. "I'll be fine."

Ignoring his bravado, I clean the scrapes.

It gives me something to focus on—something other than the awful images in my mind.

Felix cringes when alcohol touches the cuts, but doesn't faint or cry out.

Come to think of it, he didn't even faint at the sight of a burned body. Proximity to me seems to be desensitizing my usually squeamish roommate.

"Take this." I hand Felix two Tylenol pills.

"Thanks, Mom," he says but takes them, chasing them with fancy sparkling water from the limo's bar.

We buckle up and fall silent. With the adrenaline rush subsiding, everyone is processing what happened.

Focusing on meditative breathing, I cradle my knees with my hands and rock back and forth.

My thoughts spin around like a centrifuge in a lab.

If Nero didn't send the limo for me as promptly as he did, we would've taken Kit's car to JFK.

It would've been our charred bodies on the asphalt instead of poor Bentley's.

The relief I feel at being alive is poisoned with guilt and more than a little fear.

Someone tried to kill me.

Again.

Me, Felix, and Kit, to be precise.

The explosion flits through my mind again, and white-hot anger ignites underneath the shock.

If this was Baba Yaga's doing, she'll answer for it—and everything else.

If Vlad doesn't get her, I will.

Her and Koschei.

In fact, I think I might enjoy *his* death even more.

Taking a breath, I consider if the explosion could've been a hit by someone else.

Chester, for example. Perhaps he heard about my interactions with Roxy—his daughter—and decided to come after me again.

Chewing on a hangnail, I call Nero. His voicemail answers, and I leave him a message to call me back as soon as he can.

We ride the rest of the way to JFK in silence, pretending not to hear the sobs coming from the driver's side of the limo.

Thalia is definitely not as heartless as she appeared during my training.

That, or she and Bentley were especially close.

The car stops at the drop-off area, and the partition separating us from the driver slides down.

Thalia shows us her phone's screen, where she wrote:

I assume you're headed for the Otherlands.

"Yes," Kit says without batting an eye at the strange mode of communication. "Buyan is our destination."

I've exiled myself to Earth, Thalia writes. *I'd be breaking my vows if I left.*

She doesn't seem to realize she'd spoken out loud after the explosion, breaking her vow of silence, and I'm not about to remind her.

"You can't leave a car here anyway," Felix says. "Not if you plan to keep it."

"We got this. Don't worry," I tell Thalia as reassuringly as I can. "You might help us most if you stay nearby and give us a lift back when we return. Something tells me this limo is bulletproof." I knock on the tinted window.

Nero told us it was, Thalia writes, then looks away as tears glimmer in her eyes.

I guess she realized that the "us" doesn't include Bentley anymore.

"We'll see you later then," Kit says to the nun.

Thalia reaches for my phone, puts in a number, and dials.

When her own phone rings, she hangs up and turns the missed call into a contact in my phone book.

Handing the phone back to me, she waves us goodbye.

We briskly walk into the airport and head for the secret passages.

"Let me see if I remember the way," I tell them once we start to traverse the corridors that lead to the hub.

"Go for it," Felix says.

I lead the way, and no one has to correct me.

"Good job," Kit says when we enter the giant room. "Want to follow my map the rest of the way?"

I take out the diagram she drew and walk up to a purple gate in the south corner of the room.

"That's it," Kit says and steps through the gate.

"After you," Felix says, so I follow Kit.

The hub on the other side is a cave.

At least I assume it's a cave. The place smells earthy, like wine cellars and basements, and the "sky" is covered by luminescent critters of some kind.

"How can I tell where west would be?" I pull out my phone, but it's going berserk.

"It's not a true west," Kit explains. "When it comes to these maps, the convention is to assume you're facing north when you exit any gate. That's one of the many flaws with this methodology and why Hekima came up with his own system."

I walk up to the green gate in the "western" corner, and Kit gives me a round of applause before she jumps inside.

Felix and I follow.

The hub we end up in is in the desert.

At least I think that's what it is.

I always imagined some kind of life exists in every desert, no matter how dry, but the desolation here seems total and complete, without even a dried-up cactus in sight.

A red gate is next.

The hub on the other side is teaming with Cognizant—who set up a bazaar right there between the gates.

The smell of unfamiliar spices teases my nostrils as I push through the strange crowd to the gate we need.

The next gate looks a lot like the one at JFK.

The one after that is inside a tree, like in the *Avatar* movie.

Going though world after world like this reminds me of the Orientation lecture the other week, when Dr. Hekima used his powers to give the class a taste of the Otherlands.

The final gate brings us to a hub located in the middle of a forest meadow.

Though to call this a forest is like calling Mount Everest a hill. The trees are reminiscent of birches, but are tall enough to touch the clouds.

"This way." Kit wades through shoulder-height grass toward the edge of the meadow, where a sky-high oak tree is covered by an enormous golden chain—like the neck of a giant rapper.

I make out a small figure as we get closer to the oak tree.

The size of a panther, the black tomcat (I assume) looks like a very big Siberian domestic cat.

Oh, and there are pince-nez-style glasses on his flat fluffy nose.

I exhale loudly.

The cat stops pacing around the tree and looks at us with uncanny intelligence.

"Are there hallucinogens in the air here?" I ask Felix under my breath.

"Doubt it," he whispers back. "I've heard bedtime stories about this. Every Russian child has. Now I wonder if Pushkin—the famous Russian poet—was one of the Cognizant just as my grandfather had always claimed."

Kit walks up to the tree and says something to the cat in what I assume to be Russian.

"She just asked the cat if he knows the way to the Golden Hare Inn," Felix translates.

The cat moves the glasses higher up his nose with a fluffy paw, then uses the same paw to point to a rickety road to the left of us.

Then, to add insult to injury, he starts talking in a deep baritone, speaking what might be Russian.

I rub my temples.

An honest-to-goodness talking cat.

We're definitely not in Kansas anymore.

"I can barely make sense of his dialect," Felix whispers. "But I think he said it's that way—and to be careful of something."

"That's my understanding as well," Kit says. "He also offered to give you head."

"I don't think that's what he said." Felix takes a step back. "I think he said 'you have a big head.'"

"I'd like to float my hallucinogen idea again," I say. "I'll accept vampires, zombies, and a telepathically communicating chinchilla who can turn into a monster, but I draw the line at a giant talking cat. With glasses."

Felix chuckles while Kit says something to the cat, then turns to face us. "It's far. I better give you a ride."

Felix and I exchange confused glances, and by the time we look back, Kit is no longer standing there.

Instead, there's a beautiful black mare.

"Kit?" I look over the horse, with its intricate saddle and jewel-studded reins.

The horse nods its head.

"You want us to... ride you?" Felix asks, blushing.

Kit/horse winks a green eye at him.

"Give me a boost," I tell Felix.

In stunned silence, he helps me get on Kit's back, then hands me the reins.

I give Felix a hand, and he gets on behind me.

"Hands on my waist and nowhere else," I tell him without turning, and I can almost feel his blush intensify as his hands grasp my midsection.

"No pony-play jokes either," I add. "Whatever happens in Buyan, stays in Buyan."

Felix's laugh sounds borderline hysterical.

Kit snorts, then leaps into a whiplash-inducing gallop.

The bumpy ride isn't my biggest problem, though. Since I'm sitting in the front, birch branches spank me as though I were a hardcore banya enthusiast.

We reach a three-way fork in the road. A big stone stands there prominently, with something etched on it in a pretty font in what I assume is Russian—there's a reversed R there and everything.

Felix squints at the writing. "This dialect is even harder to discern in written form, but I think it says: if you go left, you lose your horse but save yourself. If you go right, you lose yourself but save your horse. If you go straight, you lose yourself and your horse."

Kit turns left.

Seeing how *she's* the horse, I guess it's her choice to make.

Then I realize we're no longer riding a horse.

Kit sprouts horns and grows taller underneath us.

"She's turned herself into a reindeer," Felix whispers in case I didn't figure that out yet.

"No jokes about Kit being horny," I whisper back.

Felix chuckles for a while, then eventually quiets down.

I bet his butt is as numb as mine.

When we exit the forest, we finally understand what the cat was talking about.

A giant head is in front of us.

CHAPTER FORTY

IT'S A MAN'S HEAD.

At least I hope so. It has a long beard, a strong nose, and a prominent chin.

A pointy helmet the size of a cistern adorns the head, and from this vantage point, it's unclear if the head is just sprouting from the ground, or if there's a giant man stuck in a huge ditch.

"Was the gold chain around that tree once on this dude's neck?" I ask under my breath.

No one replies.

As we get closer, it becomes clear the head is agitated.

And it has a reason.

A dozen chainmail-clad dudes on horseback are attacking it with bows, arrows, and swords.

"Bogatyrs," Felix whispers in my ear. "They're like these really powerful knights from Grandfather's stories."

The head blows on the closest bogatyr.

The hurricane-strength wind sends the warrior tumbling to the ground, his neck bent at an impossible angle.

A few moments later, he resurrects in a very familiar manner.

"Your bogatyrs must be the same type of Cognizant as Koschei," I say over my shoulder to Felix.

"Interesting," Felix mutters back. "Hopefully, there are enough of them here for someone to have figured out a way to kill them for good."

I hover my hand next to my gun, in case the bogatyrs decide to bully someone their own size for a change.

The giant head gets attacked again.

The poor thing doesn't seem to have a way to permanently kill its enemies—which might be why it eats the horse of the second attacker, along with the man's leg.

What would happen if the giant swallowed an immortal warrior whole? Would the guy resurrect inside the giant's stomach over and over?

Assuming the head has a stomach, that is.

One of the bogatyrs catches my attention. He's holding an oblong object that looks like a small snow globe filled with fire.

"I think that's a firebird egg," Felix whispers in awed fascination. "I guess it makes sense *this* would be the world they get smuggled from."

I lift my eyebrows. "Firebird?"

"That's a Russian version of the Phoenix," Felix says. "Grandfather said their eggs are the ultimate weapon against vampires and their vicious cousins—the upirs. I've heard that if the Enforcers catch you in possession of a firebird egg, a deadly accident is likely to occur to you during your 'arrest.' It's rumored that the Council has a bunch of these and other cool weapons stashed below their castle."

With a battle cry, the warrior tosses the firebird egg at the giant head.

The head's flying-saucer-sized eyes widen; then it desperately blows at the egg.

The gambit works. The firebird egg flies back at the thrower, hits his shield, and explodes into a huge ball of all-consuming fire.

Flesh and chainmail melt as the bogatyr and his horse scream in agony.

Feeling nausea coming on, I look back at Felix. "Could these firebird eggs be the weapon we need to defeat Koschei? The bannik mentioned a duck egg, but maybe—"

Felix points a pale, shaking finger back at the no-longer screaming bogatyr.

I turn just in time to see the ashes of the burned-up guy resurrect as if nothing happened.

There goes that idea.

The closer we get to the fighting, the more I worry about becoming collateral damage.

Kit must realize this too because she gets off the road, making a wide circle around the whole mess.

Though the roundabout makes an already bumpy ride intolerable, neither Felix nor I complain.

When the poor head is behind us, the road leads us into a bucolic farming village.

We pass by empty streets.

"People are either working in the fields or hiding out in those wooden huts," Felix whispers.

"Or the giant head ate them all," I reply. "Or—"

I stop talking because I see a big, wooden hut-like structure in the middle of the village.

As we get closer, I spot a hare drawn in gold paint above the door.

"I bet that's the Golden Hare Inn," Felix says.

Kit stops and kneels.

We get down, and she turns back into her sarafan-clad self.

Swaying her hips, she strolls confidently into the place.

Felix and I follow warily, and I get that "walking into a Wild West saloon" vibe as a bunch of strange beings stare at us from their tables.

"I think that's a kikimora," Felix whispers when he sees me gazing at a wraith-like monstrosity wearing a ratty version of Kit's dress. "And that's probably a leshy," he adds when I look at the most frightening creature in the place—a naked something that looks as though DC's Swamp Thing had a child with Marvel's Groot before raising it in Chernobyl.

Kit takes a seat at an empty table in the middle of the dining area, and we join her.

A human-looking waitress walks up to our table and hands everyone wooden slates with Russian writing burned into them.

Kit and Felix scan theirs.

"There isn't a duck egg on this menu," Felix says without looking up. "Now what?"

Kit says something very loudly in Russian.

The place goes dead silent, and the waitress pales.

The leshy stands up and lumbers to our table.

With a wooden fist the size of Felix's head, he whacks the table—smashing it into little pieces. Then, grinning to reveal moss-covered teeth, he looks us over with hunger in his swampy eyes.

CHAPTER FORTY-ONE

I YANK out my gun and point it at the creature's head. "Don't move or I'll shoot."

The thing clearly doesn't speak English, or if it does, it might not understand what a gun can do.

He reaches for Kit's neck with a gigantic paw.

I squeeze the trigger.

The gun makes an unusual sound, but nothing else happens.

Despite the hand on her neck, Kit stands up, but she's no longer herself. She now looks like our attacker, with one important and disturbing detail.

She's the female of that species.

At least that's what I assume based on the large breasts.

The leshy's reaction supports my theory. He falls instantly in lust with Kit.

There's no mistaking *that* tree-trunk development.

The gender binary is wonky for the leshys, it seems,

because Kit is two standard deviations taller than our very male attacker.

Instead of flirting, she too grabs him by the throat, then almost playfully tosses him at the inn's wall.

The wall breaks into shards, and the horny leshy flies a few more feet before landing in a heap inside a chicken coop.

Kit says something in Russian in the booming voice of a leshy.

"Anyone else wants to mess with me?" Felix translates, but I could've guessed as much.

Kit's threat calms everyone down.

The waitress bows almost to the ground and runs away.

I look at my gun in confusion.

"There's a reason some Otherlands are stuck in medieval times," Felix whispers. "Sometimes, gunpowder doesn't work right in those places, and other times, something else is wonky, like electricity."

"Must be those differences in the laws of physics Dr. Hekima mentioned at Orientation," I whisper back.

Felix nods, and we sit for a few minutes in an extremely uncomfortable silence.

Eventually, the waitress comes back, carrying a small Fabergé-style egg in her hands. I have no idea what real duck eggs are supposed to look like, but I bet this is an artist's interpretation.

Kit turns back into her usual shape and takes the egg. Then she says something to everyone in Russian and heads for the missing wall.

Felix and I sprint after her as if the kikimora is about to leap at us—because that's probably the case.

"I'm sure glad I asked Kit to tag along," I whisper to Felix. "If it were just us, we'd be digesting inside that leshy's belly."

"I doubt you would've gotten farther than the cat," Kit says, then pockets the egg and turns back into a horse.

Felix and I get back on, and we gallop back.

Mere minutes after we pass the still-raging battle with the giant head, a whole battalion of bogatyrs starts chasing us.

"Where did these come from?" Felix mutters in my ear, holding on to my sides for dear life as Kit swerves off the road and picks up speed.

"Maybe they're the backup for the head-killing crew," I say, trying not to bite my tongue as we jump over a boulder. "Could've decided we'd make better sport."

Felix tightens his grip on me. "Maybe. Could also be a squad specializing in people who came to steal the only weapon that can hurt these dudes." He sounds like he's about to pass out.

Kit leaps over a ditch at full speed, her hooves pounding the ground like a drum.

The bogatyrs are still catching up.

An arrow whooshes by my ear.

"Kit, this isn't good," I shout over the battle cries and the hammering hoofbeats. "I hope you have a plan."

A firebird egg explodes two feet away from us, the heat wave nearly singeing my eyebrows.

If we could just make it to the giant forest in the distance, we'd have a chance.

Kit must've come to the same conclusion because she speeds up so much it feels as though she's flying.

Which is when I see countless bogatyrs come out of the forest in front of us, blocking any chance for escape.

Stomach sinking, I glance back at our pursuers—and wish I hadn't.

Dozens of firebird eggs and enough arrows to blot out the sky are flying our way.

This is it.

We're about to turn into well-done shish kebabs.

CHAPTER FORTY-TWO

THIS IS when I realize that it doesn't just *feel* like Kit is flying.

She is actually flying—a fact highlighted by the frantic beating of her giant wings.

"Is she one of those Great Eagles from *Lord of the Rings*?" I mutter as I watch us fly above the projectiles.

"No," Felix whispers in a petrified voice. "I think she's the roc."

I look at Kit's wingspan.

Yep.

She could easily be the roc—an enormous bird of prey from Middle Eastern mythology. Like with the firebird, the legends about the roc must be based on something in the Otherlands.

Those pre-Mandate Cognizant must've loved to brag. Especially about weird birds.

"I didn't realize Dwayne Johnson was one of the

Cognizant," I say, hoping that a bad joke might calm Felix and myself down. "Nor did I know *The Rock* could fly."

Felix squeezes my midsection without so much as a chuckle.

I allow myself a breath of relief when we fly into the forest.

Miraculously, we dodge all the trees in our way.

When we eventually reach the meadow hub and land, the giant cat looks at us with opened-mouthed fascination.

The roc is clearly not native to Buyan.

We get off, and Kit turns back into herself.

Massaging my aching posterior, I give myself a solemn oath to never, under any circumstances, get on top of a horse, or a reindeer, or a bird, or Kit, ever again.

"Here." She hands me the Fabergé egg. "You earned it."

Hearing angry shouts of the approaching bogatyrs in the distance, I decide it's best to drag the still-hyperventilating Felix through the gate and let him recover on the other side.

Once he's able to breathe normally, we traverse our route backward through the hubs at a brisk pace.

When we finally exit in JFK, I turn my attention to the egg.

The latch to open it is easy to spot for my escapist-trained eye.

Inside the egg is an intricate needle made out of some silvery metal.

"A needle," Felix says, wiping away the sweat from his forehead. "That makes more sense than a neem or a neep."

"I was thinking he was about to say something related to food or an inn," I say defensively. "Needles do not have anything to do with those things."

"What do we do with this?" Kit asks, studying the needle as she takes the open egg from me to pocket it again.

Felix pulls out his phone and taps the screen a few times.

"According to Yandex.ru and assuming our Koschei is in any way related to the one from Russian legends, we might want to break the needle." He waves his phone. "Though I'm not sure how much we want to trust such a source."

I take the needle and try to snap it in half.

It doesn't even bend.

"Let me try," Felix says and takes the needle from me.

He can't break it either.

"Can I try?" Kit asks, and by the time I hand her the needle, she's turned herself into a giant orc.

The orc tries to break the needle.

No luck.

She puts the needle in her mouth and crunches on it.

No result—which is impressive, considering an orc once bit through my gun.

Kit turns back into herself and hands me the needle. "Ask Nero to break it," she says. "His strength is legendary."

"Good idea," I say and pretend to swallow the needle in the same manner as during my needle-swallowing effect.

Kit looks stunned, so I open my mouth to let her see it empty.

"You hid the needle inside a specially designed hollow tongue piercing," Felix says without looking inside my mouth. "When did you swap it for the usual set of lock picks you carry there?"

Kit spots my tongue jewelry and looks disappointed.

I resist both the desire to choke Felix for revealing two of my most cherished secrets and the urge to beg him to tell me how he could possibly know what no one was supposed to ever find out.

Best guess—Felix somehow hacked the computer of my guy in Vegas. We'd agreed he wouldn't keep any copies of the designs, but the greedy weasel must've done so anyway.

Looking smug, Felix strides to the hub exit.

I take out my phone and let Thalia know we'll be out soon.

On the screen are over a dozen messages and voicemails from Nero, the timestamps on which make no sense until I look at the clock and realize something.

Otherland time dilation has played a cruel trick on me.

It's already late Monday morning.

I'm supposed to be at work.

CHAPTER FORTY-THREE

A REPLY from Thalia arrives as I start checking Nero's messages, most of which amount to, "Call me ASAP."

Nero wanted you in the office half an hour ago, Thalia's text says.

Sure enough, that's what Nero's latter messages and voicemails are about.

I make everyone jog to the limo, where Thalia and I agree that the situation calls for serious speeding to work.

"Sashimi, anyone?" Kit asks after loudly rummaging through the food bar in the limo.

"I'm not eating raw fish from a car that circled JFK all night long." Felix wrinkles his nose. "Not everyone can turn their stomach into that of some kind of carrion eater."

Kit chuckles, then bravely gobbles down the sashimi.

I make myself and Felix a bagel with peanut butter

and jelly, and by the time we're done with breakfast, the limo stops next to my work building.

To the shock of employees passing by, Nero personally opens the door for me—a billionaire turned valet.

"My condolences, again," Nero says to Thalia with genuine emotion on his face. "Once you drop off Kit and Felix, please take as long as you need to grieve. I'll watch over Sasha personally in the meanwhile."

Thalia nods solemnly.

I get out, and Nero shuts the limo door.

"Buyan?" He turns toward me, his expression quietly furious. "Really?"

I shrug. "We had Kit with us, and it's not like you would've helped anyway, with your precious contract and all."

His jaw flexes violently; then he seems to take himself in hand. "Tell me everything," he orders, shepherding me into the building. "I need to know exactly what happened, so I can figure out who blew up that car and why."

I describe everything that happened from the pier onward as we walk to the elevator; then, at his urging, I tell him in detail about our trip through the Otherlands.

I'm so absorbed in narrating our bizarre journey through Buyan that I don't realize where Nero's leading me until he herds me into my new safe/cell/office.

"This place?" I glare up at him. "After everything that's happened, you're going to lock me up again?"

"I never should've let you out," he says darkly. "You're lucky to have made it out of Buyan alive."

"Are you from there?" I ask on a hunch. "Is that how you know how safe or unsafe the place is?"

Without answering, Nero starts to slam the door.

"Wait." I grab his arm. "Can I just give you my stock recommendations and go home without being held prisoner?"

He looks at my hand with such intensity that I yank it back. "No." He locks the metal door, shutting me in.

"Well, my recommendation will be the Asia Tigers Fund," I say, in case he's got his ear to the metal door on the other side. "Their stock ticker is GRR."

Nero doesn't come back—not that I expected him to.

Annoyed I'm about to do exactly what Nero wants, I nevertheless sit down to have a vision.

It's been a while since I've checked on Vlad, so I might as well do it.

Shuddering at the memory of the last time, I attempt reaching Headspace.

I fail.

Must still be out of juice from the last marathon.

Getting comfortable on the cushion, I meditate, then use the Jacuzzi, eat another gourmet meal, and take a nap.

When I test it again, I find my power is still recharging.

Pacing the stupid cell, I deeply empathize with criminals kept in solitary confinement. This is as close to torture as I've ever experienced.

After what feels like two days, my attempt to reach Headspace finally succeeds.

Once inside, I focus on Vlad.

The result is a cloud of similar shapes—meaning I'm about to get a more traditional vision of a single event pertaining to Vlad.

A very creepy-sounding event, with music that grates on my nonexistent nerve endings.

Oh well.

I have to know what he's about to do.

Cringing metaphysically, I touch the shape closest to me and fall into the vision.

CHAPTER FORTY-FOUR

VLAD STRIDES up to the chicken-leg-adorned entrance of the Izbushka restaurant.

Dressed in a black leather coat, tall boots, and dark shades despite the setting sun, the vampire looks ready for *The Matrix* cosplay.

Two burly bouncers block Vlad's path.

"The restaurant is closed," one says in a booming voice.

"Our vendors failed to deliver anything today," says the other. "The dancers didn't come, the—"

The first bouncer gives the talkative one such a baleful glare that the man shuts up and channels his anger into giving Vlad a dirty look.

Vlad lifts his sunglasses, revealing mirrored eyes. Before either can say or do anything, he orders them to sleep.

They take an instant nap, and he steps over the bodies and whooshes inside.

The marble floors look extra polished today, and someone has added a few blingy candelabras throughout.

The bouncer didn't lie. The place is empty of patrons. There are just some members of staff cleaning, and mobster-looking dudes walking about looking bored.

Still, someone must've wanted to have fun: the disco ball above the center stage is spinning, the laser show is turned on, and Russian music is blasting through the giant speakers.

The song sounds like the Russian-language version of the one by t.A.T.u. that Felix made me listen to a few years back—*All the Things She Said*.

A few heads turn in Vlad's direction as he takes out a shotgun and an Uzi from under his coat.

His Uzi sprays bullets at the nearest goons.

They fall, bleeding all over the glossy floors.

Screams ring out, and the staff bolt for the exit while the gangster types reach for their guns.

Vlad sends another burst of bullets at the gangsters.

Most fall, but a few manage to fire at Vlad—and one bullet tears into his shoulder.

Oblivious to the wound, Vlad keeps shooting until his Uzi runs out of bullets—at which point he tosses it at the nearest goon.

As though propelled by a rocket, the Uzi smashes into the man's skull, caving it in.

Using his now-empty hand, Vlad lifts his sunglasses

and stares at the remaining enemies with those ready-for-glamour eyes.

"Sleep," he orders over the sounds of music and screaming.

Everyone within eyesight of Vlad's reflective eyes drops to the ground.

Two dudes at his back don't fall, however

They raise their guns.

Vlad must sense them somehow, because he launches into the air in a backward somersault.

The goons' eyes widen.

Vlad lands behind them and punches one with his free hand while clubbing the other with the butt of the shotgun.

Broken, the goons collapse on the floor.

Which is when Lucretia, Ariel, and Gaius land as if dropping from the sky, surrounding Vlad from three sides.

CHAPTER FORTY-FIVE

VLAD REACHES into his pocket and takes out a grenade.

"At such close quarters, you're just as likely to blow up as we are," Gaius says, but steps back.

His brooding face grim, Vlad removes the pin from the grenade and tosses it at his own feet.

"Get back!" Gaius barks at Lucretia and Ariel.

They obey instantly.

The grenade doesn't explode. Instead, thick smoke pours out.

Gaius steps back in confusion.

The smoke makes it hard to track Vlad's movements. One moment, he's standing inside the cloud; the next, he's beside Gaius, aiming the shotgun at the vampire's face.

Gaius's eyes widen. "Wait—"

Vlad presses the trigger.

Gaius's head explodes.

Vlad shoots again, this time at Gaius's chest, then keeps shooting until the shotgun is empty.

Gaius's aura goes away. I guess there's a more practical way to kill a vampire.

Ariel leaps at Vlad—proving that glamour works even after the vampire who cast it is dead.

Lucretia grabs Ariel from behind—proving that the sire bond is broken.

"Get her out of here," Vlad grits through his teeth. "Both of you, leave now."

Lucretia drags Ariel toward the exit.

Tossing the shotgun aside, Vlad takes out a machete and heads for the back of the restaurant.

The smoke from the grenade reaches the ceiling.

The fire alarm starts blaring over the beats of the song.

Sprinklers turn on, but instead of water, they spray a viscous liquid that smells like gasoline.

Hospital-gown-clad Johnnies run out and head for Vlad. They clearly got here in a rush. Some of them are not wearing sunglasses, exposing their black, Baba Yaga-controlled eyes.

Vlad expertly halves two of them with his machete, like a hunter clearing away brush.

Wiping gasoline from his brow, he narrows his eyes at something behind a dozen more Johnnies.

It's Koschei. He's standing there, clutching a knife.

Vlad's machete rips through the remaining Johnnies like a hot spoon through ice cream.

When he eviscerates the last Johnny, Vlad leaps

inhumanly high and cleaves Koschei's knife-wielding arm as he lands.

Koschei screams.

Vlad chops at his enemy, again and again.

Koschei screams louder as he loses more body parts but somehow manages to stay alive.

When there's nothing else to cut, Vlad chops Koschei's head off, waits for the resurrection, and repeats the grisly work with the enthusiasm of a kid pulling wings off a fly.

When limbless Koschei is screaming and writhing on the ground like a snake for the tenth time, Baba Yaga walks out of the smoke.

"Thank you for bringing me the Council seat on a silver platter," she says in her androgynous, thousand-year-old voice. "Your seat was going to go to Gaius, but with him dead, your presence here greatly simplifies my plans."

"You shouldn't have helped Gaius kill Rose." Vlad is all but vibrating with rage.

"You talk about vengeance," Baba Yaga says, but if Vlad realizes she's quoting *The Godfather* yet again, he doesn't show it. Instead, he lifts the machete as though he plans to throw it like a knife.

Baba Yaga raises her arm, parroting Vlad's movement. Before he can even blink, black energy flows from each of her fingers into his head.

A lot of energy.

The witch seems to age another few decades under the effort of it.

Vlad's eyes fill up with black energy identical to those of the Johnnies, and the weapon does *not* leave his hand.

"Good," Baga Yaga says in a weak voice. "Now let's use that blade to slice your neck."

She strains until her face looks pained from the mental effort.

Vlad starts to move like an automaton. He positions the machete at his own throat, then lazily hacks at it.

The neck wound looks grievous.

Vlad falls to his knees.

His blood streams down, mixing with the gasoline.

"Again," Baba Yaga hisses.

Vlad slices himself one more time, and starts to fall to the marble floor.

Baba Yaga sags in exhaustion.

Vlad's body hits the floor.

A firebird egg rolls out from under his black leather coat and stops in the puddle of gasoline at Baba Yaga's feet.

"No," she gasps, staring down in horror. "Not after—"

The egg cracks open.

The fire blast turns Vlad, Baba Yaga, and the still-struggling Koschei into ash, and the gasoline ignites, spreading flames in a heartbeat.

In moments, the restaurant looks like the Seventh Circle from Dante's *Inferno*—

CHAPTER FORTY-SIX

I'M BACK in my cell, covered in a layer of sweat so dense you'd think I was actually in a burning restaurant a moment ago.

Leaping to my feet, I head straight for the monitor keypad device.

The clock shows 1:49.52—the remaining time on my work allotment.

With a trembling finger, I key 911 into the number pad.

The screen blinks red at first; then a videoconference app comes on.

Blinking in confusion, I accept the call.

"You don't look like you're having a medical emergency," Nero growls. "I thought I explained the consequences of—"

"Vlad's about to die," I blurt out. "We have to go save him. The fire—"

"Slow down." Nero gets closer to the camera. "How and why is Vlad going to die this time?"

My voice unnaturally shrill, I tell him what I just foresaw.

"It was sunset when he got to the scene, and the sun sets around six p.m. this time of year." I wave my phone. "It's 3:45 right now, and it could take over two hours to get to Brighton Beach at this time of day. We have to—"

"I can't step foot in Brighton Beach." A muscle ticks in Nero's temple. "I've told you that."

"Isn't the contract only valid while Baba Yaga is alive?"

"Yes."

"Well, I saw her die in my vision. Can't you—"

"No. It doesn't work like that. If anything, that's an excellent argument *against* going. Doing so can change the vision and result in Baba Yaga's survival."

"But don't you also have the right to attack her if she goes after me?"

His eyebrows snap together. "She just confirmed that she didn't try to kill you with that explosion—and she was telling the truth again."

"That's bullshit." I smack the monitor in frustration. "Let's see how she doesn't try to kill me when I go there to save Vlad."

"You're not going anywhere." Nero reaches for his computer, about to disconnect.

"Wait!" I shout. "Please. I promised Rose I'd take care of Vlad."

The phrase "take care of Vlad" seems to awaken something dark in Nero's eyes. Something frightening.

"Don't you see that this was Vlad's exact plan?" His tone is sharp enough to cut glass. "He knows Baba Yaga has the power to take someone over. The gasoline in the sprinklers, the smoke grenade, the firebird egg—they're all part of a suicide mission. Vlad *wants* to die. Losing someone you love can—"

"Vlad isn't thinking rationally."

"Neither are you," Nero snaps. "Your work allotment is now doubled for today."

With that, he hangs up.

I bang a fist at the safe-like metal door to no avail.

The clock shows up on the screen again, now showing 9:45.12.

Resisting the urge to punch it, I type in 911 again.

The screen goes red, and the video conference app starts up but instantly disconnects.

Nero doesn't even pick up to tell me I doubled my "work allotment" again—the clock just shows 15:44.59.

I almost rip the screen off the wall, but I need it.

Since I can't rely on the bastard's help, I must figure out the passcode.

Praying to my seer intuition, I type in my best guess: 5317. According to Felix, if you write 5317 on an old-school calculator and turn it upside down, it will read as LIES.

The screen blinks red, and an annoying beeping sounds rings out—but the door stays shut and the clock changes to show 55:44.48.

What?

He did say he'd double my week's work allotment if I put in the wrong passcode, but I didn't expect the bastard to do it like this.

My head is ready to explode, and it takes all my willpower to calm myself enough to think.

If my powers don't serve up a passcode, I'm screwed. Assuming the code is four digits, there are 10,000 possibilities to try. If I enter one per second, it will take 166 minutes to go through them all—or about two hours and forty-two minutes.

That's assuming I don't get locked out after too many wrong guesses for security reasons, as with smartphone passcodes.

Either way, Vlad doesn't have that kind of time.

If only I had reception in this place. Then I'd call Felix, and he would figure out a way to hack this lock.

Thinking of Felix gives me an idea.

Back when we were trying to hack Nero's computer, Felix had suggested a way to use Headspace to guess a password. At the time, I had no clue how to do what he described, but I might now.

"I'm going to guess the passwords," I tell myself so confidently that I actually believe it. "I'll punch in 0001, then 0002, and so on and so forth, until I get to 9999."

To really seal in the deal, I punch 0001.

It doesn't work, and I get forty more hours on my allotment clock.

I punch in 0002.

Same result.

Instead of typing in 0003, though, I launch myself into Headspace.

––––––

IGNORING the default shapes around me, I focus on my situation in the cell—particularly the password-guessing game that I've started.

A cloud of vision-shapes appears in front of me, all as similar to each other as I've ever encountered.

If I'm on the right track, these are so alike because the only difference between them is which digit I press into that keypad.

I focus on reaching out with multiple wisps, as I'd done for the Vlad visions. Only this time, it's not a dozen or so that I need to sprout but ten thousand.

The feeling of getting ripped apart is exponentially stronger as I get pulled into thousands of directions—but then I feel myself in ten thousand places at once and the visions begin.

––––––

I TYPE in 0003 into the keypad without success.

––––––

I TYPE in 0004 into the keypad without success.

––––––

I GET visions of myself failing while pressing 0005, then 0006, and on and on, until I get to 7734.

———

I TYPE in 7735 into the keypad. Green light winks at me, and the cell door unlocks.

———

I GET visions of myself of futilely pressing 7736, then 7737, and on and on, until I get to 9999 and the visions stop.

———

I'M BACK in the room, the metal walls spinning around me as I jump from foot to foot in excitement.

I did it.

I used my power to brute-force the stupid lock.

At least I hope I did.

Index finger trembling, I type in 7735 into the keypad.

Green light winks at me, and the cell door unlocks.

Finally.

Now I just have to get out of the building before Nero can stop me.

CHAPTER FORTY-SEVEN

I SPRINT to the elevator as though chased by a team of zombie IRS agents.

The elevator seems to take a thousand frantic heartbeats to get to me, and when I get inside, I stab the ground floor button hard enough to hurt my finger, then bite my nails all the way up.

The doors open.

Nero isn't there.

Phew.

I sprint out of the elevator and through the lobby.

My coworkers give me confused looks, but no one stops me.

I bump into a woman as I exit the door. She looks familiar, but I pass her too quickly to register where I might know her from.

Spotting an empty yellow cab, I jump in front of it and frantically wave my arms.

The driver stops, rolls down his window, and yells something unintelligible about my sanity.

"I'll give you two hundred dollars to get me to Brooklyn," I yell back. "Three hundred if you manage to do it before sunset."

He unlocks the door for me, and we speed away.

As we turn the corner, I catch a glimpse of Nero running out of the building.

Too late, asshole.

I pull out my phone and dial Felix.

"Sasha," he says. "How are—"

"No time. Put me on speaker so Kit can hear."

Felix does as I ask, and I start explaining what happened, lowering my voice to a whisper when I touch on the supernatural bits.

"Did you realize that the password you cracked is another one of those upside-down calculator words?" Felix says when I finish. "It's SELL—which is *so* Nero, don't you think?"

I squeeze my eyes shut. "We don't have time for that. I called because I was hoping you could send your robot to help me. It might be the only way to get to Baba Yaga without getting snared by her mind-control juju."

"It does sounds like a good use for Golem," Felix says. "Let me set him up and get ready."

"Only Golem, not you," I clarify. "For this to work best, I need you to control it from the safety of our apartment; otherwise, someone can get to you before the robot gets to Baba Yaga."

I only twist the truth slightly. I also don't want to expose him to more horrors.

"That makes sense," Felix says with noticeable relief in his voice.

"What about me?" Kit asks.

"Can Baba Yaga take *you* over?" I ask.

"Probably," she says. "But, like Vlad, I would be very difficult for her to control, meaning if she tries, she'd be weakened, which could give you a critical opening."

"In that case, I'd love it if you volunteered to go," I say. "But I'd totally understand if you'd rather not risk it."

"Does this mean we're friends now?" she asks cheerfully. "I have so much fun hanging out with you and —"

"Yes." I'm glad Kit can't see me roll my eyes. "We're friends without benefits whether you join this mission or not. But if you want to enjoy having me alive as a friend for much longer, please join."

"Good point," Kit says. "You do still owe me a vision."

"Yep," I say, for once grateful to be owing a favor.

"Okay, then," Kit says. "I'm in. But keep in mind, I will *not* kill anyone under the Mandate. Nor can I bring the Enforcers with me, or do anything else in my official capacity as a Councilor."

Crap.

Baba Yaga, Koschei, and Gaius are all "under the Mandate"—meaning Kit's hands will be tied.

"Kit can still help out with the Johnnies and the

other goons," Felix says. "I think it's still worth your while to take her."

"I agree," I say. "Our main goal is to get Vlad, Lucretia, and Ariel out alive. Revenge is an optional gravy."

"Fluffster wants to add something," Felix says. "He says, 'Don't you dare die.'"

"Tell him I'll do my best," I say. "Now, to save time, can Kit and Golem meet me on Broadway? This way, my cab can pick them up without turning onto our street."

"No problem," Kit and Felix say in unison.

"Okay, hurry," I say. "We'll be there soon."

They hang up, and I watch the cab navigate the rush-hour traffic with nervous anticipation.

To stay sane, I spend a few minutes doing meditative breathing; then, when I'm calmer, I try to get into Headspace.

It doesn't work, which I guess makes sense.

Though the visions that helped me hack the passcode were short, there were ten thousand of them, so it's feasible I ran out of juice.

If I'm lucky, I'll be able to recharge by the time we arrive at our destination. And if there's one kind of seer experience I could use more of, it would have to be power management.

I see my friends standing on the corner from a block away.

"Pull over next to that lady in a ninja outfit," I say to

the driver, pointing at Kit as we get closer. "The one next to a robot."

Shrugging, the cab driver pulls up where I requested.

Jaded New Yorkers don't seem to care about a metallic creature getting itself into a cab, but a few tourists gawk at Golem in fascination.

The driver cares even less than the city natives. He simply presses on the gas, and we screech forward.

Belatedly, it occurs to me that I should've asked Kit to bring my Focusall, in case my powers came back in time.

Oh well, I guess I'll have to rely on my training.

"Put this in your ear." Kit hands me a familiar-looking earbud.

"Figured we'd communicate the same way as during Ariel's rescue," Felix's voice says from inside the earbud. "Tap the earbud to mute it, or tap it again to speak—or you can just speak to Golem. I'm using his eyes and ears as my own."

"Sounds good," I say to Golem. "You'd make a fortune if you could manufacture robots like this for the general public."

"You need to have my technomancer powers to control Golem at the moment," Felix says disappointedly. "But maybe I could make something everyone can use someday."

"I tried calling and texting Vlad to stop him from going into that restaurant," Kit says. "No luck."

"Oh, I'm glad you did that." I redden. "I was in such a rush I forgot to try such a simple solution."

"I doubt he would listen anyway," Felix says through the buds.

My phone rings.

It's Nero.

I click "Ignore."

A notification about a voicemail pops up, then a text message.

Surprise, surprise. It's a combination of threats and pleas.

Nero doesn't want me to go to Brighton Beach.

I don't return the call or the text.

I'll deal with my boss if I survive.

"I almost forgot." Kit hands me an energy bar and a bottle of water. "Fluffster was worried you might not have eaten."

"Fluffster was right," I say and attack the sustenance with enthusiasm.

Eating and drinking keeps me busy half of the way. The second half, I spend attempting to reach Headspace, over and over—without any success.

At 6:04 p.m., we turn onto Brighton Beach and park.

"We better hurry," Kit says, throwing cash at the driver as she exits the vehicle.

The robot and I rush out after Kit.

The sun is already setting.

"Put this on." Kit hands me a black mask and puts one on herself at the same time. "No Enforcers to wipe memories after we're done, so we have to worry about witnesses."

Feeling like a robber from a heist movie, I put on the itchy mask and sprint for the chicken-leg-adorned entrance of the Izbushka restaurant.

Kit and Golem follow close behind.

The two burly bouncers are on the ground already, sleeping.

"Shit," Kit says, catching up with me. "We may already be too late."

CHAPTER FORTY-EIGHT

PULLING OUT MY GUN, I rush inside.

"The t.A.T.u song is still blasting through the speakers," Felix says in the earbud. "That tells me you're not *that* late."

I take in the place.

Felix is right.

We arrived early enough.

Vlad is standing in the middle of the room with a shotgun and an Uzi in his hands.

"Don't move," Felix says in my earpiece needlessly. "We know he's going to be fine, but if you get into the line of fire, you can die."

As though to highlight Felix's words, Vlad sprays out bullets at the nearest goons, just like he did in my vision.

The goons fall, bleeding all over the glossy floors.

Desperate screams ring out, and we dodge the staff stampede as best we can.

Just like before, the surviving gangsters reach for their guns.

Vlad sends another burst of bullets at them, as predicted.

Most fall, but a few manage to fire at Vlad—and one bullet tears into his shoulder again.

Oblivious to the wound, Vlad keeps shooting until his Uzi runs out of bullets.

"Now we run," I say and launch into a sprint, jumping over the bleeding bodies in my way.

Vlad throws the empty gun at the nearest goon, caving in his skull, like before.

Both Kit and I look down when Vlad lifts his sunglasses and orders everyone in the range of his weaponized gaze to sleep.

All but two goons fall.

In my vision, this would be when Vlad launches into that awesome-looking backward somersault.

This time, though, Golem smacks the two dudes on their heads with his giant metallic arms.

The impact is not as bad as when Vlad did the same thing, but it does the trick: the two men drop to the floor.

"Vlad, it's me and Kit," I shout. "Please don't shoot!"

"Sasha?" Vlad looks at me like I've sprouted two heads. "Kit?"

"Watch out!" I yell. "They're about to attack."

Just like they did in the vision, Lucretia, Ariel, and Gaius land as if dropping from the sky.

Except we changed the future when we arrived here and had Golem kill the goons.

Changed it for the worse.

Since Vlad never performed that somersault, he's standing in a different location from where he was in my vision—and Gaius kicks the shotgun out of Vlad's hands as he lands.

The shotgun slides out of reach on the blood-drenched floor.

"Take him," Gaius orders Lucretia and Ariel.

Leading by example, he throws a punch at Vlad's face.

CHAPTER FORTY-NINE

"KIT, grab Lucretia. I'll get Ariel," Felix shrieks in the earpiece as the robot leaps for our roommate.

Kit sprouts extra height and muscles and jumps at Lucretia.

Gaius's punch causes Vlad to fly back a few feet, but he instantly recovers.

Gaius scowls, then follows Vlad so fast that my eyes have trouble tracking him in the dim, laser-show light.

Vlad reaches into his jacket and pulls out the grenade.

Gaius slaps it out of Vlad's hands.

The grenade rolls impotently on the floor and stops near the shotgun.

Was Gaius right when he boasted before? Is he more powerful than Vlad when Rose's boosts are taken out of the picture?

Vlad throws a punch at Gaius's face.

Gaius ducks the blow, and lands his own in Vlad's midsection.

I cringe. If Gaius's fist hits the firebird egg, they and anyone nearby will go up in blazes.

Of course, if that grenade had gone off, initiating the gasoline sprinklers, a firebird egg explosion would've killed everyone.

Vlad flies backward again.

Gaius races after him.

I raise my gun and shoot where I hope Gaius will be in a moment.

I hit the disco ball instead of Gaius.

The two vampires are now standing too closely for me to risk shooting again.

They exchange more blows.

"Ariel, I don't want to hurt you," Felix says with Golem's robotic voice to the side of us.

I spare a glance there.

The robot is holding Ariel's hands behind her back, but Ariel is twisting and thrashing as if in an exorcism.

Lucretia must've put up a fight, too. Kit's mask is in tatters. However, Kit now has Lucretia in a tight, inescapable hug.

I look back in time to see Gaius punch Vlad so hard the vampire flies back a dozen feet.

Gaius sprints forward.

I shoot—and miss the super-fast vampire again.

Vlad reaches into his coat, pulls out the machete, and swings it at Gaius's head.

Gaius catches Vlad's wrist and performs an Aikido-like maneuver.

The machete pierces Vlad's thigh, causing him to grunt in pain.

I rush toward them. If I shoot point blank, I have a smaller chance of hitting Vlad.

When I'm a foot away, I raise the gun.

Gaius must've sensed me coming, because he swats me like a fly.

I feel like a baseball that met Babe Ruth's bat. My gun flies in one direction, and I fly in the other.

Something cracks when I slam into a wall, and air vacates my lungs as I slide down the bloody marble.

My nerve endings go nuclear, and I think I pass out.

When I come to my senses, all I want to do is lie in a heap and recover, but I can't.

Vlad needs me.

With an effort of will powerful enough to finish two marathons, I crawl into a pushup position.

This is when I notice where I landed: a few feet from the grenade and the shotgun.

Through the pain, a desperate outline of a plan forms in my head. Not even a plan, just a thought.

When Vlad won in my vision, it was under the cover of smoke, and he did it by shooting Gaius in the face. Would the future fall into place if the same variables were in play?

I crawl over and grab the grenade and the shotgun. Using the shotgun as a crutch, I rise onto wobbly feet.

Sucking in a breath, I take a shuffling step in the direction of the fighting vampires.

Then another and another.

Gaius stole the machete from Vlad and is hacking away.

Vlad only manages to dodge half of the swings; the rest leave Vlad's clothes and flesh in tatters.

There are numerous deadly-for-humans wounds on Vlad's body.

I prepare to throw the grenade at them to give Vlad some cover, but then I recall that the smoke leads to gasoline from the sprinklers—which won't go well if Gaius hits the firebird egg... or if Vlad falls.

I try to peek into the future to see if using the grenade will be safe, but no luck.

Either I'm failing to get the needed Headspace focus, or I haven't recharged my power yet.

Pocketing the grenade for now, I attempt another step, then another and another.

Soon, I declare my walking apparatus functional. Here's to hoping that means nothing major was broken.

After a dozen more agonizing steps, I get within swatting distance of Gaius again.

I'm gambling on him being too busy trying to pull out the machete from Vlad's shoulder.

Quietly, I aim the shotgun, but then I hesitate.

A pellet can hit Vlad. Then again, that probably won't be as bad as getting another blow with that machete.

Unless a pellet hits the firebird egg. If that happens, all three of us will be burnt toast in an eye blink.

Oh well. As Felix says, "She who doesn't risk never gets to drink champagne."

Holding my breath, I squeeze the trigger.

CHAPTER FIFTY

A GAPING hole explodes in the middle of Gaius's chest.

Vlad seems fine—if by "fine," I mean cut up savagely with a machete, but shotgun-pellet free.

Leaving the weapon in Vlad's shoulder, Gaius clutches his chest.

"How is he still standing?" Felix whispers in my earbud.

With a grunt, Vlad grasps the machete in his shoulder with both hands and rips it out—spewing a fountain of blood.

Gaius's eyes widen and he starts to move back, but it's too late.

Vlad chops Gaius's head off.

The head rolls away as the body drops to the floor, and the Mandate aura disappears.

Vlad also slumps. There's a puddle of blood at his feet.

I hope he stays upright enough to keep that egg in check.

"You can let me go," Lucretia says in a hoarse voice. "I'm not following Gaius's commands any longer."

I look back.

Just like in my vision, Gaius's death broke the sire bond for Lucretia, but not Ariel's glamour.

Kit lets go.

"I think you broke my ribs," Lucretia mutters.

"Are you okay?" I ask Vlad.

"I'll survive," he grits out, blood pouring from his mouth. "I'm not sure I can fight, though."

I look at Lucretia. "Can you drag him out?"

She solemnly nods, and rushes to grab Vlad under his armpits.

"Kit," I say. "Help Golem get Ariel out of here while I cover our exit."

"If I remember your vision correctly, there are Johnnies in the back," Felix says. "And Koschei and Baba Yaga."

"That's *why* I said I'm going to provide cover fire," I grumble, then shuffle over to get my handgun.

Kit runs to help Golem.

A hospital-clad Johnny shows up from the back of the restaurant just as I lift my gun and shoot.

The Johnny runs for me.

I clearly missed him.

I shoot again—and this time, I get the Johnny between those black eyes.

Another one gets the same treatment, then another.

Something jerks my head back so suddenly I get whiplash.

I duck down, leaving my mask in the hand of the Johnny who grabbed me before putting a bullet in his brain.

"Everyone is outside," Felix says in my ear. "Lucretia is holding down Ariel, and Kit is giving Vlad blood so he doesn't die. I'm sending Golem back to help you."

"Thanks," I say as another Johnny leaps down from the dance stage.

I shoot him also, then wonder if I should toss the smoke grenade to provide myself and the robot with some cover.

Does that mean I'll start a fire when I shoot my gun in the resulting gasoline downpour? It wasn't the case when Vlad shot Gaius in my vision, but he might've been lucky that time.

Then again, Vlad didn't care if this place burned to the ground with him in it, and I care about that scenario very much.

If only I could see the future. Then I'd be able to make this decision for sure.

Taking in a deep breath, I channel all my practice into an overwhelming need to reach Headspace.

A Johnny breaks my concentration and pays with his life.

Then another pops up.

In a lull between the killings, I try focusing again.

To my shock, it works.

For the first time ever, I get Headspace access in the middle of a gunfight.

———

FLOATING BETWEEN THE SHAPES, I catch my metaphysical breath and enjoy not having to defend my life for a moment.

Though I'm fairly sure that no time passes in the outside world while I'm in Headspace, I still want to get this over with as quickly as I can.

So, what do I focus on?

The grenade?

Thus far, I've had better luck targeting visions using people, or when I relied on the default shapes around me.

I dubiously examine the black, ice-cold, bitter-tasting, pyramid-like snowflakes that surround me.

The music they play does not bode well for this vision.

Which is exactly why I should see what future they'd bring.

Thus decided, I reach out to a single target to save power for later, then let my wisp do what it's meant to do—and plunge in.

CHAPTER FIFTY-ONE

BABA YAGA IS STANDING above a familiar, broken-looking female body sprawled like a corpse at a crime scene. Only the chalk outline is missing.

There's a giant iron-cast skillet in Baba Yaga's hand with blood smeared on it. A welt on the head of the limp body matches that part of the skillet.

"Thanks to this attack, you voided my contract with Nero," Baba Yaga says to the body. "Now I can take care of you for good."

Though I don't usually feel emotions in this state, an arctic chill permeates through my bodiless being.

No wonder that body is familiar.

It's mine.

In fact, I've seen myself this way once before—during the fight with Beatrice, after she killed me inside a vision. That time, I was able to prevent that fate by changing the circumstances that led to it.

Hopefully, I can do the same thing this time around.

Someone steps on a piece of metal behind Baba Yaga.

It's Kit.

She's aiming a shotgun at Baba Yaga's head.

Before the old witch can turn, Kit presses the trigger.

The gun clicks futilely—must be jammed or out of bullets.

"Looks like I get *your* Council seat, after all." Baba Yaga spins around to stare at Kit with a carnivorous smile. "I had my people try to shoot you, then blow you up to no avail. Now you come to me voluntarily—and I get to make everything look like a legitimate suicide. How—"

Without finishing the tirade, Baba Yaga tosses the heavy skillet at Kit's head.

Kit must've been caught off guard by Baba Yaga's confession because she doesn't dodge the projectile, and the skillet smacks her in the head.

Kit staggers.

Just like in the vision about Vlad, Baba Yaga lifts her arm.

Black energy forms on each of her fingertips.

She seems to age a few decades under the effort before the energy shoots out.

Only it doesn't fly at Kit.

It arcs from Kit to the unmoving Sasha on the floor.

Why shoot there?

Then I see it.

The Jubilee necklace with that giant stone.

It's still on my neck, and it absorbs Baba Yaga's energy—the way a ring Rose once gave me did.

Of course. This is why Rose asked me to bring it.

She knew who Koschei works for, and what might happen after her death.

Leave it to Rose to exact one last revenge from beyond the grave.

Kit recovers from the hit and smirks, seeing the situation.

Then she grows and morphs into a drekavac—a nightmarish xenomorph-meets-dementor creature we learned about at the last Orientation.

"No," the weakened Baba Yaga pleads. "Just shoot me. Don't—"

Drekavac-Kit stalks up to Baba Yaga and reaches out with multiple pustule-infested limbs.

Baba Yaga's tortured scream isn't recognizable as coming from a throat. It sounds more like some hellish string instrument playing a single, glass-shattering note.

Writhing and twitching so hard she probably tears her own ligaments, the old witch collapses on the ground.

Kit looms over her victim.

A horrific-looking tongue slowly snakes out of the drekavac's maw.

Wherever the thing licks Baba Yaga's skin, it melts away as though it never existed, leaving behind raw meat.

"Getting killed by a drekavac is the worst fate that

can befall anyone," Dr. Hekima had said, and clearly, he hadn't exaggerated.

If I had a body, I'd be vomiting.

On the third lick, Baba Yaga's throat produces one last agonized scream; then she slumps, blissfully dead.

Kit turns herself into an orc, kicks Baba Yaga's remains to the side, and walks up to my unmoving body.

Carefully picking me up, the orc strides toward the restaurant exit.

CHAPTER FIFTY-TWO

I'M THRUST BACK into the reality of the gunfight, and now that I have a body, I have to breathe deeply in order not to throw up from what I just saw.

What Kit did to Baba Yaga in that vision is going to haunt me more than Bentley's burned body—and I didn't think that was possible.

Speaking of poor Bentley: it seems the car bomb that killed him was aimed at Kit, not me. Same goes for that attack in the bathroom—Gaius was helping Baba Yaga when he lured Kit to the hotel with the promise of sex. That's why Baba Yaga was able to honestly tell Nero she wasn't trying to kill *me*. It was true. I just happened to be near Kit when Baba Yaga struck.

If I hadn't been so self-centered, I would've guessed it earlier.

The more I think about the recent events, the more I realize Baba Yaga deserves the fate she got in the vision.

She killed Rose. She killed Kevin and Bentley. In the vision, she even got to me—or will.

Yeah.

Will.

Maybe my top priority should be preventing myself from ending up as that unmoving body?

But how? I didn't see what led up to it, so I need more data.

Trying to go back into Headspace fails.

Either I'm too stressed out after what I saw, or I don't have enough juice.

A Johnny jumps out from the back of the restaurant, and I put a bullet in his head on autopilot.

Another one leaps out, and I shoot him too.

"I saw the most horrible vision," I say for Felix's benefit. "I need to do something to prevent it, but—"

I don't finish my sentence because I see him.

Koschei.

He's holding the knife, and his green eyes gleam with deadly determination as he leaps for me.

I shoot him in the head.

The gun clicks empty.

I raise the shotgun, but it's too late.

Koschei smacks it out of my hands, then tosses me at the nearest wall like a Frisbee.

I hit the wall with my injured back and slide to the floor, again.

My consciousness flees.

CHAPTER FIFTY-THREE

I BLINK my eyes open to the sight of Koschei's knife arcing at my chest.

This is it.

I'm done for.

CHAPTER FIFTY-FOUR

A METALLIC ARM grabs Koschei's wrist before he can finish the stabbing motion, and a giant metal fist smacks into his jaw with an audible crack.

Koschei flies back.

Golem leaps at him.

Koschei slices at Golem's torso with the knife, leaving a deep groove in the metal and breaking off the blade.

He then tosses the remnants of the knife at the robot. The impact dents the metal carapace with a clank; then the pieces drop to the floor.

Golem kicks Koschei in the shin.

There's a sound of a bone cracking.

Golem kicks the same spot again.

Koschei's leg snaps, a jagged piece of bone sticking out as he falls.

The robot stomps on him so hard that a few of its leg bolts fly in different directions.

Hissing in pain, Koschei nevertheless tries to catch the metal foot.

Golem kicks his head like a soccer ball.

Koschei dies, but instantly resurrects and punches the robot in the midsection.

Metal bends and bone breaks.

I inhale a deep breath and nearly pass out from the pain.

My ribs might be broken.

Possibly other things too.

Gritting my teeth, I roll over and begin to crawl for the shotgun.

The sounds of metal and bone clashing grow louder and more disturbing.

It sounds like Koschei is breaking himself apart over and over to win.

I spare a quick glance back and see Koschei rip out Golem's right leg.

Golem falls to the side.

Koschei rushes toward me, but Golem races at him with the three remaining limbs, like a wounded *Terminator*.

In a heartbeat, a metal arm clutches Koschei's ankle.

Koschei uses the ripped-off leg like a club, delivering a devastating blow to Golem's head.

Adrenaline overrides pain as I crawl toward the shotgun with renewed determination.

The sounds of robot being torn apart intensify.

I crawl faster.

The sounds stop.

I'm a foot away from the weapon when rough hands roll me over, slamming my damaged back against the marble.

I yelp in pain.

Leering, Koschei grasps my neck with one hand and lifts me into the air.

CHAPTER FIFTY-FIVE

SADISTIC PLEASURE GLEAMS in Koschei's green eyes as he watches me dangle in front of him.

His grip on my neck is cutting off all air and crushing my trachea.

Based on my encounter with drowning and my training for a water escape, I know I don't have much time.

Desperately channeling all my martial arts lessons, I aim a punch at Koschei's face with my right fist.

My knuckles connect with his jaw, and my hand feels like I broke it.

Wincing, he tries to smack me with his free hand.

Just as Thalia had taught me, I block his blow with my right forearm. Something cracks, but I ignore the pain and punch him with the left fist at the same time as I kick with my legs.

Face contorted by an ugly grimace, Koschei

squeezes my neck even harder. I think he intends to break it in order to speed up my demise.

Leaning in, he whispers, "I didn't think I'd enjoy this so much. You're—"

I'll never know what he was going to say because I choose that moment to attempt one last gambit.

Just as I've practiced so many times for my needle-swallowing effect, I spit out the needle from Buyan, aiming for the bastard's right eye.

The needle goes into Koschei's iris like an icepick into Jell-O—and as soon as it does, the still-exposed part of the needle begins to glow.

CHAPTER FIFTY-SIX

LETTING GO OF MY NECK, Koschei roars like a wounded bear and drops to his knees.

Falling to the ground on all fours, I grit my teeth against the agony and crawl for the shotgun.

Koschei's screams intensify.

Using all my remaining strength, I pick up the weapon.

Koschei's Mandate aura seems to be flickering.

I put the shotgun point-blank against the needle protruding from his eye and squeeze the trigger.

Half of Koschei's head disappears, and glowing needle shards spread through the rest of his body.

"This is for Rose," I hiss and put a hole in his torso. "And this for Kevin."

I shoot until the gun clicks empty, and Koschei is lying prostrate on the ground.

The shiny needle shards seem to absorb what

remains of his aura; then his body turns into ash in front of my eyes.

A second later, the ash disappears without a trace.

Staring at the empty spot on the floor, I toss the now-useless shotgun away.

Wait a minute. An empty shotgun was in Kit's hand in my vision, so does that—

"Poor Koscheiushka," Baba Yaga says from behind me as something hard slams into the back of my head. "Not so immortal after all."

I just got hit by a giant skillet, I realize dimly.

This is how I ended up in the heap on the ground in my vision.

And then all my thoughts go away as my consciousness dives into blackness.

CHAPTER FIFTY-SEVEN

I WAKE UP TO PAIN.

Horrible pain.

My head feels like my brains are leaking out, and my back is one giant spasm.

But on the plus side, I'm not dead—though I almost wish I were.

Opening my eyes, I find myself cradled in the arms of an orc, being carried out of the Izbushka restaurant.

"Kit," I croak out, then wince as my ribs scream in protest.

"You're alive," Kit's orc voice booms out. "Keep it that way."

"You were there," I rasp out, "right after Baba Yaga knocked me out with that skillet. Then you turned into a drekavac and killed her, didn't you?"

"How did you—"

"Probably a vision," Felix says in our ears. "Sasha, I'm so glad you're okay. I hope you don't mind, but I texted Nero when Baba Yaga was killed. He asked me to do it. I believe his limo was parked just out of reach of Brighton Beach, waiting for her death to be rid of the contract so he could swoop in and help."

The pain makes it difficult to parse Felix's words.

Kit exits the restaurant, her uneven stride a torture for my broken body.

Vlad is lying on the sidewalk, already looking better. Lucretia is still holding down writhing Ariel.

A limo screeches to a halt next to the curb.

Right.

Felix mentioned a limo a second ago.

The driver's door opens, and Nero jumps out with supernatural speed. A familiar-looking woman exits from the passenger side.

She's the one I bumped into on the way out of the office.

Now that I'm not running, I recognize her as Isis—the healer with prices only Nero could afford.

Pain makes it hard to think, but I still wonder what Isis was doing walking into Nero's building just as I was running out. Did he summon her ahead of time? That would make him more psychic than I am. Also, it would imply that he knew I'd escape my cell. But if that's true, why not stop me? And how could he have—

"Put her in the back," Nero growls. "Carefully."

Kit picks up her pace, and everything hurts so badly I stop thinking and pray to pass out.

The agony grows almost intolerable when Kit places me on the seat.

I must have countless broken bones, or worse.

"You'll have to quadruple the usual rate," Isis tells Nero after she gives me a quick scan. "This is going to hurt me a lot."

"Fine," Nero says without a moment's hesitation. "Hurry."

Isis demonstratively sighs, then points her hands at me.

The golden energy streams out, and I feel my wounds closing and broken bones straightening.

When she healed us the other week, Isis's skin had a healthy olive tint. Today, she's paler, and the more of her energy she sends out, the sicklier she looks. Before my very eyes, a couple of her jet-black hairs turn gray.

A pleasant warmth flows through me, and my pain morphs into pleasure.

"Make her sleep," Nero commands.

"Wait," I say, reaching into my pocket to pull out the smoke grenade. "Throw this into the restaurant and have Vlad toss in his firebird egg."

Nero takes the grenade, removes the pin, and tosses it at the glass above the door.

The glass shatters into tiny pieces, and a few breaths later, the fire alarm activates.

"Do it," Nero commands, looking at Vlad on the pavement. "Erase this place."

Grunting in pain, Vlad takes out the firebird egg and pitches it inside the restaurant.

My lips curve in an evil smile as I watch the Izbushka go up in flames.

"An hour nap will do you good," Isis whispers, shooting me a stronger pulse of her energy.

"Wait," I want to say again, but my eyelids grow heavy and I sink into a healing sleep.

———

I OPEN my eyes to find Nero holding me above my bed.

Nero in my bedroom?

"This must be a dream," I mutter as he gently lays me down.

"Yes." His deep voice is a croon. "This is just a dream."

"I like dreams like this," I say dazedly and grab his collar. "Are you sure it *is* a dream?"

Nero doesn't reply, but his limbal rings almost overtake his eyes.

Pulling on his collar, I raise myself up so that our lips nearly touch.

He doesn't pull away, but he doesn't lean down either.

That's fine. All the healing energy roaming through my body is giving me an almost superhuman strength —and the libido of a succubus.

Easily lifting myself the rest of the distance, I lock lips with Nero. They're surprisingly soft, his breath vaguely minty-tasting—

Someone clears her throat nearby. "Is this why you

wanted me here?" Isis asks. "Because I'm not sure I have enough strength left to heal her if—"

"No." Nero reluctantly pulls away from me. "Finish your job."

The healing energy makes my lids heavy again.

"Sleep tight," Nero says from far away, and the warm energy leaves me no choice but to obey.

CHAPTER FIFTY-EIGHT

I WAKE up to the feeling of something furry snuggling at my chest and back.

Wait, chest *and* back?

I lift the blanket.

Yep. There's something furry on both sides.

A cat and a chinchilla.

"Good morning," Fluffster says in my head.

"Hey, bud," I whisper back.

Lucifur looks at me with green eyes that seem to say, "If you wish to keep your intestines, vassal, you will cover me with that blanket at once."

I cover her back up, happy to see her doing better.

"How are you feeling?" Fluffster asks, standing up on his hind legs. "I heard you got really hurt."

Swinging my legs off the bed, I examine my body for damage from last night.

Nothing.

No, much better than nothing.

"I feel like I've been on a two-year vacation," I tell him. "With spa treatments, cabana boys feeding me grapes, white sand—"

"Sasha?" Felix yells from outside the door. "Fluffster tells me you're awake."

I give the traitorous chinchilla a narrow-eyed stare. "What if I wanted to nap some more?"

"It's one p.m.," Fluffster replies without remorse. "You're lucky Nero excused you from work; else you'd be so late, you'd lose your job."

"He excused me from work?" I say, perhaps too loudly. I vaguely recall a wet dream that was stranger than usual, as it featured Isis in addition to Nero.

Wait a sec. Could that kiss have been real?

If so, what did Isis mean by her weird comment? She almost made it sound like I'd need healing if we got it on.

And that leads to a question I never thought I'd ask about my boss.

Exactly how big is he?

"You're talking about Nero?" Felix says from behind the door, and I feel my cheeks start to burn. "He said you can come back to work when you feel up to it."

"Nero is being nice?" I push all thoughts of phallic sizing aside. "I must've been hurt *really* badly."

Neither Fluffster nor Felix say anything, so I get up and look for something to wear.

"We're in the kitchen having lunch," Felix says as I pull on my robe. "Join as soon as you can."

With a post-healing bounce in my step, I rush into

the bathroom and quickly take care of business before heading to the kitchen.

A whole chorus of voices greets me as I approach.

"If I were you, I'd always make myself look like one of the Batmans," I hear Ariel say. "Or at least like Christian Bale."

"No, you should look like one of the *Matrix* characters," Felix counters. "Particularly Neo."

"I get bored looking the same way for too long," Kit says as I walk in.

"Sasha!" Ariel puts down her fork, jumps up, and gives me a tight hug. "I'm so glad I caught you before I left."

"Left?" I take in her appearance. Leave it to Ariel to look ready for a cover shoot, even after yesterday's ordeal. "Just checking—you're not under glamour anymore, right?"

"No. After Gaius died—" She stops talking, her expression turning somber.

Is she actually mourning Gaius after everything that he's done? I'm tempted to ask but suppress the urge.

She probably needs some time to come to grips with it.

"She came to her senses an hour after we got home." Felix gets up, grabs an empty plate, and walks over to the stove. "Now, thanks to Nero's healer lady, she's almost as good as new."

"And I decided to go back to rehab." Ariel's face smooths out as she sits back down and resumes eating what looks like Felix's famous Mushroom Stroganoff.

I take a seat as well.

"Kit and I will take her to Gomorrah as soon as we're done." Felix puts a plate full of Stroganoff in front of me, then hands me a fork.

"So." I stare down at the food, unsure how to best put my question without insulting my friend or bringing up any painful memories. "Did Gaius—"

"I don't think I drank any more of his blood," Ariel says, her face unreadable. "Or anything else like that." She gathers a large pile of noodles on the edge of her plate, then stabs them all at once with her fork. "The cravings are much more tolerable now. I feel almost like a normal person again, which is why I think I should get away from temptation and get fully clean. Besides, Bailey's dream therapy is helping me with other stuff..." She puts the fork in her mouth, then starts gathering the noodles into a big pile again.

Felix and I exchange furtive glances. This is as close as Ariel's ever gotten to admitting her PTSD—which is great progress in and of itself. If I ever meet Bailey, I'll have to thank her.

"I'll go with you guys." I spear a heaping serving of Stroganoff with my fork. "Just let me finish."

"Sorry, but no," Felix says without meeting my gaze. "Nero asked me to make sure you take it easy today."

"Nero isn't the boss of me," I say. "Neither are you."

"Well, strictly speaking," Felix says. "He is your—"

"Just chill at home for a bit," Ariel says conciliatorily. "Nero might hurt Felix if your bodyguard sees you leave the building."

Fuming, I stick the fork in my mouth and chew violently.

"Speaking of Nero," Kit says and makes herself look like my boss, only shirtless. "He, Vlad, and I made a deal that concerns you all." She turns into a shirtless Vlad. "If the Council ever learns about all the murders we partook in—and that's an unlikely 'if'—Vlad will assume responsibility for it all, even Koschei and Baba Yaga, if you catch my drift." She looks at me with Vlad's piercing eyes.

I finish chewing and swallow. "This is so that I don't get into trouble for killing Koschei, a Cognizant under the Mandate, and same for you and Baba Yaga?"

"Exactly," she says. "It's just a precaution because no one should even realize they're dead."

"Oh?" Felix says curiously.

"Pada visited the burned-up restaurant, cleaning up the remains," she says. "And I'll use my powers to make sure all the dead blip on the Council's radar from time to time." She briefly makes herself look like one of the Enforcers Vlad killed on the pier, then even faster like Gaius, Koschei, and Baba Yaga.

Seeing the last two sends a shiver down my spine, even though I know it's just Kit. I'll have to talk to Lucretia about this.

Assuming new vampires do therapy, that is.

"We can make it look like Baba Yaga and Koschei took a trip back to Russia," Felix says excitedly. "I can even create an electronic trail."

"That's good," I say with a grin. His proposal

reminds me of a magic effect, and nothing cheers me up like designing a good deception. "Gaius also could move someplace. Then, in a while, a rumor could spread about how they all went on a trip to an Otherland with a weird time flow."

"That could work." Kit's sneaky expression rivals mine. "Vlad and Lucretia already glamour-wiped the memories of the surviving humans, but we can have them go back and implant memories consistent with this story. Same with any human cops looking into this."

"I'm sorry to interrupt the fun, but I'd really like to get going." Ariel puts down her fork. "Even that casual mention of vampires…"

"Say no more." Felix stuffs the rest of his food into his mouth, and Kit follows suit.

"We'll be back soon," Felix says, getting up.

"When you see Lucretia, can you please thank her for convincing my med school program to give me a deferment?" Ariel stands up as well. "I don't know if I'll ever feel safe talking to her face to face."

"Of course," I say. "Funny it should take glamour to get that deferment."

"That's what I said." Felix chuckles and heads out of the kitchen.

Kit clears her throat and looks meaningfully at Ariel.

"Oh, right," Ariel says with an almost imperceptible eye roll. "Kit can crash in my room until I need it."

"We should burn the sheets after," Fluffster says mentally—presumably to everyone but Kit.

"I'll see you at the funeral." Ariel gives me a peck on the cheek and follows Felix out of the kitchen.

I sit there, stunned, my appetite gone without a trace.

Ariel meant Rose's funeral.

An event I've put out of my mind, probably to stay sane. Now that—

"I'll come back with Felix." Kit interrupts my thoughts with a peck on my sauce-smeared lips.

They leave, and I poke at the rest of my meal in gloomy contemplation while Fluffster eats his hay.

When we're both done, I clean up the kitchen, which makes me feel a little better.

That is, until I return to my room and see yesterday's tattered clothes neatly folded on the chair.

Huh.

I woke up naked and didn't even question it, but I probably should have.

Did Nero undress me?

My cheeks turn hot again, as do other parts of my body.

Pushing away the X-rated movie in my mind, I rummage through the pockets of my bloodied pants, take out the map that leads to Buyan, then toss the rags into the garbage.

"Are you about to play with Headspace again?" Fluffster asks when I take a seat and start meditative breathing.

"Sure," I say, though I was just trying to calm myself.

Fluffster jumps onto the bed to better observe me. A feline eye looks at him hungrily from under the blanket, but to my surprise, Lucifur doesn't attack.

"The cat is a quick learner," Fluffster says smugly in my head. "Now if I could train her to like a less expensive brand of cat food, she'd be perfect."

Shaking my head, I attempt to access Headspace.

My power must be fully recharged because it works right away.

———

I FLOAT THERE FOR A WHILE, just enjoying the weightlessness-like sensation.

Not having a body can be rather soothing—especially when I know I'm not fighting for my life in the outside world.

It has never occurred to me before, but Headspace is an excellent place to get away to think. In fact, because time doesn't seem to pass in the outside world, I can do thinking without wasting precious moments of my life.

Hey, maybe the next time I need to think up a magic effect, I will do so in Headspace. Maybe this is how I'll invent a show that would impress the Cognizant. After all, if Nero really liked my cheat-at-cards demonstration, other supernatural beings might also.

I float for a moment, trying to figure out what I

should do with this current Headspace session, when something dawns on me.

It's been a while since I tried to make a Headspace call to Rasputin—my biological father.

Reaching him should be easier now that I learned more about him during Nero's rare moment of candor.

Yes, that's it.

I should've started with this.

Imaginative, Nero had called him, and I bet Rasputin is that—assuming he purposefully crafted the mystery-man persona in the human histories.

Quirky—that was another epithet Nero had given him, and that makes sense too. When I think about the bearded picture of the man, quirky and eccentric are definitely terms that come to mind.

Nero had also called him resourceful. This is easy to believe as well. According to history, my father had been excellent at manipulating the Russian royal family —so much so that people eventually wanted to kill him for it.

The only description of Nero's that I don't agree with is loyal. How could that be true for a man who had abandoned me, his daughter, to be raised by strangers in a foreign land?

Nevertheless, I do my best to focus on the essence of the man—including *everything* Nero had said.

To my huge surprise, it works.

Or at least I assume it does because a Headspace entity turns up next to me.

One that isn't Darian or the bannik.

The entity pulses with equal measure curiosity and dread.

I reach out to him/it.

The entity reluctantly returns the favor.

Perhaps it's my imagination, but the mutual metaphysical touch brings to mind scenes of family members hugging each other after a long time apart.

Our minds meld, and I prepare for a wild ride.

CHAPTER FIFTY-NINE

I'M SITTING ON A BED, brushing a woman's hair with an ornately designed brush.

My hand is strong and masculine—evidence I might be in Rasputin's memories, or those of some other male seer.

The woman is turned away, so I can't see her face. Her pale shoulders and graceful back remind me of a ballerina, and the way she moans and purrs in pleasure when he/I groom her is the kind of seductive that borders on pornographic.

Could this be my mother?

Am I about to see a memory of my own conception?

That would be like walking in on your parents, but exponentially weirder.

Or is this their post-coital bliss?

"I love how unpredictable you are," I say in Russian in a deep male voice. The language is another clue that this is my father's memory.

"That's not the only thing you love about me," the woman answers, her voice soft and lilting.

Though she says the words in Russian, I understand them—a perk of being inside the head of a native Russian speaker. I can even tell she has an accent when she speaks—though what kind is unclear.

She starts to turn, but before I see her face, the memory changes.

———

I'M STANDING IN AN OPULENT, onion-domed building filled with gold decorations and religious icons in the style of the Russian Orthodox Church.

If I really am in Rasputin's memories, this might be a church inside the Winter Palace.

Nero stands next to a fancy candelabra dressed in clothes that seem to have jumped out of a black-and-white photo taken in Russia circa early 1900s. Rasputin must be *very* tall—I'm looking down at Nero, which is an odd experience.

For someone who will become my boss a hundred years from now, Nero looks exactly the same. Well, except for that perfectly trimmed beard that brings to mind an overzealous hipster.

"If we follow this course, she will have a peaceful life all the way to her twenty-fourth year," Rasputin/I say. "I can't see further than that—though I *can* tell something will happen that year that will splinter her futures beyond reckoning."

"I'll be extra vigilant when I get there," Nero says. "Now about—"

———

THE MEMORY SWITCH HAPPENS AGAIN, and the hustle and bustle of JFK surrounds me on all sides.

He/I am holding a little girl by her tiny hand.

Her skin is pale, and her big blue eyes are looking up with a frightened expression.

I recognize that face.

This is what I look like in the first pictures my adoptive parents took of me.

"How can I leave my child?" is a thought that swirls through his head, and the pain he feels is overwhelming. "It's the only way," he then tells himself, over and over. "It's the only way I could think of," he whispers to the girl.

Some sadistic part of me actually likes it that he's upset.

He's about to abandon me like a bag of trash.

He should feel like shit.

He/I look at the nearby bar.

Younger-looking Mom and Dad are sitting there, drinking cocktails.

"They shall be good parents to you," he/I say to the mini me in Russian. "It's the only—"

———

MY/RASPUTIN'S eyes are closed.

I recognize the constriction in the wrists and around my chest from my escapist training.

This is what it feels like to be tied to a chair with rope.

If I could, I would wrinkle my nose. Wherever we are smells like an underground morgue.

Then a fist slams into my stomach.

Well, Rasputin's, not mine, but the pain makes me forget who is who for a moment.

Air escapes our lungs and we gasp for air—but keep our face as placid as is possible under the circumstances, with our eyes closed.

"When *this* torturer sees the pain, the beatings are much worse," Rasputin thinks, resisting the temptation to squeeze his hands into fists.

The next blow is to the kneecap—and the pain is so intense he fails to keep in a pained gasp.

Ow, ow, ow.

I need a way to disconnect from this memory, fast.

The pain is all too real.

"I deserve this," Rasputin thinks as another blow makes him want to scream. "Everything they do to me I deserve for leaving my child."

CHAPTER SIXTY

I FIND myself in a vacuum-like blackness for the third time, facing a synapse-hologram of a man I do not recognize.

Bald and beardless, at first he looks nothing like the images of Rasputin I saw online.

Except for those eyes.

The eyes look the same.

And there's his now-exposed chin.

It looks just like the one I popped pimples on as a teen.

My chin.

"Grigori Rasputin?" I ask tremulously.

Every possible human emotion seems to kaleidoscope on his translucent face as he nods and points at me. "Sasha?" he asks, pronouncing my name in that Russian manner that Felix's parents do.

I nod.

He rattles out something in rapid-fire Russian and floats down.

"I don't understand." I float to his level. "I don't speak Russian."

The pain in his eyes seems to intensify.

"*Ya ne govoryu po-angliyski*," Rasputin says very slowly and points at himself, then at his mouth, then at my mouth.

"You don't speak English," I guess.

He shrugs.

If he doesn't speak English to the point where he doesn't know *that* phrase, his English must be as bad as my Russian.

Or maybe worse. Felix taught me how to say hello and a couple of versions of goodbye in Russian—and at least a few curse words.

"*Opasno*." Rasputin points at our surroundings, then at the entities, himself, and me. "*Opasno*." He repeats it a few times.

"*Opasno*," I parrot, and he nods.

"I have no idea what that means, but I'll find out as soon as I'm out of here," I tell him.

He shrugs and repeats the word one more time.

"How do I find you?" I ask. Pointing at him, I pantomime legs walking with my index and middle finger. "I want to meet you."

"*Nyet*." He shakes his head vigorously, then points at me, then at himself. He then does the walking gesture and makes a cross with his arms.

The message is loud and clear.

He doesn't want me to come find him.

"Why not?" I demand. "Where are you? Who was torturing you? Why?"

"Proschay," he says solemnly, and I feel myself getting ripped away from him.

Felix taught me that word.

It means goodbye—but the type of goodbye that has connotations of never meeting again.

"No. Wait!" I shout, but the feeling of getting ripped apart intensifies until something disconnects, and I'm thrust back into the real world.

———

I SIT THERE RECOVERING for a moment. My father must've used a burst of power to disconnect from me—a seer's version of hanging up.

I pull out my phone and search the word *"opasno."*

It translates to "danger."

Okay. What did he mean by that?

He was pointing around when he said it, so maybe he was telling me the same thing as Darian, about how dangerous it is to speak in Headspace that way.

I get up and begin to pace around the room.

"What's the problem?" Fluffster asks. "Did you see a disturbing vision?"

Feeling silly that I forgot he was even there, I tell Fluffster what happened—and when I'm done, he confirms that *opasno* indeed means danger, and that *proschay* is farewell.

"Maybe those conversations are dangerous because they make your future harder to predict?" Fluffster cocks his head. "Darian said no one could foresee those, so—"

"Maybe," I say, my eyes falling on the map to Buyan. "Hold on a second."

I stare at the map as if seeing it for the first time.

Something about it has been gnawing at me ever since Kit drew it, and the current context seems to help.

Yes. It has always reminded me of something—something to do with Rasputin, I now realize, though I still have no idea what.

On a hunch, I unlock my phone and start browsing through the pictures there, and as I do, I finally recall where I've seen this kind of map-meets-Venn diagram before.

And how it ties to Rasputin.

Swiping past the photos of the contract between Nero and my father, I find it.

It was in my phone this whole time.

A picture of something else in Nero's safe.

Another Otherland map in the style Kit had utilized.

A map that Nero kept in the same folder as everything else pertaining to Rasputin and me.

Could it be?

Have I found a way to my father?

Something—probably seer intuition—fills me with the certainty that I have.

Yes.

I *know* I have.

Just as I know something else.

Wherever Rasputin is, he's being tortured—and his coping strategies imply that it's something that happens to him often, maybe even every day.

Which leaves me with only one course of action.

No matter what he told me, I can't stay away.

He's my father.

That he didn't raise me was his choice, and this will be mine.

One way or another, I will find him.

Even if this map leads me into the very depths of hell.

Thank you for reading! I hope you're enjoying Sasha's story! Her adventures continue in *Paranormal Misdirection (Sasha Urban Series: Book 5)*. To be notified of new releases of my books, please visit www.dimazales.com and sign up for my mailing list.

Love audiobooks? This series, and all of my other books, are available in audio.

Want to read my other books? You can check out:

- *Mind Dimensions* - the action-packed urban fantasy adventures of Darren, who can stop time and read minds
- *Upgrade* - the thrilling sci-fi tale of Mike Cohen, whose new technology will transform our brains *and* the world
- *The Last Humans* - the futuristic sci-

fi/dystopian story of Theo, who lives in a
world where nothing is as it seems

- *The Sorcery Code* - the epic fantasy adventures
of sorcerer Blaise and his creation, the
beautiful and powerful Gala

I also collaborate with my wife on sci-fi romance, so if
you don't mind erotic material, you can check out *Close
Liaisons*. Visit ww.annazaires.com for more
information and to get your copy.

And now, please turn the page for an exciting excerpt
from *The Thought Readers.*

SNEAK PEEK AT THE THOUGHT READERS

Description

Everyone thinks I'm a genius.

Everyone is wrong.

Sure, I finished Harvard at eighteen and now make crazy money at a hedge fund. But that's not because I'm unusually smart or hard-working.

It's because I cheat.

You see, I have a unique ability. I can go outside time into my own personal version of reality—the place I call "the Quiet"—where I can explore my surroundings while the rest of the world stands still.

I thought I was the only one who could do this—until I met *her*.

My name is Darren, and this is how I learned that I'm a Reader.

Excerpt

Sometimes I think I'm crazy. I'm sitting at a casino table in Atlantic City, and everyone around me is motionless. I call this the *Quiet*, as though giving it a name makes it seem more real—as though giving it a name changes the fact that all the players around me are frozen like statues, and I'm walking among them, looking at the cards they've been dealt.

The problem with the theory of my being crazy is that when I 'unfreeze' the world, as I just have, the cards the players turn over are the same ones I just saw in the Quiet. If I were crazy, wouldn't these cards be different? Unless I'm so far gone that I'm imagining the cards on the table, too.

But then I also win. If that's a delusion—if the pile of chips on my side of the table is a delusion—then I might as well question everything. Maybe my name isn't even Darren.

No. I can't think that way. If I'm really that confused, I don't want to snap out of it—because if I do, I'll probably wake up in a mental hospital.

Besides, I love my life, crazy and all.

My shrink thinks the Quiet is an inventive way I

describe the 'inner workings of my genius.' Now that sounds crazy to me. She also might want me, but that's beside the point. Suffice it to say, she's as far as it gets from my datable age range, which is currently right around twenty-four. Still young, still hot, but done with school and pretty much beyond the clubbing phase. I hate clubbing, almost as much as I hated studying. In any case, my shrink's explanation doesn't work, as it doesn't account for the way I know things even a genius wouldn't know—like the exact value and suit of the other players' cards.

I watch as the dealer begins a new round. Besides me, there are three players at the table: Grandma, the Cowboy, and the Professional, as I call them. I feel that now almost imperceptible fear that accompanies the phasing. That's what I call the process: phasing into the Quiet. Worrying about my sanity has always facilitated phasing; fear seems helpful in this process.

I phase in, and everything gets quiet. Hence the name for this state.

It's eerie to me, even now. Outside the Quiet, this casino is very loud: drunk people talking, slot machines, ringing of wins, music—the only place louder is a club or a concert. And yet, right at this moment, I could probably hear a pin drop. It's like I've gone deaf to the chaos that surrounds me.

Having so many frozen people around adds to the strangeness of it all. Here is a waitress stopped mid-step, carrying a tray with drinks. There is a woman about to pull a slot machine lever. At my own table, the dealer's hand is raised, the last card he dealt hanging unnaturally in midair. I walk up to him from the side of the table and reach for it. It's a king, meant for the Professional. Once I let the card go, it falls on the table rather than continuing to float as before—but I know full well that it will be back in the air, in the exact position it was when I grabbed it, when I phase out.

The Professional looks like someone who makes money playing poker, or at least the way I always imagined someone like that might look. Scruffy, shades on, a little sketchy-looking. He's been doing an excellent job with the poker face—basically not twitching a single muscle throughout the game. His face is so expressionless that I wonder if he might've gotten Botox to help maintain such a stony countenance. His hand is on the table, protectively covering the cards dealt to him.

I move his limp hand away. It feels normal. Well, in a manner of speaking. The hand is sweaty and hairy, so moving it aside is unpleasant and is admittedly an abnormal thing to do. The normal part is that the hand is warm, rather than cold. When I was a kid, I expected people to feel cold in the Quiet, like stone statues.

With the Professional's hand moved away, I pick up his cards. Combined with the king that was hanging in the air, he has a nice high pair. Good to know.

I walk over to Grandma. She's already holding her cards, and she has fanned them nicely for me. I'm able to avoid touching her wrinkled, spotted hands. This is a relief, as I've recently become conflicted about touching people—or, more specifically, women—in the Quiet. If I had to, I would rationalize touching Grandma's hand as harmless, or at least not creepy, but it's better to avoid it if possible.

In any case, she has a low pair. I feel bad for her. She's been losing a lot tonight. Her chips are dwindling. Her losses are due, at least partially, to the fact that she has a terrible poker face. Even before looking at her cards, I knew they wouldn't be good because I could tell she was disappointed as soon as her hand was dealt. I also caught a gleeful gleam in her eyes a few rounds ago when she had a winning three of a kind.

This whole game of poker is, to a large degree, an exercise in reading people—something I really want to get better at. At my job, I've been told I'm great at reading people. I'm not, though; I'm just good at using the Quiet to make it seem like I am. I do want to learn how to read people for real, though. It would be nice to know what everyone is thinking.

What I don't care that much about in this poker game is money. I do well enough financially to not have to depend on hitting it big gambling. I don't care if I win or lose, though quintupling my money back at the blackjack table was fun. This whole trip has been more about going gambling because I finally can, being twenty-one and all. I was never into fake IDs, so this is an actual milestone for me.

Leaving Grandma alone, I move on to the next player—the Cowboy. I can't resist taking off his straw hat and trying it on. I wonder if it's possible for me to get lice this way. Since I've never been able to bring back any inanimate objects from the Quiet, nor otherwise affect the real world in any lasting way, I figure I won't be able to get any living critters to come back with me, either.

Dropping the hat, I look at his cards. He has a pair of aces—a better hand than the Professional. Maybe the Cowboy is a professional, too. He has a good poker face, as far as I can tell. It'll be interesting to watch those two in this round.

Next, I walk up to the deck and look at the top cards, memorizing them. I'm not leaving anything to chance.

When my task in the Quiet is complete, I walk back to myself. Oh, yes, did I mention that I see myself sitting there, frozen like the rest of them? That's the weirdest part. It's like having an out-of-body experience.

Approaching my frozen self, I look at him. I usually avoid doing this, as it's too unsettling. No amount of looking in the mirror—or seeing videos of yourself on YouTube—can prepare you for viewing your own three-dimensional body up close. It's not something anyone is meant to experience. Well, aside from identical twins, I guess.

It's hard to believe that this person is me. He looks more like some random guy. Well, maybe a bit better than that. I do find this guy interesting. He looks cool. He looks smart. I think women would probably consider him good-looking, though I know that's not a modest thing to think.

It's not like I'm an expert at gauging how attractive a guy is, but some things are common sense. I can tell when a dude is ugly, and this frozen me is not. I also know that generally, being good-looking requires a symmetrical face, and the statue of me has that. A strong jaw doesn't hurt, either. Check. Having broad shoulders is a positive, and being tall really helps. All covered. I have blue eyes—that seems to be a plus. Girls have told me they like my eyes, though right now, on the frozen me, the eyes look creepy—glassy. They look like the eyes of a lifeless wax figure.

Realizing that I'm dwelling on this subject way too long, I shake my head. I can just picture my shrink analyzing this moment. Who would imagine admiring themselves like this as part of their mental illness? I can just picture her scribbling down *Narcissist*, underlining it for emphasis.

Enough. I need to leave the Quiet. Raising my hand, I touch my frozen self on the forehead, and I hear noise again as I phase out.

Everything is back to normal.

The card that I looked at a moment before—the king that I left on the table—is in the air again, and from there it follows the trajectory it was always meant to, landing near the Professional's hands. Grandma is still eyeing her fanned cards in disappointment, and the Cowboy has his hat on again, though I took it off him in the Quiet. Everything is exactly as it was.

On some level, my brain never ceases to be surprised at the discontinuity of the experience in the Quiet and outside it. As humans, we're hardwired to question reality when such things happen. When I was trying to outwit my shrink early on in my therapy, I once read an entire psychology textbook during our session. She, of course, didn't notice it, as I did it in the Quiet. The book talked about how babies as young as two months old are surprised if they see something out of the ordinary, like gravity appearing to work backwards. It's no wonder my brain has trouble adapting. Until I was ten, the world behaved normally, but everything has been weird since then, to put it mildly.

Glancing down, I realize I'm holding three of a kind. Next time, I'll look at my cards before phasing. If I have something this strong, I might take my chances and play fair.

The game unfolds predictably because I know everybody's cards. At the end, Grandma gets up. She's clearly lost enough money.

And that's when I see the girl for the first time.

She's hot. My friend Bert at work claims that I have a 'type,' but I reject that idea. I don't like to think of myself as shallow or predictable. But I might actually be a bit of both, because this girl fits Bert's description of my type to a T. And my reaction is extreme interest, to say the least.

Large blue eyes. Well-defined cheekbones on a slender face, with a hint of something exotic. Long, shapely legs, like those of a dancer. Dark wavy hair in a ponytail—a hairstyle that I like. And without bangs—even better. I hate bangs—not sure why girls do that to themselves. Though lack of bangs is not, strictly speaking, in Bert's description of my type, it probably should be.

I continue staring at her. With her high heels and tight skirt, she's overdressed for this place. Or maybe I'm underdressed in my jeans and t-shirt. Either way, I don't care. I have to try to talk to her.

I debate phasing into the Quiet and approaching her, so I can do something creepy like stare at her up close, or maybe even snoop in her pockets. Anything to help me when I talk to her.

I decide against it, which is probably the first time that's ever happened.

I know that my reasoning for breaking my usual habit—if you can even call it that—is strange. I picture the following chain of events: she agrees to date me, we go out for a while, we get serious, and because of the deep connection we have, I come clean about the Quiet. She learns I did something creepy and has a fit, then dumps me. It's ridiculous to think this, of course, considering that we haven't even spoken yet. Talk about jumping the gun. She might have an IQ below seventy, or the personality of a piece of wood. There can be twenty different reasons why I wouldn't want to date her. And besides, it's not all up to me. She might tell me to go fuck myself as soon as I try to talk to her.

Still, working at a hedge fund has taught me to

hedge. As crazy as that reasoning is, I stick with my decision not to phase because I know it's the gentlemanly thing to do. In keeping with this unusually chivalrous me, I also decide not to cheat at this round of poker.

As the cards are dealt again, I reflect on how good it feels to have done the honorable thing—even without anyone knowing. Maybe I should try to respect people's privacy more often. As soon as I think this, I mentally snort. *Yeah, right.* I have to be realistic. I wouldn't be where I am today if I'd followed that advice. In fact, if I made a habit of respecting people's privacy, I would lose my job within days—and with it, a lot of the comforts I've become accustomed to.

Copying the Professional's move, I cover my cards with my hand as soon as I receive them. I'm about to sneak a peek at what I was dealt when something unusual happens.

The world goes quiet, just like it does when I phase in... but I did nothing this time.

And at that moment, I see *her*—the girl sitting across the table from me, the girl I was just thinking about. She's standing next to me, pulling her hand away from mine. Or, strictly speaking, from my frozen self's hand—as I'm standing a little to the side looking at her.

She's also still sitting in front of me at the table, a frozen statue like all the others.

My mind goes into overdrive as my heartbeat jumps. I don't even consider the possibility of that second girl being a twin sister or something like that. I know it's her. She's doing what I did just a few minutes ago. She's walking in the Quiet. The world around us is frozen, but we are not.

A horrified look crosses her face as she realizes the same thing. Before I can react, she lunges across the table and touches her own forehead.

The world becomes normal again.

She stares at me from across the table, shocked, her eyes huge and her face pale. Her hands tremble as she rises to her feet. Without so much as a word, she turns and begins walking away, then breaks into a run a couple of seconds later.

Getting over my own shock, I get up and run after her. It's not exactly smooth. If she notices a guy she doesn't know running after her, dating will be the last thing on her mind. But I'm beyond that now. She's the only person I've met who can do what I do. She's proof that I'm not insane. She might have what I want most in the world.

She might have answers.

Visit www.dimazales.com to learn more!

ABOUT THE AUTHOR

Dima Zales is a *New York Times* and *USA Today* bestselling author of science fiction and fantasy. Prior to becoming a writer, he worked in the software development industry in New York as both a programmer and an executive. From high-frequency trading software for big banks to mobile apps for popular magazines, Dima has done it all. In 2013, he left the software industry in order to concentrate on his writing career and moved to Palm Coast, Florida, where he currently resides.

Please visit www.dimazales.com to learn more.